Praise for Books by Yasmine S. Ali, MD

What readers are saying about *The View from the Cliffs*:

"A lovely, tender, careful and rich novel. Ali has plaited intricately the history of three regions, and of three vivid touching characters, with politics and medical science and human passions, and achieved a powerfully integrated outcome . . . I was engrossed, and filled with admiration, for the structure, dialogue, and rich characterisation. Ali's creative words embody hope—for patients, for medical science, for human conflict, for human interactions and passions and deep connections. May her words, her hopeful philosophy, be what guides our future."

—Justice Edwin Cameron, South Africa

"I cannot remember the last time I read a book this quickly. I was fascinated by the characters, and Ali packs considerable meaning in relatively few words. She truly has a beautiful gift."

—Dennis Caffrey, Ret. Colonel, US Air Force

"The writing is AMAZING, as usual. Ali is a GREAT writer and I thoroughly enjoyed reading this book! Her command of the English language and her use of words to evoke scenes is AMAZING, too! I loved the characters and want to see more of them! . . . This book is in a class by itself."

—Nadia, beta reader

"I felt I was back in Ireland again. [Ali's] writing took me back home."

—John, Irish beta reader

"I've spent most of my free time in the last two days immersed in this book. I'm still wiping the tears away . . . I was totally caught up in the book's cadence and wrapped into the characters. It's a romance and yet it's not. I love all the cultural references. The comparison and contrast of the Irish and Palestinian people was fascinating and thought-provoking. And the ending is so powerful."

—Vicki, beta reader

"The people sitting next to me on the plane were probably worried about me. I was crying too hard when I got to the final chapters, and I had to save the last pages till I got home! I do LOVE the book—and it just got better and better. It felt like such a privilege to be among the first readers."

—Kelly, beta reader

"I finished reading this book yesterday, and I can't stop thinking about it! Such a beautiful and epic story. Bravo!!"

—Sarah A. Samaan, MD

"The book is lovely. Such great detail—I don't know how [Ali] does it! Very descriptive. Congratulations to the author—she is amazing! Beir bua!"

—Mary, Irish beta reader

"LOVED IT! This novel was a delight to read. I cared about the characters and what happens to them, learned a lot, and thoroughly enjoyed it from start to finish."

—Jane, beta reader

"Such vivid characters. A lovely novel. And a remarkable love story."

—Amy, beta reader

"A heartfelt novel for anyone who loves to read and loves to travel. This book will rekindle your capacity for hope, too."

—H, beta reader

Praise for *Walk through Fire: The Train Disaster that Changed America*

As seen on ABC, CBS, and C-SPAN

Listed in MDLinx's "5 Great Books to Read" in 2024

A 2023 Reading Club selection by the Network of the National Library of Medicine

Selected for the 2023 Southern Festival of Books

AEMO Library's Book of the Month, February 2024

"A poignant account of the 1978 Waverly train disaster . . . The book's greatest strength are the intimate accounts from first responders . . . Ali vividly captures how quickly the community came together in face of catastrophe. This is a fitting tribute to everyday heroes."

—*Publishers Weekly*

"In the author's narrative voice, which is simultaneously empathetic and authoritative, the facts are the backdrop to a story about grace . . . Ali, a cardiologist and medical writer, has a gift for translating her scientific knowledge into clear prose, complemented by her deep knowledge of the place where she grew up and her affection for its people."

—*The Nashville Scene*

"The Waverly Train Disaster, which happened just minutes from where I live, was one of the worst events ever to happen to the people of Waverly, many of whom I have been honored to know, and this amazing story of how they dealt with it has important lessons for all of us. Like me, Dr. Yasmine Ali is from this part of the world, and this book shows her dedication to sharing and honoring the history of her hometown."

—Country Music icon and bestselling author of *Coal Miner's Daughter*,
  Loretta Lynn

"*Walk Through Fire* captures a pivotal, life-altering moment in history that forever shaped our policy and our government and crystallized the irreplaceable role of the community hospital. Dr. Yasmine Ali gives voice to the small-town heroes who overcame unimagined adversity when the lives of their neighbors and loved ones were on the line."

—Former US Senate Majority Leader Bill Frist, MD

"Using first-person accounts, local documentation, and primary-source research, *Walk through Fire* is a riveting in-depth examination of a deadly 1978 tank car explosion that devastated a city and triggered sweeping changes in the railroad industry and in emergency response."

—Carl Swanson, editor *Trains* magazine

"One of the best books I've ever read . . . Dr. Ali does an excellent job weaving history into the stories of the individuals who were there that fateful day. Their story, this story, absolutely needed to be told. I thought I would like this book because I knew some of the individuals in it. I didn't know that I would be so deeply moved and LOVE the book because the writing would be so excellent and the depth of the story would be so deep."

—Patti Hoehn Damesworth, reader

"This is so much more than a book. This is bringing healing to the past from this tragedy. Very powerful."

—Heather Fork, MD, Founder and CEO, The Doctors Crossing

"I was hooked on the first line . . . I read for a couple of hours when I got home and finished the book the next afternoon. I don't know how [Ali] completed all the research and the interviews, and did such a great job. I felt as though I knew or worked with some of the people. I was saddened by all they went through and happy for those who have lived on to have successful lives."

—Fred Ramsey, reader

"I am so touched by this narrative . . . [Ali] did a wonderful job of opening my eyes and my heart to those who were so affected by this tragedy . . . It is very apparent how many hours have gone into her research—the final product is such an outstanding piece of Tennessee history and glimpse into the lives of the people of Waverly."

—Edna London, Coordinator, Lewisburg Study Club

"I just want to compliment [Ali] on her book, *Walk through Fire*. I just finished reading it—in less than a day because it was so interesting and intriguing I had a hard time putting it down . . . All in all, I found the book to be excellent in every respect and hope many others read it."

—D.F., Former Hazmat Shipper/Handler

"I just finished *Walk through Fire* and it was incredibly good . . . I've encouraged all my network of followers to buy and read it as a must-read for rail hazmat specialists. We must never forget our history. Thank you, Dr. Ali, for writing this book."

—Michael Lunsford, chemical safety consultant and former Hazmat Director for CSX

"I just finished Dr. Ali's book and thoroughly enjoyed it. As a train fan, firefighter/paramedic and member of our county hazmat team, this book was riveting."

—D. C., reader

"I thoroughly enjoyed the book. [Ali's] skills as a storyteller combined with her interdisciplinary mastery of medicine, law, commerce, and history made it a wonderful read."

—Bill, reader

Also by Yasmine S. Ali, MD

Walk through Fire: The Train Disaster that Changed America
(Get your autographed copy at www.LastSkyWriting.com !)

Be first to hear about all of Dr. Ali's new books, products, and merchandise as soon as they're released—subscribe to her _Positive Vibes_ newsletter today and never miss an update!

Subscribe for free to _Positive Vibes_ at https://yasmine-ali-author.beehiiv.com /subscribe or scan the QR code:

Find Dr. Ali's books and merchandise at www.LastSkyWriting.com, or scan the QR code:

The
View
from the
Cliffs

A Novel

YASMINE S. ALI

LastSky Books
An imprint of LastSky Writing, LLC
Ashland City, Tennessee
www.YasmineAliMD.com

Be the first to learn about new releases from Yasmine S. Ali! Visit www.YasmineAliMD.com and sign up for her acclaimed *Positive Vibes* newsletter on the home page. You'll get a regular ray of sunshine in your inbox, plus behind-the-scenes insights and the chance to enter reader giveaways and to receive subscriber-only deals and discounts on books, merchandise, events, and more!

For information about special discounts for bulk purchases, please email Info@LastSkyWriting.com

Library of Congress Control Number: 2024923662

ISBN: 978-1-966259-00-8 (trade paperback)

Second printing

For Dr. Kelly Lynn Moore, who understood Ranya's motivation even better than I did.

For my mother, who read aloud to me and I to her.

and

In loving memory of Raniyah Ramadan, who was beautiful in every way.

"Think you're escaping and run into yourself. Longest way round is the shortest way home."

—James Joyce,
Ulysses

Author's Note

THIS BOOK WAS CONCEIVED and written from 2015 to 2019, and its internal timeline covers the two decades from 1996 to 2016. Had it been written today or with a more recent timeline, it would have been a very different book.

Keeping that historical context in mind, it is my hope that you will grant me a modicum of grace and allow yourself to go back in time with the characters as you read this book.

PROLOGUE

IN THE CENTER DRAWER of his old oak desk lay a photograph. He opened the drawer and took it out now, for the time had come.

Every element of this photograph was, to his eye, devastatingly beautiful. He had long ago ceased counting the number of times he had opened that drawer, ceased measuring the eternity he had spent studying this one snapshot, immersed in the layers of memory that saturated the very air around him, embracing and suffocating him both at once and without distinction.

The desk creaked as he rested his elbows against it and ran his hands through his silvering hair. A February wind rustled the shutters, but he paid it no mind, his attention consumed by the photo before him. For the millionth and the last time, he allowed himself to become lost again in the image and all it represented. All the pain, all the joy. All the captivation. The woman standing on the cliffs at the edge of the world, the gales of the Atlantic whipping her long, unruly black curls into the air around and above her, despite her futile attempts to hold them down. The corners of his lips turned upward wistfully, and he felt that old, familiar ache return to his chest.

There she was, he thought again, always trying to bring order out of chaos. She wore that fantastic smile, and the gorgeous green of the cliffs stretched out into infinity behind her.

God, he missed her.

He looked again at the orange-and-white urn atop his desk, and sighed heavily. He couldn't believe he was going without her.

PART ONE

CHAPTER ONE

"All the things do depend upon the motional pulsation of the heart: To the heart is the beginning of life, the Sun of the Microcosm . . . and author of all."
—William Harvey,
On the Movement of the Heart and Blood in Animals

July 6, 1996
Saturday

RANYA KNEW A STROKE WHEN SHE SAW ONE.

Nancy, the Coronary Care Unit nurse who had called her to Mr. Williams' bedside, was telling her how she had just stepped in to take his vital signs and discovered that he couldn't move his right arm, but Ranya was no longer listening. She knew when she stepped through the door of that room that she would be calling a Stroke Code.

The hospital had recently instituted this kind of Code for situations just like this one. There was a new drug, a clot-buster known as tPA, in the infancy of its use for strokes, but the medical team had to act fast, and not every stroke patient would do well with it, so the final decision was up to the neurologist on call.

Ranya calmly interrupted Nancy's report. "We need to call a Stroke Code. Would you do that now, please?"

Ranya was well aware that it was a Saturday; moreover, it was the first Saturday of July, a time when all academic hospitals across the country were flooded with a new wave of interns and residents, many just out of medical school. Fresh recruits, one might say. And this university hospital in Nashville, Tennessee, was certainly not immune to the annual phenomenon.

She was already losing her patience with the inefficiency that seemed to descend upon the hospital at this time year after year. Well, this was one time when she hoped against hope that someone somewhere on the neuro service had thought to leave an experienced attending in charge.

In the hospital cafeteria, Gabriel had taken the first bite of his bland turkey sandwich when he heard the Stroke Code announced on the overhead speakers. He groaned. Always bad timing, but was there ever a good time for a stroke? His greater concern was that this was yet another green intern-and-resident team who wouldn't know a real stroke if it walked up and shook their hands. Waste of yet another good Saturday afternoon. Fine, then; he would be sure to turn it into a teaching opportunity.

When he arrived in the Coronary Care Unit, he marched up to the central nurses' station, demanding, "Who called a Stroke Code here?"

Several fingers pointed in unison to the room directly across the hall.

Gabriel looked toward the room indicated, and could discern through the curtained glass wall the bottom of a doctor's long white coat—probably a female doctor, judging from the shoes. Although they were sensible flats, they were definitely not a man's. She was standing at the right side of the patient's bed, and as he approached the room he could see and hear that she was speaking rapidly to the nurse on the other side of the bed, pointing toward some piece of equipment just outside his field of vision while holding her stethoscope in the other. *Blood pressure cuff*, he surmised instantly; *she wants the blood pressure cuff*.

Gabriel strode into the room and stood at the foot of the bed. He always stood at the foot of the bed first, because that was where, as he had learned over the years, a good doctor could grasp in one glance the patient's overall condition—improving, mildly ill, or really sick; urgent or time for a pleasant chat. And the presence or absence of that unexplainable yet unmistakable sense of Death in the room.

But this time, standing there was different. Looking back later, he would feel that he must have known it then, must have known in that very moment that his life was changed forever.

For as long as he lived, Gabriel would never forget the first impression he had of the woman standing at the bedside as she turned to face him. She was absolutely striking. Tall, with olive skin and glorious, almost arrogant, black curls that cascaded down the shoulders and back of her doctor's coat. And her eyes. Large, almond-shaped eyes the color of liquid midnight.

She was the most beautiful woman he had ever seen, and he drew his next breath on the sudden certainty that she always would be.

Patient, Gabriel, patient. You've been called here to attend a patient. His mental detour had taken only a fraction of a second, but his self-admonition snapped his mind back to the present situation in a way that was almost physical, and he leaned forward to place his hand on the bed rail, as though stopping himself from freefall. Or was he bracing himself? He would later wonder if there was a difference.

The female doctor extended her right hand to him while speaking rapidly and matter-of-factly. "Hi, I'm Dr. Ranya Abbasi. Thank you so much for coming quickly. Mr. Williams here had an MI two days ago and was to be moved to the floor later today or tomorrow, but now we've found him to have right hemiparesis. His last known normal was ten to fifteen minutes ago."

So this was no green intern. Looking more carefully at her badge, Gabriel saw that she was a cardiology fellow—actually, the Chief Cardiology Fellow. Well, well. Brains as well as beauty. Thank heavens. But it was even more than that. Her presence filled the room. She had an air of . . . competence, that was it. She stood there with the self-assurance of one who had worked hard all her life to get there, and knew exactly what she was doing.

Patient, Gabriel, patient. She has just told you that this patient—now your patient—came in with a heart attack and now is having a stroke. A stroke, Gabriel, a stroke!

"Well, clearly you've done the right thing," Gabriel heard himself say after clearing his throat. "Radiology's already been alerted. I'll just do a quick exam and we'll be on our way down to head CT, okay?"

He switched places with her, moving to the patient's right side while she watched from the foot of the bed. He could feel her eyes upon him, observing his exam, and he became conscious that he was performing an even more thorough neurological exam than usual. It also seemed to him that she had the uncanny ability to simultaneously watch both him and the cardiac monitor above the patient's head.

He wondered about her name; it sounded Arabic. Or Pakistani? No, Arabic, he felt certain somehow, in spite of the absence of any accent to clue him in. If anything, he thought he might have detected a faint drawing-out of some terminal syllables in just a few of her words, hinting at the slightest of Southern accents. He made a mental note to ask his best friend, Rasheed, about her. If anybody would know, he would.

CHAPTER TWO

"Life is short, the art long, opportunities fleeting, experiment treacherous, and judgment difficult."
—Hippocrates

RANYA HAD HEARD THE BROGUE in the neurologist's rich baritone—Irish? Scottish? She could never tell. And it wasn't as though one could ask. Not that it really mattered. Whatever he was, he wasn't inexperienced. Good. Finally. Maybe this day would turn out better than she had otherwise anticipated.

He seemed to do a more detailed physical exam than most of the neurologists she had encountered thus far. She wondered where he had trained and why she didn't recall seeing him before. Rasheed might know; he seemed to know everybody and then some.

She remained silent, not wanting to distract the neurologist from his assessment, but her mind was working in overdrive. She knew that Mr. Williams' heart had taken a bad hit from the heart attack and wasn't pumping well at all; could blood have pooled and clotted in the bottom of his heart, and now a piece of that clot had traveled to his brain? All of the body's blood supply cycled through the heart, after all, and that included the circulation to the brain. So a clot there could easily be the culprit for this stroke. She would have to be sure that another echocardiogram was ordered to look for it. After the neurologist was finished with his tests, of course.

Or maybe the clot was present on his first echocardiogram when he came in to the hospital and we didn't catch it. Ranya felt a leaden sensation fill her stomach.

Her silent fretting was interrupted by the neurologist asking her about her patient. "Was he responding to you earlier? And has he been able to maintain his airway, swallowing okay and all that? Anyone see him gurgling or trying to cough?"

There was an urgency in his voice, a hint of alarm even, and Ranya caught it. Then, as she was about to answer him, out of the corner of her eye she caught something else: an almost imperceptible change in her patient's breathing. She glanced toward the head of the bed, at Mr. Williams' face and at his chest. She was aware of the neurologist looking first at her, then sharply at Mr. Williams, who had suddenly made a strangled sound that was between a cough and a gasp. Before the alarms on his cardiac monitor started beeping, Ranya was already one step out of the room and yelling, "We need help in here!"

In the second that it took her to re-enter the room, the monitor had flatlined.

CHAPTER THREE

"Our greatest glory is not in never falling, but in rising every time we fall."
—Oliver Goldsmith

RANYA WAS IN CHARGE.

As alarms, beeps, and whistles went off all over the room and all over the telemetry floor, and as the overhead speakers trumpeted the repeated call of "Code Blue" across the hospital, Ranya was issuing orders, rapid fire.

She pointed one index finger at the neurologist and uttered a one-word command, the most crucial one of all: "Compressions."

Her right index finger moved next to Nancy with her second command: "Airway."

And as help from the rest of the floor nurses and the code team began filling the room, Ranya began directing them, too. She found an unusual calm in the conducting of a Code; although she had seen many others panic during resuscitations, she had never done so. She could see no point in panicking; how would that help the patient? To her, there could be no simpler, no more straightforward goal: to follow the science-based algorithm that stood a chance of bringing her patient back to life. Stay focused and in control, and the patient had a chance of living. Lose focus or allow incompetence to creep in, and it was all over.

It took less than a minute for everyone to start getting into place under Ranya's guidance. Defibrillator pads were placed on Mr. Williams' chest, the first dose of epinephrine was pushed down the intravenous line that emanated from his right arm, and the anesthesiology resident prepared to intubate.

Ranya went through her routine of checking all the crucial roles, surveying the scene before her, chaos coalescing into order. And in her survey, she moved to the other side of the bed and took note of the neurologist's chest compressions. He didn't seem to be compressing Mr. Williams' chest quickly or deeply enough every time. Not surprising: he was a neurologist, after all. How often were those docs called upon to perform CPR, anyway?

She placed two fingers on the side of Mr. Williams' neck, feeling for the carotid artery, palpating to see if they were getting a pulse with those compressions. And the answer was just as she had suspected: only erratically.

"Doctor," she said to the neurologist, leaning close enough to his ear so that she could be heard in a low voice, "we need more effective compressions."

And then, more loudly, pointing to one of the cardiac nurses in the room, "Sam, please get ready to switch off with the doctor here."

Having taken care of that to her satisfaction, Ranya turned her eyes to the cardiac monitor as the next round of epinephrine went in. It was only moments before she was rewarded with a change in the lines dancing across the monitor. In a louder but still controlled voice, she announced to the room, "We have V-tach. Charge the defibrillator."

She followed this by commanding, "All clear! Everybody clear!"

Her peripheral vision registered the image of the neurologist being shoved unceremoniously into a corner of the room as everyone scrambled to avoid the defibrillator shock that was coming. After checking quickly to ensure that no one was touching the patient or the patient's bed, Ranya announced, "Shocking!" and pressed her index finger to the "Shock" button on the defibrillator.

Two shocks later, and Ranya felt her shoulders relax, her breath exhale. She reported to the entire room, "Sinus tachycardia. We have a return to sinus rhythm. And—" she paused to check Mr. Williams' carotid pulse, "—we have a pulse."

Ranya allowed herself a very small smile. Mr. Williams was alive again.

CHAPTER FOUR

"A man who carries a cat by the tail learns something he can learn in no other way."

—Mark Twain

RANYA LET THE METAL CHAIR scrape against the cafeteria floor as she pulled it out to sit down for her dinner, which consisted of a hospital salad that had gone limp. Resting her elbows on the cold table, she lightly touched her fingers to her temples. It had been a very long day.

She thought about Mr. Williams, whom she had met for the first time in the emergency department less than three days ago. Such a nice guy. She had now gone over those first echocardiogram images three times. She had even asked one of the more experienced cardiology professors to look at them with her.

They had not missed anything on the cardiac ultrasound. There was no clot, at least not when he first came in. He would still need to have another echocardiogram done—maybe he had developed a clot in the interim since his admission. Maybe he had the irregular heart rhythm of atrial fibrillation, known to cause clots that can go to the brain. But Ranya could not recall seeing any evidence of atrial fibrillation on his cardiac monitor at any time.

She sighed. She would have to be sure to go through the telemetry records, too. And maybe he had a history of atrial fibrillation from earlier and no one had known it. Or maybe he just had incredibly bad luck.

Why did it always seem that the nicest people were the ones to have the worst complications? Mr. Anthony Williams was a sixty-seven-year-old retired general contractor with an East Tennessee accent unique to Knoxville. She knew his details by heart. He had the kindest manners and kept a sense of humor about him, even as Ranya and her team were evaluating him for the chest pain that had brought him to the door of their emergency department in the first place.

And then there was his wife, who had stood beside him all the way, with a worry in her eyes that he tried to joke away. Well, it turned out his wife had been right to worry so much after all. The worst part of Ranya's day had been breaking the news of Mr. Williams' stroke and ensuing cardiac arrest to his dear wife.

Her mind was about to replay that gloomy scene when she noticed a tall man approaching from the far end of the dining hall. About six feet tall, full head of chestnut hair, face appearing clean-shaven in spite of the evening hour. It was the neurologist from earlier. But he wasn't wearing his white coat now; just the blue Oxford shirt and tie, black slacks. And shiny, polished black shoes. *Heh*, she thought with absent-minded amusement, *a doctor who takes care of his shoes.*

He was standing at her table now. Lightly drumming his fingertips on its far corner, he cleared his throat and began with, "Ah, hello there."

Ranya folded her hands and sat back in her chair, looking up at him expectantly. "Yes, hello."

The neurologist tugged at his tie. "Very nice job with that code today. Impeccable performance, actually."

Ranya blinked at him.

He continued, "No doubt you already know that the head CT confirmed a stroke. Given the circumstances of the code and the—um—traumatic chest compressions, I did not feel it wise to administer tPA, given the serious risk of bleeding and all that, you know."

"But," he went on, seeming to want to lighten this less-than-ideal report, "surprisingly, it doesn't appear to be an overly large stroke territory on the CT scan, and we'll continue to observe and do what we can. I'll be following right along with you in Mr. Williams' care. Be there with you every step of the way."

Ranya nodded her head, looked down at the table, then looked back up at him. "Thank you," was all she said, nodding again.

But the neurologist didn't leave then. "So," he said after a brief pause, "you're the lucky one on call tonight?"

"Uh, no, I was the lucky one on call when Mr. Williams came in." And involuntarily, her shoulders sank.

She could feel the neurologist's alert eyes upon her, examining her face before dropping his gaze to the table between them. "Ah, well then," he began, and then paused, making space for silence. After a reflective moment, he raised his eyes to hers and began again, "Well, you know, I find that a drink or two can do wonders on a Saturday night like this one—care to join me?"

Ranya studied him for a second. Then she stood up, gathered her belongings, and faced him squarely. "I don't drink," she said. And then, unable to keep the weariness from her voice any longer, she said, "Good night, Dr. . . . ."

He filled in quickly, "O'Brien. Dr. Gabriel O'Brien. But you can call me Gabe."

"Good night, Dr. O'Brien." She walked away, leaving him standing in silence.

CHAPTER FIVE

"Palestinian are her eyes . . ."
—Mahmoud Darwish,
"A Lover from Palestine"
(translated from the Arabic by Yasmine S. Ali)

"I no longer physically live in the place we had set out from. Yet I very much live there, because this place is no longer just a mere geographical entity, but my idiom, my ethos, my laughter."
—Fawaz Turki,
The Disinherited: Journal of a Palestinian Exile

ON A FLIGHT OVER THE MEDITERRANEAN, Rasheed was sitting in a window seat in the first-class compartment, looking forward to returning to Nashville after his visit to Ramallah. As he stared out the plane window at the bright blue sky, he found himself thinking of Ranya.

Would she be upset with him for falling out of touch for a few days? It was not always easy to get a call through, especially with the eight-hour time difference and her hectic schedule. Not to mention his constant family obligations, trying to get to everyone who wanted to see him before he left. But he was certain she remembered when he would be returning. She'd be there to pick him up at the airport, she had said. Ranya always remembered.

He imagined how busy she must be with the start of another new medical year, her Chief Fellow year. Such a high achiever, that Ranya. He recalled how he had met her last year at a joint department party of the whole cardiovascular service. He'd thought then, as he still did now, that she was gorgeous, just gorgeous, sharp as a whip, and, best of all, Palestinian. Well, okay, so she was Palestinian-American, having been born in America, but she always seemed proud of her heritage, and seemed to have a good grasp on the history of the region. And that thrilled Rasheed to his core. A reverence for heritage, and even more, an understanding of the history of that heritage—their *shared* heritage—meant everything to him.

He thought now of the West Bank city of Ramallah from which he was returning, the hometown that was always with him in his heart and soul, wherever else in the world he found himself. *Ram Allah.* The mountain of God. From the Aramaic and the Arabic. He, Rasheed Haddad, was named after its founder, who had overseen the building of the town in the mid-1500s on a mountain that overlooked the plains of west Palestine.

Just ten kilometers north of Jerusalem, the one-mountain town of Ramallah eventually became the sprawling city that consumed the seven or eight surrounding mountains, and from those mountains, one could see all the way to the port of Yaffa with its night lights illuminating the Mediterranean Sea.

So a small town it was no more. It wasn't even the town of his boyhood any longer. Almost since its founding, Ramallah had been a majority-Christian town—specifically, Greek Orthodox. But that, too, had rapidly changed in recent years.

The loud, ever-present hum of the jet engines enveloped him in a cloud of white noise, and Rasheed closed his eyes and tried to rest, but found himself thinking of the cardiothoracic surgeon, the only one for kilometers around, who had inspired him to become a heart surgeon himself. That surgeon hailed from one of the oldest Ramallah families, and, wow, the stories he could tell.

But Rasheed had his own stories now, stories of a different kind. He had shared with his mentor a couple of the new heart valve techniques he had learned in the States, told him about the hospitality of the American South. He might even have mentioned meeting Ranya.

Then again, if he were being honest with himself, the fact was that he couldn't stop mentioning Ranya.

His family's home in Ramallah filled his mind's eye . . . the house in which he grew up, with its rough-hewn rock exterior that kept out the heat of the day, and the cool marble-floored interior covered in Persian and Egyptian rugs. He had found nothing like it in America, at least not yet. And he had always thought he would go back, bringing his much-needed skills to his people and his hometown. But it wasn't that easy now. And meeting Ranya had changed all that anyway.

He found that he had to agree with Ranya: her hometown of Nashville was a beautiful place to live, as was the rest of Tennessee. He smiled to himself as he thought of Nashville's four seasons. Ramallah had them, too, but to a milder extent, and with more predictability to the weather. Nashville's summers were humid beyond reason, but given that most of his days were spent in the sterile coldness of the operating room, it didn't really seem to matter.

It might be a shock to Gabriel's system, though, now that he thought about it. He wondered if Gabe was ready to wilt, or kill him, or both, now that he was in the middle of his first Nashville summer. But still he felt it fortunate that he'd been able to convince Gabe to take that neurology position in Nashville. It would be good to see him again, too.

CHAPTER SIX

"I love you—I am at rest with you—I have come home."
—Dorothy Sayers,
Busman's Honeymoon

RASHEED WAS A TALL MAN, and Ranya had no trouble spotting him in the stream of disembarking passengers, even before he made it off the jet-bridge and into the terminal at the Nashville airport. He was a sight for sore eyes after being away for three weeks. She made no effort to keep from grinning like a fool when his stunning green eyes locked with hers and his face lit up with recognition and excitement. His long stride quickened as he made his way toward her.

They embraced. Tightly. "How was your flight?" she asked.

"Which one?" he laughed. They both knew what a long, arduous journey it was to travel from Nashville to any destination in the Middle East. In fact, she didn't know how he managed to look so good after all that flight time.

"How are your parents, your family?" she asked as they walked together toward baggage claim.

"Doing well, thanks. I told them all about you. I couldn't help myself."

He smiled at her and took her hand in his. She felt her cheeks flush.

"And listen, Ranya," he continued as he squeezed her hand, "I'm so sorry I wasn't able to phone you for the past few days. With the time difference and not being sure when you were on call, plus all the family around trying to wish me farewell and see me off . . . I mean, you know how it is—"

"Of course," she said. "Don't worry about it. How was Ramallah?"

"It was really good. Really good. It's not like when I was growing up there, you know, but what place is? Everyone sends their regards, by the way. And you know what I realized? Ramallah is actually a lot like Nashville!"

"What? Really? How so?"

"Well, the hospitality, for one thing. The emphasis on honor and pride of place. And," he chuckled, "how there are genteel ways of saying 'no' without ever using the word itself."

"Ah, now, Rasheed," she teased, "how could anyone ever say no to you, in any language?"

CHAPTER SEVEN

"Fortune favors the bold."
—Virgil,
The Aeneid

"But Rasheed, it's a once-in-a-lifetime opportunity," Ranya said, her voice rising. "A great opportunity to learn from the best in the world, from the father of structural heart interventions!"

"It's just that . . ." Rasheed ran a hand through his hair. "I mean, good grief, Ranya—France for a month? I just got back from Ramallah last week, and I was hoping we could spend some time together. You know?"

"Well, all the approvals just came through, and I'm so lucky to have this opportunity. Surely you must see that, Rasheed. This could change my life."

I was hoping I *could change your life,* he thought, but held his tongue. He wondered if this would always be the case: would Ranya's career always be her life? Would anyone or anything else ever get to come first?

He made himself swallow, hoping the touch of bitterness he felt would go down with it. Maybe he wasn't being fair. From what she had told him about her parents, all that had happened, he could understand a good bit of her relentless drive and ambition. And he couldn't say he wasn't proud of her for it; that drive was one of the features that had most attracted him to her in the first place, and still did.

Plus, she was right: it was a great opportunity. Wouldn't he have taken it, if the same sort of chance had come his way?

He liked to think that he was talented, skilled, but he knew that he was nothing compared to Ranya. She was truly gifted. He couldn't let himself stand in her way.

But he also feared that he was nothing *without* Ranya. He wanted to be sure she knew it, too.

They were standing in the middle of his living room and, letting impulse get the best of him, he took both her hands and lowered himself onto one knee.

"Rasheed, oh my God, what are you doing?!"

He made himself go on, in spite of the shock on her face. "Ranya, I will always support you in whatever you do and whatever path you choose. Please know that, beyond the shadow of a doubt. I just want to be the one to walk beside you on that path."

"Um, Rasheed, I—"

"No, Ranya, please, just hear me out. You don't even have to give me an answer right now. But I can't bear to have us be apart for so long, again, without at least letting you know how serious I am about you. Would you marry me? At least consider it?"

The words coming out of his mouth sounded like babble, even to him. This wasn't how he had wanted it to go. He didn't even have a ring for her yet. And in the middle of his living room, in the middle of an argument, no less. He promised himself he'd have a proper do-over later. Now, he just wanted to get his feelings across to her, and, hopefully, get her to commit to him once and for all.

"Goodness, Rasheed, it's just for a month. I'll be back, you know. I'm not abandoning you." She gave him a half-hearted smile. "Hey, just think of it as a chance for me to practice my French."

He held his position and continued to look up at her.

"Rasheed, please get up. Please. *S'il vous plait?*"

"Not until you say you'll think about it."

"Okay, okay. Of course I will. I'll think about it."

Rasheed stood up and pulled her close. "I love you, Ranya," he murmured in her ear.

She leaned back, her hands on his shoulders, and looked him in the eye. "I love you too, Rasheed."

CHAPTER EIGHT

"She prized the frank, the open-hearted, the eager character beyond all others . . . She felt that she could so much more depend upon the sincerity of those who sometimes looked or said a careless or hasty thing, than of those whose presence of mind never varied, whose tongue never slipped."

—Jane Austen,

Persuasion

GABRIEL LEANED BACK IN HIS SEAT and closed his eyes. It was a short flight to Atlanta, and then there'd be the longer one to Dublin.

No sooner had he begun to relax than the urgent voice of one of the flight attendants caught his attention.

"Is there a doctor on the flight? If so, please press your flight attendant call button to identify yourself to the crew."

Gabriel sighed and reached up to push the button. No rest for the weary, it would seem.

As he followed the flight attendant, it became apparent that he was not the only physician on this flight, because he could see someone else up the aisle, already moving into position beside the patient. He would still offer his help; it never hurt to have an extra pair of eyes—and another brain—brought to bear on such a situation.

His own heart nearly arrested at the sight of the head of black curls that came into view as he got closer. She was not the patient, he was happy to find, but had answered the call for medical assistance, too—one step ahead of him. How she had gone through the airport in Nashville, and then boarded the same plane, without him ever noticing, must be a testament to his mind's preoccupation with the news about his grandfather. So make that two steps ahead. He was beginning to think he would never be able to catch up with her.

"May I be of assistance?" he inquired upon reaching his destination, at her elbow.

Ranya jerked her head upward, her eyes widening in surprise upon meeting his.

"We've got to stop meeting like this," he quipped, then immediately wished he hadn't.

She stared at him. "Yeah," was all she replied. Then, without further delay, she filled him in on the details of the passenger who had been experiencing trouble with his breathing. Gabriel could see that the flight crew had already placed a nasal cannula under the man's nostrils to deliver oxygen, and Ranya had her fingers on his wrist, monitoring his pulse.

They took over the seats next to him for the rest of the flight, and Ranya continued to reassure him that he would be all right, that they would make it to Atlanta, where he would be met by an ambulance and a medical team. She counseled him about his heart condition, told him that she was a chief cardiology fellow, and that alone seemed to calm him and ease his breathing.

A passenger from across the aisle, once things had calmed down, leaned over and touched Ranya's shoulder. "Where do you work? I want you to be my doctor."

Well, guess I'm chopped liver. But Gabriel had to admit that he was proud to be with her, even though he hardly knew her. He would have to rectify that upon his return to Nashville.

Once they touched down in Atlanta, an ambulance was there to greet them, just as Ranya had promised. As they walked into the terminal together, Gabriel found himself chatting to her, telling her about his grandfather's passing and his connecting flight to Ireland so he could attend the funeral. It felt good to be able to talk about it with her, and she showed genuine concern, the most emotion he'd gotten out of her yet. He just wished it could have been under different circumstances. It made him all the more eager to know everything about her.

They said farewell as they went in different directions to catch their connecting flights, and as he watched her walk away, Gabriel realized that he hadn't even asked her where she was going.

CHAPTER NINE

"Let us not waste our energies brooding over the more we might have got. Let us look upon what it is we have got."
—Michael Collins

October 1996

RASHEED'S CALLER ID WAS flashing Ranya's number. Happily, he picked up the phone. "Hello, *Habibti*," he said, hoping that the broad smile he was wearing could be heard in his voice. He had been delighted to have her back after her trip to Paris, which, to hear her talk, was successful beyond her highest hopes.

She was happy, and that made him happy.

Ranya wasn't one for endearments, though, and as usual, she launched right into the purpose for her call. "Rasheed, how would you like to see this movie with me on Friday? It looks really good. It's called *Michael Collins,* and it's about the Irish revolutionary and freedom-fighter who brought down the British and got independence for Ireland. The start of the IRA, I think, and all that, you know." Rasheed was a little surprised at how excited she seemed. She sounded breathless.

"Michael Collins, huh?" Rasheed replied. "Never heard of him, but definitely sounds interesting. Mind if I bring a good friend? I think this'd be right up his alley."

"Yeah, sure, of course. Bring whomever you want"—and now Rasheed could hear the teasing smile in her voice—"as long as it's not another pretty woman." He could almost see those long lashes winking at him.

"You're the only one for me, *Habibti*, you know that," he said. "See you soon."

He hadn't pushed her on his marriage proposal since her return; she had said she would think about it, and she was clearly committed to him, and that was good enough for him. For now.

And anyway, he'd been so preoccupied with work and dealing with hospital politics, he didn't feel up to facing or creating further drama in his personal life. He had been so busy, in fact, that he had only found a chance to say hello to Gabriel once in passing. Rasheed had called him when he'd learned that his grand-father had died, but the only available conversation was with Gabe's answering machine, and he knew that Gabe had taken time off to be in Ireland.

So Rasheed saw Friday night as a good opportunity not only to see a movie with Ranya, but to see his best friend again for more than two seconds in a hospital hallway. From Ranya's description of the movie, it sounded as though Gabe would definitely be interested, and anyway, Rasheed felt sure that he would enjoy meeting Ranya.

When Gabriel stepped into the lobby of the independent movie house where *Michael Collins* was showing, the first claim on his attention came from the mouth-watering smell of corn popping; the second came from the sight of his best friend standing side by side with the most beautiful woman in the world.

The good doctors were waiting for him in front of the movie poster beside the entrance to Theater 1, with Liam Neeson looming formidably behind them, his stylized figure suspended above an exuberant crowd, hands clenched and gesturing forcefully into the air in his role as Michael Collins.

Rasheed's sleek leather running shoes gleamed against the deep-brown parquet flooring, squeaking as he moved animatedly in conversation with Dr. Ranya Abbasi. Rasheed was tossing back his full head of wavy black hair now, laughing that full-throated, gregarious laugh of his, and Gabriel marveled once again at how readily his friend could seem at ease with almost anyone.

But the woman at his side was not just anyone; she was the one woman Gabriel had been hoping every day to meet again, the one woman he had not been able to get out of his mind in over three months. And now here she was.

She was as lovely as he had remembered, if not lovelier. His heart rate quickened and he felt a sudden thrill at the prospect of finally being able to be in her company again. Maybe this time would be different. They were going to a movie, not another medical emergency, after all.

He took a deep breath before waving to them. As he approached, Rasheed reached out one arm excitedly and said, "Ah, here he is! Ranya, meet one of my very best friends, Dr. Gabriel O'Brien."

Ranya granted him a brief smile. "Dr. O'Brien, we meet again," she nodded her head as she shook his hand.

"Please, as I said before, call me Gabe. Or Gabriel, at the very least."

"So you two have met?" said Rasheed, looking from Gabriel to Ranya with an expression of great interest.

"Yes," answered Ranya, turning to Rasheed but still glancing at Gabriel as she added, "a few months ago, I believe, in a Stroke Code."

Gabriel was surprised that she did not mention their episode on the flight to Atlanta. There must be more going on here than he had surmised. He could have brought it up himself—he had about two seconds in which he could still do so tactfully—but he let those seconds elapse and committed himself to following Ranya's lead . . . possibly forever.

"Well, Gabe, this is my amazing girlfriend I've been wanting you to meet," Rasheed said proudly.

And there it was. Gabriel's gut absorbed the punch, and he fought hard against the sudden wave of nausea that threatened to overtake him. He felt the rush of heat to his face, tried to keep it down. And, giving thanks for small triumphs, finally managed the thinnest of smiles. But that turned out to be the best he could do on a moment's notice, as a verbal reply utterly failed him.

Rasheed, irrepressible fellow that he was, simply proceeded on, waving his arm and gesturing them both in to the theater. "C'mon, guys, let's get our seats, yeah?"

Rasheed found them good seats in the theater, slightly left of center, and with a surgeon's grace folded his six-foot-two-inch frame into the seat between Ranya and Gabriel. When the movie's opening text appeared on the screen, briefly detailing Ireland's long struggle for independence and self-determination, Rasheed leaned over to Ranya and whispered—too loudly, Gabriel thought—"Sounds like the Palestinians."

Ranya simply held out her open palm toward the screen, silently mouthing, "I told you so."

As the movie went on, Gabriel had to admit that it was well done. It was an admirable and well-executed effort that truly brought to life the history of the time, highlighting one of the masterminds of the Irish War of Independence, and Liam Neeson as Michael Collins was at his very finest, to be sure. A mighty performance. It was uncanny how much he seemed to resemble the Big Fella himself.

Gabriel cast the briefest of glances in Ranya's direction. She seemed fascinated and totally absorbed in the history, his country's history, playing out on the screen. From the Easter Rising to the War of Independence to the Civil War that followed the signing of the Anglo-Irish Treaty.

And he noticed, too, how the fingers of her right hand were lightly and comfortably intertwined with those of Rasheed's left. He looked away.

They sat in reverent silence through the closing credits, and when they finally rose from their seats, Rasheed was the first to speak. "Thirty-one years old. He was younger than I am when he died," he said, shaking his head in wonder.

"Aw, now, you're ancient anyway," Gabriel teased.

"It's incredible, isn't it? Just unbelievable," Ranya said, eyes wide with wonder. "What a great movie."

Ranya continued talking as they queued to leave the theater. "I am just so fascinated by this Michael Collins character and his story," she commented to Rasheed. "What a genius he was. What a righteous struggle, how he took on the British. What a life!"

Rasheed nodded his head. "What an unlikely triumph of the underdog." Turning to Gabriel, who stood in line behind him, he said, "You Irish never cease to amaze, do you?"

Gabriel just smiled at his friend.

"I need to know more about this," Ranya declared to the air as they exited the theater. "I have to know more about Irish history now."

Well, that was a task Gabriel was up to. Irish history was a rollicking ride, and he could tell her all about it. He was already contemplating how to get more information to her when Rasheed proposed they all hit Sunset Grill for dinner.

Gabriel hid his surprise at being invited along for the next portion of the evening; given that Rasheed and Ranya seemed to be eager to continue their discussion of the movie, surely that was reason enough to justify his presence. A conversation about Ireland and its politics—Gabriel, God save him, was always up for that.

While waiting in line for a table, their dialogue continued. Rasheed was frowning, expressing his displeasure that the movie was "too violent." Gabriel, who had his hands in his pockets, now put his shoulders back in a gesture that served to broaden his chest as he raised his eyebrows and scoffed, "Are my ears deceiving me? Did I just hear a Palestinian say this movie was *too violent*?"

Ranya laughed, saying, "You know, Rasheed, I have to say I was thinking the same thing. It wasn't all that bad. And it wasn't like it was gratuitous violence. I think every one of those scenes served a purpose."

Gabriel agreed, "Yeah, you know, those were violent times. Very much so. Still are in the North at times. It doesn't really serve anyone to look past that, you know? It's just reality."

Gabriel went on, warming to his subject, "And, like, how many Bloody Sundays are we gonna have? You know that scene in the movie where the British tanks roll into the Gaelic football match at Croke Park and open fire on the crowd? On a Sunday in the fall of 1920? Dublin was playing Tipperary, and I know so many people who had relatives who were there. In the crowd, watching the game. There was news that Collins had sent out his Twelve Apostles and members of the IRA's Dublin Brigade to assassinate multiple British agents that morning—you saw that depicted in the movie, too. Well, that was the same day as the Croke Park massacre, with the assassinations in the morning and the massacre in the afternoon. A bloody Sunday indeed."

"Wow, wow, wow," murmured Ranya, shaking her head. "You know, my great-uncle died fighting the British in Palestine, during the Arab revolt of the late 1930s. My father thought so much of that, he broke with tradition and named my brother, his only son, after that uncle instead of after my grandfather."

Gabriel held her gaze and nodded his approval.

Rasheed turned to Ranya and remarked, "Huh. I didn't know that."

Ranya, seeming not to want to dwell on it, attempted to bring the discussion back to the movie by asking Gabriel, "So the movie really was pretty accurate historically, do you think?"

"Well, of course, there were some Hollywood-ish elements and some changes that were made in the making of the film, to make it seem more dramatic, I suppose," Gabriel replied.

"Yeah, like who knows if that love triangle was really true?" Rasheed asked, making a cynical face.

"Oh, no," Gabriel said, glancing down at his menu, "that part was, in fact, absolutely true. The love triangle was real."

Gabriel looked up and met their eyes. "Harry Boland loved Kitty Kiernan and wanted to marry her, but she ended up engaged to Collins."

"So are you suggesting that Collins didn't really love her, but Boland did?" Rasheed asked.

"Oh, no, no, no—by all accounts, Michael Collins deeply loved Kitty," Gabriel answered.

Ranya exclaimed, "You know so much about this, Gabriel!"

Good God, maybe I've finally impressed her. "Well, if you'd like to know more, I have a number of good books I can lend you, including a great biography of Collins," he said.

He felt Rasheed staring at him. "Or, uh, I could just leave them with Rasheed next time I'm by his house."

Ranya rewarded him with a gracious smile. "Thank you, Gabriel."

"You know," Rasheed broke in, "something that strikes me is the similarity between the split in Irish sentiment upon the signing of the Treaty with Britain, and the reaction we've seen among Palestinians since Arafat signed the Oslo Accords."

Ranya nodded. "Yeah, there are so many that say Arafat just totally sold out when he did that—just like they said about Collins, apparently. I mean, they wanna know: what was Arafat thinking? What about the Palestinian right of return, among so many other things, you know?"

Rasheed was about to speak, but she waved him off so she could continue. "But now that I've seen the movie, I wonder if he also wants it to be a stepping stone—just as Michael Collins did. Both hoping that their compromises would finally bring peace. And oh, boy, look how that turned out!"

Gabriel mused, "Irish nationalists, Palestinian nationalists—not so very different, are they? And I think we could say the same of any nationalist movement anywhere in the world."

Rasheed retorted, "But it's more than just a 'movement,' Gabe. We're talking about people's countries here. We're talking about people's lives. And their God-given right to determine how their lives should go."

Gabriel scrunched up his face and began, "You think it's God-given, do you? I mean—"

But Rasheed cut him off. He put both hands up, closed them into fists, then opened them again. He pursed his lips and spoke hesitantly at first, then seemed more decisive about sharing his next statement aloud. "You know . . . well, you know that scene in the movie where Collins and Boland are on a ferry together, and Collins makes the remark that he hates the British 'for making hate necessary'?"

Gabriel and Ranya both nodded and murmured their recognition. Rasheed continued, sober-faced, "Well, I get that." He straightened his back as they looked at him with dawning understanding. He repeated, as if it would explain everything: "'I hate them for making hate necessary.' I get it."

CHAPTER TEN

"We have always found the Irish a bit odd. They refuse to be English."
–Winston Churchill

ON THEIR SUNDAY MORNING walk through Nashville's Edwin Warner Park, Ranya asked Rasheed about Gabriel.

"Ah, yeah, I've known him since we were residents in training at the same hospital in Boston," Rasheed told her. They had been there for one another through thick and thin, becoming the best of friends even as they pursued very different specialties.

"Got the brain of a neurologist—pun intended—gotta think everything to death, you know. But he's a good man, that Gabe. Like a brother to me," Rasheed said. "Salt of the earth. The kind of man who would take a bullet for you."

Rasheed stopped in his tracks then, looked up at the autumn sky and squinted. When he turned back to Ranya, one eye still squinting, he added, "And I guess I would do the same for him."

"Well, then," Ranya said, "I guess I have to be thankful there aren't a lot of bullets flying around Nashville!"

They were coming upon a series of rolling green meadows now, and in the distance they could see a figure running with two dogs across a wide-open field. As they got closer, Ranya saw that the dogs had gorgeous coats of rich mahogany that gleamed in the sunlight. Rasheed was the first to recognize their owner, and when he did, he let out a great laugh and said, "Well! And the devil appears!"

They heard Gabriel call out to his dogs, "*Tar anseo,*" and watched as the two canines returned swiftly and happily to him. One dog sat on either side of him, and he put a hand in front of each of their noses and commanded, "*Fan.*" The dogs stayed right where they were.

Ranya strode over and asked, "Are those Irish Setters? A friend I grew up with had one. I really loved that dog."

Gabriel knelt down between his dogs, put a hand on the back of each and ruffled the fur there. "Oh, these are the nicest dogs you'll ever meet. You'll never meet an unfriendly Irish Setter."

He looked up with a mischievous grin and added, "Can't say the same for all Irishmen, I'm afraid." He winked at them both.

Rasheed laughed and Ranya smiled—how could she hold back a smile in the presence of those beautiful dogs?

She asked Gabriel, "What was that you were saying to them earlier?"

"Oh, that was Irish."

"Irish?"

"Yes, the Irish language, you know."

Rasheed bumped Ranya with his elbow. But Ranya, undeterred, stood with her arms akimbo, and said defensively to Rasheed, "Well, I'm not trying to be disrespectful. I just thought the Irish spoke English."

Rasheed raised his eyebrows at her and said, "Now think about that, Ranya, what you've just said, after the movie we just saw."

Gabriel interjected, not unkindly, "Like all the peoples of the world, we have our own language, but it was suppressed for hundreds of years as part of the oppression of the Irish people. You may have heard it referred to as Gaelic."

Gabriel stood to his full height then. "Come, let's walk, eh? And I'll tell you all about it." He issued another command to his dogs, "*Ar aghaidh leat,*" and they bounded forward.

The deciduous trees were putting on a brilliant display that autumn, their changing colors contrasting with the ever-faithful deep green of the eastern red cedars. Competing gently with the sounds of the forest, Gabriel explained how Irish was a Celtic language similar to Scots Gaelic, Welsh, and Cornish.

Ranya could hear the pride in his voice as he continued. "It really is an ancient language, because when the Celts introduced the original language, known as Primitive Irish, to the island of Ireland, it was maybe as far back as 2,500 years ago. Pretty cool, right?"

"Wow, yeah, I didn't know all that," Ranya replied, keeping her eyes trained on the dogs that continued to run ahead of them.

"But then," Gabriel went on, his face darkening, "occupation by the English made the English language the primary and official language, required for all legal transactions. And then with the Protestant Reformation came this idea that Irish was a barbaric language, and so English continued to gain ground as the language to be used in books and documents and to be spoken by all 'civilized' people."

Rasheed grimaced at this and shook his head. "Just like some people think of Arabic as 'barbaric.'" He shook his head again and added with disdain, "Idiots."

"Yeah," Gabriel chuckled, "but we Irish have always been stubborn enough to know ourselves, and to refuse to be told what to be, especially by the likes of the English."

"A stubborn Irishman, huh?" Rasheed joked. "I'm sure I wouldn't know anything about that."

Gabriel pursed his lips and lightly punched Rasheed's arm.

"Okay, okay, so what about now, Gabriel? Clearly the language survived. Does everyone in Ireland speak Irish?" Ranya asked.

"So, yeah, the Irish language survived, even as it was driven underground at times, and now, it's a requirement that it be taught in all our schools, and under the Irish Constitution, it's recognized as the national and first official language of Ireland."

Gabriel beamed at them both, and took a little bow. And then he invited them over to his apartment for tea.

CHAPTER ELEVEN

"Being Irish, he had an abiding sense of tragedy, which sustained him through
temporary periods of joy."
—William Butler Yeats

RANYA STOOD IN GABRIEL'S living room, fixated on the display above his
mantel. A flag of three vertical bands of color, green and orange on either side of a
white center, occupied prime real estate on the textured brick wall. She knew now
that this was the flag of the Republic of Ireland. Its presence there reminded her
of the Palestinian flag that hung over Rasheed's mantel. But just below Gabriel's
flag, there were two wooden sticks, one crossed diagonally over the other. They
looked a bit like hockey sticks, but not quite. Ranya asked Gabriel about them.

Gabriel reached up and took down one of the sticks. Handing it to Ranya as
she stood beside Rasheed, he said, "That, my friends, is a hurley. It is what we use
to hit the ball in the uniquely Irish sport of hurling."

Ranya, who had been turning it over in both hands, made to give it to Rasheed,
but he declined, shrugging his shoulders. "I already know what it is." Rasheed
jutted his chin in Gabriel's direction and said, "But he's the one who knows how
to use it."

So she gave the hurley back to Gabriel, who demonstrated to her the wrist motion used to wield it properly. He smiled broadly and said, "Every self-respecting
Irish boy knows how to play hurling."

Ranya asked, "And how do you play hurling? I mean, what sort of game is it?"

"Oh, that's another story for you," Gabriel replied. "But first, let me get the kettle on.

"Now, I know from Rasheed that you Arabs have all sorts of teas and tastes in tea and coffee, and so on, so I think you'll enjoy this rather special treat—well, I think it's rather special, having just brought it back from Ireland with me—it's Barry's tea, and I hope you'll love it as much as I do," Gabriel chattered as he moved to the kitchen. They both moved with him, as did the dogs, one of whom appeared to be glued to Ranya.

He continued talking, animated now, as he set his stainless-steel kettle down on the gas stove. "Tea is a big deal in Ireland, of course, but this is just what I have here, and I find it to be all right."

Was it Ranya's imagination, or did Gabriel seem nervous? She wondered if he was naturally such a chatty type.

Rasheed waved his hands in the air. "No worries, Gabriel, I've had that tea before, and I'm sure Ranya will love it," he said.

Turning to Ranya then, Gabriel brought his conversation back to the sport of hurling. "Okay, so hurling, like the Irish language, is of ancient Gaelic origin. We think it's been played for at least 3,000 years or something like that. It's kind of like ice hockey on grass, but the only protection worn is a plastic helmet. You use that stick, the hurley, to hit a small leather ball called a *sliotar* between the goalposts of the opposing team. There are different points awarded for how it goes through the goalposts, either over or under the crossbar. Over the crossbar gives you one point, but under the crossbar is a net guarded by a goalkeeper, so that's considered a goal and is worth three points."

He paused, as if deciding how much detail was really necessary. Ranya hoped her eyes weren't glazing over, but it was a bit too much to follow. She was more of a visual learner.

As if he had read her mind, Gabriel's next remark was, "Um, it's probably best if you see it in action, because as with any game, it has a lot of its own rules, which can seem complicated. But just know that it's pretty much the Irish national sport and incredibly popular with us."

He paused again, and then, as if he just couldn't resist, added proudly, "It's regarded as the world's oldest and fastest field sport. Some have called it 'the fastest game played on grass.' It really is very exciting."

"Sounds like it," said Ranya, trying to be kind. "So do you still play?"

"Oh, no, not now," Gabriel replied. "I haven't played since I entered medical school."

"Did you go to medical school here in the States?"

"No, University College Cork. I was born in Navan, in County Meath, but my family moved to Cork City when I was a child."

Rasheed leaned over to Ranya and added, "Gabe did his first residency training in Ireland."

"And now here I am, after another residency in America, an attending neurologist, at your service," Gabriel finished, inclining his head.

The dog at Ranya's side nudged and licked her hand, and Ranya glanced down at him.

"Shamrock is quite taken with you," Gabriel observed.

"Oh, so that's his name—Shamrock? That's great!" Ranya knelt down and ran her hands over the dog's long, soft ears. "Hi, Shamrock," she cooed, "nice to meet you."

"And the other is . . .?" Ranya asked, directing her gaze toward the dog leaning against Rasheed's leg.

Gabriel started to answer, but Rasheed beat him to it. "This is Maggie. She's the smarter one, clearly, because she likes me more. She knows greatness when she sees it."

Ranya laughed. "Well, I don't think it's a competition."

"That is true," Gabriel said. "Because there can be no competition, not when it comes to the Resplendent, the Most Regal, the Most Radiantly Remarkable Rasheed. You are without peer, my friend. Tell me, is the air gettin' thin up there in your high tower? A bit lonely at the top? 'Cause I wouldn't know."

They were all laughing now, but Ranya knew that every joke contained at least a kernel of truth.

Gabriel invited Ranya and Rasheed to sit together on the black-and-white couch in his living room, and he pulled around a tall, wicker bar stool to face them. He sat upon it with one leg bent and the other outstretched, so that the tip of his impeccably-white sneaker grazed the beige carpet. Ranya had been amused to see Maggie abandon Rasheed in favor of lying down beside Gabriel's foot, and Shamrock trotted over to her and threw himself down at her feet. She reached out and once again stroked the soft, smooth fur of that glorious coat she so admired.

"Look, Gabe," Rasheed was saying, "I know it's been a pain to get to this point, but compared to all you've gone through to get here, it'll be relatively smooth sailing from now on. And you like Nashville so far, right?"

"Oh, sure, lovely place, 'tis grand really," Gabriel responded, setting his teacup down on the breakfast bar behind him to give Rasheed a thumb's up.

"And I've only been here in Nashville for a few months," Gabriel added upon further reflection. "No doubt there is much more to discover and enjoy once I've completely got my bearings."

Ranya was certain it wasn't her imagination this time. He was trying not to look at her. He was making a valiant effort of directing his gaze at Rasheed.

"Although, you know," he went on, folding his arms across his chest, "I don't think I'll ever get used to all the madness of Americans in certain areas of life. It's as bad here as it was in Boston, if not worse."

"Madness?" Ranya asked, forcing him to look her way.

He shifted in his seat and said, "Oh, God, yes—the cars are huge, the malls are huge, the guns are huge, even the roads are huge! And I have to say to you both—and Rasheed, I know you've heard me say this many a time before—in

Ireland we treat the patient, not the chart, and I'm afraid that here it's going the other way 'round."

He went further, "That's just one of many concerning issues with American medicine, I fear. I don't know that the overall practice of medicine in this country is headed in the right direction; in fact, I think it's definitely not."

They all sat in silence for a moment. Then Gabriel spoke again, his face brightening as he added, "But who knows what the future may hold?"

Ranya decided to seize this opening to change the subject, and asked him, "So, why neurology? What drew you to that as a specialty?"

Gabriel's face completely changed, his eyes growing wider and more earnest as an almost childlike look of wonder came over him. "Because it's like magic," he said in a reverent tone. "If you're good, and observant, and really know your physical exam, you can tell where a lesion in the brain is hiding from something as simple as the way a person's big toe turns up or down, or from the way their eyes move. Or have them close their eyes and hold their hands out in front of them, and get a glimpse of their cerebellum. What other specialty can say that?"

"Gabe the magician," Rasheed said, smiling at him.

"And I know you cardiac types," Gabriel wagged his finger at both of them, "think that the heart is the center of the universe, but we are who we are because of the brain. In all its endlessly complicated glory."

"But, goodness, neurologic diseases are so tragic, and there's very little in the way of cure or even treatment for any of them," Ranya lamented. "I mean, Parkinson's, multiple sclerosis, ALS . . . stroke." She raised her eyebrows and looked pointedly at him.

"Yes, but we'll get there, Ranya. We will get there. And never underestimate the healing powers both of reassurance and of proper diagnosis. Even when we do get there, those will always remain fundamental."

Ranya suddenly wished he had been her dad's neurologist. She also knew that she envied Gabriel's students and residents. She saw that he must be an extraordinary teacher as well as an excellent clinician. And that combination was few and far between.

CHAPTER TWELVE

"It is not a bad thing to have a courageous, quiet man for a friend, even if it has gone out of fashion."
—Arthur Miller,
An Enemy of the People

NEARLY EVERY WEEKDAY AT 1:05 p.m., Ranya crossed the light-filled skywalk that connected the hospital to the medical school. Her destination was the little, brown-walled café tucked just inside the entrance to the med school, which also happened to be her alma mater. The café served only coffee, and Ranya did not drink coffee, but she had discovered that she could get a cup of steaming hot water there, and that was all she needed for the tea packets she carried in a pocket of her white coat.

She was pleased with the herbal teas that Rasheed had brought back for her from Ramallah. There was *miramiyyeh,* a sage tea that always settled her stomach after lunch, and za'atar tea, a thyme blend that was believed to help clear the respiratory tract. There was even a rose tea that she loved just for its exotic and complex blend of flavors. There was nothing else like it.

She smiled to herself as she thought of Rasheed. She had never told him this, but she had admired him as a cardiac surgeon long before being formally introduced to him at the department party. He ticked off all the boxes on her "tall, dark, and handsome" checklist, and she loved the way the ebony waves of his hair contrasted with his striking, jade-green eyes. His skin tone was a golden olive that seemed to glow from within, an outward reflection of his inner vitality.

She loved so many things about him, she had to admit, from his ready smile that could light up an entire room, to his calm and skill in the operating theater, to the confident assuredness with which he conducted himself, remarkably absent of arrogance or bravado. His confidence was authentic and well-earned, not a veneer to hide insecurity. In fact, "insecure" was the last word she would associate with Rasheed. He was superbly competent, and she found that she herself felt secure in his presence. And that was saying something.

So, armed with Rasheed's teas, she looked forward to her daily sojourn to the little café. And this particular Tuesday would have seen no change in her routine, except that this Tuesday, she ran into Gabriel as she was crossing the skywalk. It had only been two days since she and Rasheed were sitting in his living room, but his expression seemed to suggest an eternity had passed.

"Well, hello there!" he boomed, grinning from ear to ear.

After exchanging the usual pleasantries, Gabriel learned that Ranya was headed to the café for her tea, the very place from which he had just come. Without a second thought, he altered course and returned there to join her at an elevated table in the far corner.

He reserved the little round table for her as she went to get a cup of hot water, and while doing so, he could not help noticing the thin book she had set down on the table. A Queen of Hearts playing card was tucked inside for a bookmark, and this caused him to smile. Absolutely perfect.

When she returned, he pointed to the book and said, "So you're reading Joyce, then?"

Ranya blushed ever so slightly, and explained, "Well, yes; I thought I would start with *Dubliners* for an easier introduction to his work. I guess I've been bitten by some sort of Irish bug!"

The allusion was not lost on Gabriel, who smiled broadly.

"Anyway," Ranya continued, "I think one of the best ways to learn about a people and their country is through their literature, you know? So I picked up this book at Davis-Kidd last evening, and I also got that Coogan book you told me about, the one on Michael Collins. I'll read that next."

Gabriel was nodding and smiling the entire time; he couldn't have been more pleased. "Isn't that a great bookstore?" he asked, delighted to have finally found an inroad to making small talk with Ranya. "One of my favorite places in Nashville!" he said with enthusiasm.

"Yeah, mine too," Ranya said. She held up her cup of tea. "And they have a much better café, I have to say."

Gabriel laughed. "Oh, yeah, a good beverage, a good book, and a good slice of cake at their Second Story Café. Now that's the way to spend a Sunday afternoon."

In his limited encounters with Ranya thus far, she always seemed reserved at first, but Gabriel was discovering that once a topic caught her interest, she warmed to it, opening up like a beautiful flower in the light of day. He could certainly understand that, being one who liked to observe far more than he liked to participate.

He knew that some saw his reticence as a tragic weakness, but he had learned to use it as a strength, and he felt that it was this very power of observation, this keen ability to notice the nuances, that made him such a good neurologist. And being good at what he did was a matter of great pride to him.

Now Ranya was returning to one of those topics that seemed to have grabbed her attention, a topic near and dear to his Irish heart. She leaned across the table like a conspirator and asked him, "So, did you hear that there's to be a discussion of the Michael Collins movie tomorrow evening, led by one of the university's history professors?"

"As a matter of fact, I saw the flyer this morning. Are you going?"

"I am. Should be interesting."

"Well, I'll see you there, then!" And with that, Gabriel left before there could be any protest.

Gabriel and Ranya gathered with a dozen other attendees around a long conference table in an anonymous, windowless room in the basement bowels of a gray-stoned university building, awaiting the start of the Michael Collins movie discussion. Gabriel knew how much Ranya was looking forward to whatever wisdom and insights could be brought to bear by one of the university's professorial legends. Although neither of them had heard him speak before, his name was well known to them and to the campus at large, and he was reputed to be a thoughtful historian.

Gabriel struggled to hide his surprise, then, when the professor began the discussion in what was clearly the Queen's English. Gabriel glanced at Ranya, saw her eyes widen with disbelief. He fidgeted in his seat and Ranya crossed her arms as they endured an hour-long lecture, with very little actual discussion, on what the professor viewed as the major flaws of the movie in particular and of Michael Collins and the Irish revolutionaries in general. When he got to the point of proclaiming that Collins was in actuality a psychopathic terrorist who needlessly brought a perfectly good British colony to ruin, Ranya stood up and walked out. Without a word, Gabriel immediately followed.

"The audacity of it!" Ranya exclaimed once they were outside. She thrust her hands in her pockets and paced back and forth on the broad top step of the long brick portico. Her face was a study in livid frustration.

Gabriel hadn't been thrilled with the presentation himself, but he instinctively sought to soothe Ranya's fury. "You know, Ranya, there are some very good histories of Ireland written by Brits."

She halted her pacing and stared at him. "Oh, right. The oppressor writing the history of the oppressed. Now there's a new one."

"Um, well, maybe we shouldn't seek to paint things in just black and white, eh? Surely we have a few more colors at our disposal? And bitterness has never done much to advance our causes, has it?"

Ranya regarded him for another long moment before heaving a sigh and shaking her head, visibly trying to let it go but not succeeding. She pulled her burgundy jacket closer around her in the cool night air. "Well, there's an hour of my life I'll never get back," she muttered as she turned to go. "Good night, Gabriel."

Gabriel found that he could say nothing of use, so he held his tongue and waved, two short shakes of his hand against the autumn night. He watched her stomp down the steps, her black curls bouncing around her shoulders. For him, in spite of the disappointing content of the lecture, it had still been an hour at Ranya's side. And that was not a bad way to spend an evening.

CHAPTER THIRTEEN

"So completely is the history of the one country the reverse of the history of
the other that the very names which to an Englishman mean glory, victory and
prosperity to an Irishman spell degradation, misery and ruin."
—Cecil Woodham-Smith,
The Great Hunger: Ireland: 1845-1849

WHEN GABRIEL ENCOUNTERED RANYA on the skywalk the following Thursday
afternoon, he asked about her weekend plans, not out of any expectation that he
would be a part of them, but as a way to make conversation. So he tried to inquire
as casually as possible.

"Well, I have a bar mitzvah to go to on Saturday, and then I'm on call on
Sunday," Ranya said.

"A bar mitzvah, huh? I've never been to one of those," he said.

"Well, you can come with me if you like," Ranya said in an annoyed tone,
surprising him. "You might as well, since Rasheed is refusing to go as my guest.
Libby invited me 'plus a guest,' that's what her invitation said, on behalf of her
son."

"Is that Libby Gold, do you mean? The cardiology fellowship program director?"

"The one and only." Ranya smiled.

Gabriel tread carefully now. "And why won't Rasheed go?"

"Because she's Jewish—well, obviously, since it's a bar mitzvah—and Rasheed seems to have this stubborn inability to see individuals as just that: individuals. He wants to lump all Jews, all over the entire world," she gestured expansively with her arm, "into the same category, saying things like 'you know, they took our land.' As if every Jew on earth is responsible for the occupation of Palestinian territory. That sort of thing."

She shrugged. "It's not just Rasheed. There are many in my own family who feel the same."

"But you don't?" Gabriel was still trying to understand Ranya, in all her many dimensions.

Ranya shrugged again. "Look, I can understand the anger, but it's misdirected. Putting the weight of his pain and resentment on Libby Gold is certainly misplaced. She's my friend! In fact, I have several Jewish friends, and I don't hold any of them responsible for anyone's actions but their own. To do otherwise would be ridiculous."

"Well, now, there's a principle that *can* be broadly applied," Gabriel said, smiling in agreement.

Ranya returned his smile and continued. "And as I said, you know, Libby Gold is my good friend and mentor. Would she befriend me if she thought all Palestinians were horrible? It goes both ways, you know. And at some point, we have to be able to get past this."

She sighed. "But I guess Rasheed is not at that point yet. Maybe he won't ever be. His experience has been different from mine."

She looked up at Gabriel with a resigned expression. He looked out the windows of the skywalk for a moment, saw that the sun was breaking free of the clouds, and looked back at her. With half a smile, he said, "There's always hope." And then he added, "Maybe don't write Rasheed off just yet."

Gabriel caught up with Rasheed at Houston's on West End Avenue for their late Thursday night drink, a tradition they had reinstated that fall as a means of keeping the meat on the bones of their longtime friendship.

Once they had settled into their usual small booth in the raised bar area, bottles in hand, Gabriel opened up with no warning. "So, I am drinking with a terrorist."

"Excuse me?" Rasheed blinked.

"All Pals are terrorists. True or false?"

"Come on, Gabe, obviously you know that's false. What game is this?"

"Ranya told me you refuse to even consider going to Libby Gold's son's bar mitzvah with her. So you blame all Jews, the world over, for your plight? The plight of your people? Your people's people? Is that what this is? And, while we're at it, is it your plight, really?"

"Ranya told—" Rasheed began, then apparently decided to let that part go. "If you're referring to the plight of the Palestinians in general, then yes, as a Palestinian, I consider that to be my plight, too. Of course. But—"

Gabriel interjected, "So, speaking in generalities, then, all Palestinians are terrorists? Or cockroaches, as some have called them? Or nonexistent, even?"

"Because," Gabriel went on, "you see, this is the trap we fall into when we allow ourselves to live in generalities, my friend. There is no end to it and no escape from it."

"Gabe," Rasheed said in an exasperated tone, "what on earth has this to do with whether or not I go to Libby Gold's son's bar mitzvah?"

"My point exactly." Gabriel took a drink.

"Sorry?"

"So Libby Gold is now to blame for the occupation? For the need for the Intifada? For 'making hate necessary'? Have you ever spoken to her on the subject?

Have you ever spoken to her at all? You know, you might be surprised how much you have in common."

"Really."

"Next thing, you'll be telling me some nonsense about the holocaust not happening." Gabriel was getting worked up now. He surprised even himself. "You know, every Jew, I'll bet every single one, knows or is related to someone who perished in, or was otherwise directly affected by, the holocaust—"

"I am sick to death of hearing about the holocaust," Rasheed interrupted vehemently, hands slapping the table. The bartender looked over at their booth, but Rasheed went on. "Palestinians have been subjected to their own holocaust, their own genocide, for decades now, perpetrated by—get this—the very survivors, and their descendants, of that holocaust to which you refer. And how often do we hear or talk about that? Huh?"

"Look, Rasheed, I get it, but—"

Rasheed cut Gabriel off again. He was hot now, and Gabriel began to wonder if he had done the right thing by initiating this conversation. "Do you know how many Palestinians became refugees in 1948 when the state of Israel was created, Gabe, do you know?" Rasheed said. "Do you know what the Palestinians call the creation of Israel? *Al Nakba*. It literally means 'The Catastrophe.'"

"And now I am to understand that Libby Gold is to be held responsible for that, too," Gabriel muttered.

Rasheed ignored him. "I know—I know personally—Palestinians in refugee camps in Lebanon who still have the keys to the homes they left in Palestine. The homes they left because Zionist paramilitary forces drove them out. Of their own homes! With no compensation, no negotiation. Just violence."

Gabriel countered, more heatedly, "And did *you* know that countries all over the world—including this one—turned away thousands of Jewish refugees who were trying to flee Hitler during World War II? Put that in your pipe and smoke it. How many governments and organizations could have stepped in, yet chose to do nothing? A genocide was happening, and no one seemed to be able—or willing—to stop it.

"So maybe you should be blaming blindness to suffering for your troubles, rather than Libby Gold. Blind eyes everywhere, it seems, always." He gave a little snort at that and looked meaningfully at Rasheed.

Rasheed said, "Yes. Exactly. I know you must see that, Gabe."

"Yes, but do *you* see, Rasheed? Can you open your eyes? Pull yourself above this? We're having this conversation because I know you can." Gabriel continued, waving the bottle in his hand, "And what is this constant refusal to recognize the suffering of the Jews, anyway? Are you afraid that, by doing so, it makes yours any less? Because let me tell you right now: there is suffering enough for everyone."

"You know what?" Rasheed said, trying to control the volume of his voice, unsuccessfully. "We hear a lot—constantly, it seems—about Israel's right to exist, and the need to recognize that. But what about Palestine's right to exist? What about *my* right to exist?" Rasheed pounded the table again with his last question.

"I'm fairly sure Libby Gold recognizes that you exist," Gabriel answered, leaning back and cracking a smile now. He put the bottle to his lips and swallowed.

"Come on, you know what I mean," Rasheed replied, but with more restraint this time. Gabriel sensed that his friend had noticed his attempt at humor, his attempt to let Rasheed know that he was being understood after all.

"I'm not trying to say that any of this is fair, my friend. Nothing is, not on this side of the grave. But look, Rasheed, if only for your own sake, you've got to try to get past this, because this is a never-ending carousel of hatred, heartache, and violence."

He paused for effect, then added, "And getting off this sick ride doesn't make you any less of a Palestinian, you know."

Gabriel sat back against the hard wooden wall of the booth. "Trust me, man, trust me. The Irish have been there."

"Well, at least you have a country," retorted Rasheed, fixing Gabriel with a piercing glare.

"Yeah, well, for the most part, anyway," Gabriel conceded. "*Sláinte agus táinte,*" he said as he raised his bottle. "To Ireland."

"To Palestine," Rasheed returned, touching Gabriel's bottle with his own.

CHAPTER FOURTEEN

"Don't let us make imaginary evils, when you know we have so many real
ones to encounter."
—Oliver Goldsmith

RANYA WAS SURPRISED TO receive a call from Rasheed the following morning, saying he would go to the bar mitzvah with her after all. But she knew
better than to ask questions. She simply told him that that would be wonderful, that she was glad he had decided to change his mind, and asked him
to pick her up on Saturday morning early enough for her to have time to
congratulate Libby personally before the service began.

When Rasheed showed up bright and early on her doorstep, he was wearing one of his best suits. Ranya placed the palm of her hand against the
freshly-shaven skin of his cheek and beamed at him, thinking how handsome
he looked, what a gentleman he was. It was entirely possible that he was
overdressed, but she didn't care. That was beside the point. Or maybe, as she
reflected later, for Rasheed it was precisely the point.

When they arrived at the synagogue, Libby was delighted to see them, and
when Ranya greeted her with "*Shabbat shalom*," Libby grinned widely and
her bright eyes grew even brighter.

Shaking hands with Rasheed, Libby warmly grasped his arm with her other hand, saying, "So this is Rasheed! I've heard so much about you! All good, of course. So glad you could make it. Thank you so much for coming."

Rasheed smiled back and thanked her for the invitation, with more graciousness than Ranya could have imagined he would muster, but then Rasheed was always one for exceeding her expectations when it mattered most. They had been mostly silent on the ride over, and so Ranya had been uneasy about how it would go after all, but that brilliant, genuine smile of his was back now, and so was Ranya's ease.

Now Libby's son Jonathan, the bar mitzvah celebrant, came up and was introduced; he looked a bit nervous, but confident. Ranya congratulated him, and congratulated Libby again. She was so happy for her friend and mentor; she knew how much this day meant to her, and she felt honored to have been invited. To have Rasheed there at her side was icing on the cake. No, it was more than that. So much more.

At the party that night, Ranya stood in a corner with Libby while kids ran around them and Rasheed stood a few feet away, conversing with another surgeon whose children were also attending the party. Libby pointed discreetly in Rasheed's direction and said, *sotto voce*, "You've got such a handsome man there, Ranya. A good man. A real keeper."

Ranya smiled and replied, "Thanks. I think you're right." She was so proud of Rasheed for even being there, for being such a trooper, and she wondered if Libby saw that as well. Probably so. There was little that Libby missed, as she demonstrated with her next remarks.

"Do you know the new neurologist who joined the faculty this summer? Irish guy. I think he's a friend of Rasheed's, right? I hear he's pretty good."

Ranya involuntarily stiffened. She forced the corners of her lips upward and avoided Libby's penetrating gaze as she answered, "Yep, seems to be. From what I can tell so far."

"Well, goodness knows, we can use a good neurologist around here," Libby whispered, folding her arms across her chest and widening her eyes at Ranya, who in turn carefully refrained from looking in the direction of the one neurologist who was present and standing in the far corner of the room, a white-bearded and bespectacled man whose incompetence was exceeded only by his arrogance. Those who dared to hope placed their confidence in the expectation that he would retire soon. But it was not until that moment that Rasheed's role in it finally dawned on Ranya. At least part of the reasoning behind Gabriel's recruitment, given what she knew of Rasheed's penchant for behind-the-scenes politicking, may have been the calculated intention of speeding that retirement along.

She looked over at Rasheed again, this time with new eyes. And found that he was looking her way.

She blushed slightly, and was aware of Libby looking at her with open curiosity. Libby changed the subject quickly, engaging Ranya on a different topic. She leaned her shoulder against Ranya's and pointed toward another tall man in the room, this one much younger and fair-haired. "So, my older son, Jacob, is heading to Manhattan soon to join a large firm as an investment banker. They take up several floors of the World Trade Center. I think it's a wonderful opportunity for him."

"Oh, Libby, I know you must be so proud." Ranya genuinely meant it. Anyone could see how much Libby's two sons meant to her, and Ranya, for her part, knew how lucky they were to have Libby as a mother. She added, "I'm sure that Jacob has great fortune in his future, too—how could he not, with you as his mother?"

Rasheed watched Ranya and Libby talking, standing side by side. They could have been cousins. Where Ranya had long, ebony hair that fell in layers of tight curls, Libby had shoulder-length, salt-and-pepper curls that were larger and looser, forming a flattering frame around her face and highlighting her sparkling green eyes. In fact, Rasheed noted, they both had bright eyes and a way of gesturing excitedly with their hands when they spoke to close friends.

Pride radiated from Libby; it didn't take a genius to see that, and Rasheed found that he was glad for her. And Ranya seemed content, which is what mattered most of all. Rasheed was finding that there was little he wouldn't do to make Ranya happy.

He walked over to the refreshments table, nodding amiably to the adults he passed. He would need time to process all this. He was at a bar mitzvah party. That morning he had been in a synagogue. He had never been in a synagogue before, never in his life thought he would be. And yet there he was. Because of Ranya. And because of Gabriel? Yeah, okay, because of him too.

When it came time to dance the *hora*, Rasheed was hesitant, but Ranya tugged on his arm and spoke in his ear, "Come on, Rasheed, you're great at dancing the *debkeh*, and if you can do that, you can do this."

Reluctantly, he acquiesced, and soon found to his great surprise that he was totally enjoying himself. He turned to Ranya and yelled above the music, "Hey, I'm pretty good at this after all, aren't I?"

"Of course you are, *Habibi*—absolutely legendary. And," Ranya added, grinning at him, "I told you so."

Rasheed's entire being filled with joy, his heart beating faster and his spirits soaring. His normally-reticent Ranya had called him *Habibi*. My beloved. And at a bar mitzvah party, no less.

CHAPTER FIFTEEN

"And now the old story has begun to write itself over there . . . Isn't it queer: there are only two or three human stories, and they go on repeating themselves as fiercely as if they had never happened before; like the larks in this country, that have been singing the same five notes over for thousands of years."

—Willa Cather,
O Pioneers!

March 1997

IT WAS LATE WHEN GABRIEL got to the sandwich shop on the corner, sometime after 8:00 p.m. He could never remember whether they closed at nine or ten, so had come before nine to be on the safe side. He had walked down the street from the hospital, knowing that he would need to return to the Intensive Care Unit at least once more that night to check on a critically-ill stroke patient. It was a pleasant enough night, with the chilly hint of spring in the air, and he did not mind the walk at all; in fact, he welcomed it.

As he crossed the parking lot and looked toward the brightly-lit windows of the small restaurant, he could make out a figure in one of the windows, a face hidden behind a curtain of black curls, the head to whom they belonged bent over a book. There was only one person he'd ever met in the entire world who had hair like that, just one, so it took no guessing on his part as to the identity of this solitary diner.

He picked up his step, looking forward to another encounter with the lovely Dr. Ranya. It had been a long, busy winter at the hospital, and outside of his Thursday night drinks with Rasheed—which Ranya never attended—there hadn't been much time for socializing. He rapped on the glass of the window beside which she was sitting, and saw as she folded the book over her arm that she was reading *Ulysses*. Goodness, she was moving fast in her review of Irish literature.

Ranya was waving at him, and that was all the invitation he needed to join her.

"So now it's *Ulysses*, eh?" Gabriel asked, pointing at the book as he sat down across from her with his sandwich.

She smiled at him—and what a sweet smile it was—and replied, "Well, they say it's one of the greatest novels ever written, so I thought I'd see for myself."

"That's fantastic," he said. "Certainly not one for the faint of heart, though. Which means you should have no problem at all."

She began asking him questions about Dublin, about the book, and about the author. They were at least twenty minutes deep into their discussion when the loud voice of a man speaking Arabic could be heard from the front counter.

They both turned to look at the somewhat-disheveled gentleman, standing there in a loosely-fitting gray T-shirt, equally loose black pants, and brown house slippers. He had about two days' worth of salt-and-pepper stubble on his face. His right arm was in a sling of white gauze, and in his left hand he held a small piece of crinkled white paper that he kept waving at the cashier, who clearly could not understand him or what he wanted.

"Can you tell what he wants?" Gabriel asked Ranya.

Ranya shook her head. "I think he's Iraqi," she said. "I can't understand his dialect—my colloquial Arabic is limited to the Levant." She stood up and went over to him. Gabriel stood up too, not knowing what else to do.

He knew from what Rasheed had told him previously that Nashville was a federal refugee resettlement location, and one of the latest waves of refugees had consisted of Iraqis and Kurds from the Gulf War. He watched from a respectful distance as Ranya approached the man, greeting him in Arabic. The man responded with a smile of relief and a greeting of his own, then waved the piece of paper at her, too.

Gabriel recognized the sounds of a word the gentleman had kept repeating over and over to the cashier; he was repeating it to Ranya now. It sounded like "enwanee," but with a guttural sound at the beginning of the word. He said it as he waved the paper in the air, and he said it again as he handed the paper to Ranya, who looked at it and then looked up at Gabriel.

"It's his address," she said. "But there's no phone number. He told me his name is Ahmed. That's all I know."

Ranya asked Ahmed something in Arabic then, but it was clear that he didn't understand her. Gabriel could only surmise that she was asking him if there were someone she should call for him, someone at home for him. She tried asking something else, and Ahmed's brow furrowed in confusion; Gabriel could tell from the look on Ranya's face that she was becoming frustrated.

She finally looked at Gabriel and said, "I think I should call Rasheed. He's the only person I know anywhere around here, this late at night, who might be able to understand him and communicate properly."

Gabriel glanced down at his watch. "If I know Rasheed, he's probably just finishing his nightly rounds. Should be perfect timing. I'll call him myself."

He pulled out his Motorola flip phone and placed the call while Ranya gestured to Ahmed to have a seat at their table.

"Hey there, Gabe," Rasheed answered. "What's up?"

"Hey, Rasheed, Ranya and I have a situation here at the sub shop; there's an Iraqi man—"

"What?" Rasheed cut in. "Ranya is there with you?"

"Uh, yes," Gabriel replied after a slight pause, cursing himself for hesitating. "Here," he said, "I'll put her on."

He handed the phone to Ranya, who explained the situation to Rasheed. She gave the phone to Ahmed, who listened attentively, then began speaking in rapid-fire Arabic. He handed the phone back to Ranya. She spoke very briefly to Rasheed again, then hung up and held out the closed clamshell phone to Gabriel, saying, "Rasheed is on his way."

It was not long before Rasheed arrived, making as grand an entrance as always, even in a mostly-deserted sandwich shop that was about to close. He strode straight over to their table, where they were all standing up to greet him, and began speaking immediately with the Iraqi man, Ahmed, who once again said the word he had kept repeating and now made Rasheed the final recipient of the slip of paper as he said it.

"I'll call him a cab," Rasheed announced without further explanation.

Taxis were not the easiest to come by in Nashville, especially on a week-night, and as they all stood in the cold outside the closed restaurant waiting together, Rasheed making small talk in Arabic with Ahmed, Gabriel wondered for perhaps the third time why they did not simply all walk back to the hospital, get one of their cars, and take the man home themselves, for heaven's sake. He was just about to suggest this when a yellow taxi pulled up.

Rasheed spoke to the driver, handing him the man's address and saying, "He doesn't speak English."

"What language does he speak?" the driver asked in a thick accent of his own.

"Arabic," Rasheed answered with a smile.

And lo and behold, the driver began speaking in Arabic to Rasheed and to Ahmed, and all of them, Gabriel and Ranya included, had a good laugh.

Rasheed took out his wallet to pay in advance, but the driver put up his hand and shook his head. "There is no need," he said in English.

Rasheed spoke to him in Arabic again, insisting and even pulling out a wad of bills, but the driver continued to refuse, and finally Rasheed relented and bowed his head to him. Gabriel chanced a glance at Ranya, who was beaming with pride. As well she should be. He was fairly proud of Rasheed himself, and of the driver too.

Gabriel thought he made out Rasheed saying, *"Shookrun,"* which he knew to be Arabic for "thank you," as he shook the driver's hand. They all waved as the car took off, Ahmed safely ensconced in the back seat.

Ranya was shaking her head as she took Rasheed's arm and said, "Smaller world than we think, isn't it?"

The three of them began walking back up the street to the hospital, and Gabriel asked Rasheed what Ahmed's story was. "So, apparently," Rasheed began, with a bitter note in his voice, "the emergency department of our illustrious hospital set his broken collarbone and sent him out into the street. He probably had no translator, and that restaurant was the first place he came to that was open." Rasheed looked at both Ranya and Gabriel, adding, "It's a good thing you two were there, or who knows what would have happened to him."

Rasheed did not ask, at least not then and not of Gabriel, why or how it happened that the two of them were there together in the first place.

CHAPTER SIXTEEN

"There is something that is much more scarce, something finer far, something rarer than ability. It is the ability to recognize ability."
—Elbert Hubbard

Autumn 1997

SINCE RANYA HAD BEGUN HER one-year interventional cardiology fellowship that July, hardly anyone had seen or heard from her, given that she spent the majority of her days—and nights—slogging away in the cardiac catheterization lab in the basement of the hospital, dressed in a lead apron for radiation protection while learning how to move the tiniest of wires across blocked coronary arteries in order to open them with a balloon or a stent.

What Gabriel didn't hear from her, though, he heard about her: word was getting around that she was really good at what she did. Really, really good. Rasheed had told him that whenever Ranya called about a patient needing coronary bypass surgery, he always knew that he could trust her judgment, and so did the rest of the cardiac surgeons.

When Gabriel himself had the occasional patient who needed her expertise, he made the time to go down to the cath lab and watch the procedure. He'd observe through the giant windows that separated the control room from the sterile environment in which Ranya stood, needing little coaching from the supervising attending at her side. Gabriel found that he was always thrilled with the process, the excellent results for his patients, and, not least of all, with the operator herself.

On one of the few occasions when Gabriel chanced upon her on the skywalk that fall, he made a point of mentioning to her that she had a growing reputation for excellence throughout the hospital; it was important to him that she knew her efforts had not gone unnoticed. "A faculty appointment will surely be yours for the taking here, Ranya, in a few months or so, don't you think?" It was not really a question.

"There aren't a lot of women in cardiology, Ranya, I know that, but you've set yourself apart in more ways than one," he said.

"Yeah, and I'm the first woman at this institution to train specifically in interventional cardiology."

"You know, Ranya, you asked me once why I went into neurology, but I never asked you the same about *your* chosen specialty," Gabriel said.

The brilliance of her smile took him off guard with its suddenness, its intensity. Clearly, he had struck a chord. "Oh, I knew I wanted to be a cardiologist from my senior year of college," she said, "when I took a human physiology course, and the section on cardiovascular physiology blew me away like nothing else in science ever had before. It just made sense to me, as if all the pieces of a giant jigsaw puzzle fell into place all at once, and there I was looking at the whole wonder and beauty of the very underpinnings of human life as we know it. The circulatory system in all its glory."

She put a hand over her own heart. "I was hooked, Gabriel, I was hooked. From that moment on, being a cardiologist was the only thing I could ever imagine doing."

And then the brilliance of her smile turned to wryness just as quickly, and she held up a finger and added, "No, no—actually, no—there was something else, just one other thing, that I once thought of doing. Just one, and just once."

Gabriel couldn't believe she was going to make him ask. "And that was . . .?"

"I once considered becoming a cardiothoracic surgeon, like Rasheed."

"Ah."

Ranya mercifully broke the moment of silence that ensued. "Yeah, but I found that I liked the internal medicine background required of a cardiologist even more. The deep thinking part, you know?"

Gabriel couldn't suppress the grin that spread across his face upon hearing this. He barely managed to keep it from turning into a burst of laughter. Everyone in medicine knew the surgeon's reputation for cutting first and thinking later, if at all. "The only thing standing between me and a diagnosis is skin," was the commonly used phrase and attitude of surgeons far and wide.

He refrained from commenting that, in his neurologist's view, the work that Ranya did as an interventionalist wasn't so far removed from the work of a surgeon. Best to keep that to himself. So he only added a nod of his head.

Ranya smiled at his reaction—at least, the part of it he had let her see. She spread her hands in an expansive gesture and continued, "Yeah, so, thinking through the differential diagnoses and all the different meds and such—I like that. And how the workings of the kidneys affect those of the heart, and vice versa."

"And the brain, too, of course," Gabriel said.

"Yes, of course. That may be the best part—the heart's highest calling—to supply blood to the brain. Together, they make us who we are, don't they?"

"Indeed they do," Gabriel said. And now his restraint left him. "But even with all you've said about the 'deep thinking' part, Ranya—and pardon my bluntness here—but you're pursuing a career as an interventionalist, which some would argue is one of the most surgical directions of one of the most surgical subspecialties in internal medicine."

"No, no, Gabriel," Ranya protested, "it is so much more than that! It's the best of both worlds, don't you see? I get to be the thinker and the doer, all in one. I love it!"

"Well, there's no doubt there, Ranya—and that must be why you're so good at it."

"Thanks, but getting back to what you were saying about the rarity of women in cardiology—yeah, it's a problem, for sure," Ranya said, the gravitas returning to her face and posture. "Can you believe there are male cardiology attendings, some of my own supervisors, who still say openly that they don't think women should even *be* cardiologists? They've said it to my face!"

Then she laughed. "I'm always amused at how the only major event I attend where the line is longer for the men's restroom than for the women's is at a cardiology conference!"

Gabriel laughed too, for a moment, but then turned serious again, allowing the earnest intensity he felt to enter his voice. "Well, don't you ever let anybody stand in your way or make you feel inferior or tell you that you can't do it. Don't let any of these short-sighted naysayers get you down. Because, Ranya, I'm not a cardiologist, but even I can see and hear tell how good—*really* good—you are. Reminds me of that old saying: you leave them in the ha'penny place."

"The ha'penny place?"

"Yeah, yeah, you heard that expression in *Michael Collins*, remember? It comes from halfpenny," Gabriel enunciated it clearly now, "and refers to an insignificant or inferior position, given the low value of half a penny, you know?"

"I see," Ranya said, her face unconvinced. Then, as her eyes widened and brightened, sending her elegant dark brows upward, Gabriel could tell that Ranya really did see. She smiled slowly and looked up at him. "Thank you, Gabriel. Thank you so much. That means a lot coming from you."

"No one can hold a candle to you, Ranya. Don't you ever forget that. And don't ever let anyone tell you otherwise."

That night, inside the bright, multicolored interior of the Green Hills YMCA, the smells of sweat and chlorine intermingled with those of rubber and vinyl as Gabriel walked down the long second-floor hallway above the indoor pool, seeking the refuge—and challenge—of the spacious, machine-filled workout area. He made it a point to stay in shape, and tried to come as often as his schedule allowed, but sometimes that meant it was late evening by the time he arrived, as it was tonight.

And tonight his conversation with Ranya weighed on his mind, the challenges she faced and the utter certitude he had about her ability and will to overcome them. That Ranya was one of a kind, wasn't she? But he had already decided that long ago.

He hoped, as he always did, to put her out of his mind for just this hour, just this one hour while he strove to tax his body to its limits so there could be nothing left to contemplate other than the simple action of putting two hands around cold steel, the all-important concentration necessary for bringing a heavy barbell down to his chest without dropping it.

As he walked by the mirrored studio that was situated at the far end of the weight room, he glanced through the glass door and saw a figure moving through what looked like martial arts forms, clearly taking advantage of the late hour and an empty studio. Although the martial artist was on the other side of the room, the flying flash of dark curls as she turned to execute her next move broadcast instantly that it was Ranya. *Of course it was.* There would be no escape from her tonight.

Gabriel was mesmerized. Every move was clean and smooth and powerful and graceful all at once, in a way he had not known was possible. Her back was still turned to him, and he did not know if she had seen him in the mirrors, so he moved back from the door and stood at an angle to watch. *Only for a moment. Don't be a creep.*

And so, for that moment, Gabriel reveled, awestruck, in the sight of Ranya kicking the air far above her head, turning in a full circle to land her elegantly-controlled fist in front of her, then turning and drawing her open hands across her body with the power of one deft movement of her hips, every part of her body stopping and landing in perfect synchrony. He watched with amazement as she later sailed through the air in a flying sidekick. He had only ever seen those done in movies. He hadn't even thought they could be real.

With great reluctance and no small amount of willpower, Gabriel pulled himself away and walked toward the resistance machines to begin his workout. As he sat there fiddling with the yellow knob that adjusted the weights, nothing had ever been clearer to him: he was in the ha'penny place.

CHAPTER SEVENTEEN

"Let the winds of the heavens dance between you."
—Gibran Kahlil Gibran,
The Prophet

July 1998

"IF YOU CAN STAND STILL in the presence of this music, you're soulless," Rasheed cajoled, grabbing Gabe's arm with one hand as he took Ranya's hand in the other.

Ranya had finally finished her long, tough fellowship, and Rasheed had invited them both to join him at the American Federation of Ramallah Convention in Birmingham, Alabama. He had noticed that it didn't take much convincing to get them to say yes to that. But he knew it would take a little more convincing to get Gabe onto the dance floor, so he and Ranya had demonstrated beforehand how to dance the *debkeh*, the legendary Arabic line dance.

They had shown Gabe how all the dancers held hands, forming a line from right to left, with the most basic foot moves as follows: left foot crosses in front of right twice, then kicks and stomps, all while moving rightward with the rest of the line dancers. *Step, step, kick, stomp.* Again and again, around and around. Simple enough, but Gabe still needed some encouraging when the music started blaring.

When that most famous of Ramallah folk songs, "*Wayn a'Ramallah,*" blasted from the speakers, Rasheed knew there was no better time. With Ranya between him and Gabe, he started the *debkeh* line, making them the first to hit the parquet dance floor. Rasheed took pride in being a master *debkeh* dancer, and those who knew him, when they saw him at the head of the rapidly-lengthening human dancing snake, ran from all corners of the ballroom to join the line.

It was only a matter of minutes before the line outgrew the dance floor and began to span the entire length of the room, so that everyone at the convention that night who was capable of a kick and a stomp was now traversing the perimeter of the ballroom.

Rasheed's pulse quickened with the rhythm of the music, and he reveled in the exhilaration he always felt when leading the *debkeh,* the sense of community and the pride of heritage it brought him. It meant even more to him tonight because Ranya was there by his side, her hand in his, keeping up with his pace, the smile on her face a mirror of his own. He felt that the connection, the bond, between them was stronger than ever. He hoped once more that he could convince his dance partner to become his life partner.

Gabriel, swept up in this and still holding Ranya's hand while she held onto Rasheed's, found that he was the only person in the room not singing at the top of his lungs, and he was grateful for the arak coursing through him as Rasheed took them all ever faster on this mad *debkeh* journey.

God bless the Arabs and their arak, he thought, suddenly hitting upon the revelation that it was akin to that fictional Star Trek concoction of Romulan ale, while simultaneously, like an out-of-body experience, watching his own feet, attached to his own legs, miraculously making the right movements at the right times, without him having any idea how they were doing so. Rasheed was doing a much more complicated and elaborate version of the dance he had taught Gabriel, but Gabriel found that if he just focused on the few steps he had been taught, he could make a passable attempt at looking like he knew what he was doing.

When the song and the applause that followed finally ended, Gabriel gratefully sat down with Rasheed at a nearby banquet table. Rasheed was still trying to catch his breath, chest puffing and face glistening with sweat. Ranya had gone to get some ice water to drink and was now, Gabriel could see, caught in a small crowd of statuesque and bejeweled women talking excitedly to one another in at least two languages. There was a surprisingly large number of Arab Americans in Birmingham who either claimed Ramallah as their original hometown or were the direct descendants of those who did, and they all seemed to be here tonight, along with many more out-of-towners, some of whom had flown across the country to be in attendance.

Gabriel turned back to Rasheed, who was now mopping his face with a white cloth napkin. "So, I must say, Rasheed: that was an experience unlike any other."

Rasheed grinned at him. "I'll make a *debkeh* dancer out of you yet, Gabe."

"Tell me, what was that song that was playing, that everybody seemed to know? I kept hearing the name of your hometown in it."

"Oh, yes, *Wayn a'Ramallah*! It literally means, 'Where? To Ramallah.' It's an old Palestinian song that is popular pretty much all over the Levant. It's about a man . . . well, I'd always assumed it was a man, anyway . . . whose lover asks him where he's going—and, by extension, why he's leaving her—and his answer is that he is going to Ramallah."

"Nice," Gabriel mused. "So, can I get you a drink?"

Rasheed tilted his head back, looking in Ranya's direction. Gabriel saw her make eye contact with his friend and he and Rasheed both surmised immediately that she needed saving. "Uh, maybe a little later, Gabe. You go ahead, though." And with that Rasheed was on his feet and headed in her direction.

Gabriel reluctantly got up and wandered over to the cash bar. So the Arabs had this drink they called arak. The Greeks had a version of it; they called it ouzo.

Supposed to have existed since the beginning of distillation itself, and in Ramallah they even had their own famed distilleries. It was potent stuff, and didn't he know it, having already partaken a couple of times—or was it more?—tonight.

Thus the Arabs, who, after all, gave the word "alcohol" to the world, had also perfected the beverage that Gabriel was right now imbibing as he stood at the bar, watching Rasheed place his hand on the small of Ranya's back, watching him guide her to the dance floor as another song started up, with a great rhythm but a bit mellower than the last. *And speaking of rhythm...* He watched, unable to move, as Ranya twisted and lifted her arms elegantly above her head, her waist and hips shifting perfectly beneath the organza of the long black gown that clung lightly to her lithe figure. Rasheed moved closer to her, clapping his hands to the rhythm. Gabriel downed his shot and asked for three more.

By the time Rasheed made it back to Gabe's table, it was nearly midnight, and several other revelers had already taken seats there as the party started to wind down. Rasheed just managed to get out an apology to Gabe for leaving him alone for so long when he was accosted by one of the other convention attendees sitting around the table, a woman who was the sister-in-law of his maternal aunt.

The woman put her hand on Rasheed's arm and said, with inexplicable urgency, "Now, Abbasi is a Muslim name. Is she willing to convert? Have you asked her? You know we come from a long line of Greek Orthodox."

She was obviously referring to Ranya, and, while her question annoyed Rasheed, it did not surprise him. Not only had this aunt-by-marriage always been nosy and unfiltered, but Rasheed had long expected someone, at some point, to make such a reference, given that most from Ramallah and the surrounding areas knew of the Abbasi's of Jerusalem.

"You know, Auntie, neither of us is religious or cares about any of that; it's really not that important," Rasheed began, trying to dismiss her with as little argument as possible, but she cut him off.

"Of course it is. You know it is! How will your children grow up?!"

Rasheed could feel his irritation rising. "Well, in this country at least, religion is a choice, not a surname," he snapped. "And the God I believe in doesn't favor one group of people over another. We are all His people."

Gabe, who until this point had appeared to be nodding off, opened his eyes and slurred, "In Ireland we have Catholics. Lots of Catholics."

Rasheed reached out a hand to pat his friend on the shoulder. "Uh, yeah, Gabe, yes, I think we know that."

Then Rasheed gave Gabe a sharper look, with his hand still on his shoulder. It was not like Gabe to let himself go. But perhaps it could not have come at a better time. He turned to his distasteful relative and said, "Excuse me, I'm just going to attend to my friend here."

He stood up and looped his arm under Gabe's in one smooth move. "Come on, Gabe, time to go," Rasheed muttered, lifting him out of his chair.

Gabe leaned against him, swaying, and waved to Ranya, who was now watching them from across the room. Gabe yelled out to her, "Night! Bedtime!"

Even from that distance, it was not hard for Rasheed to tell that her mouth had dropped open. Rasheed just waved to Ranya and made a goofy face as he escorted Gabe out of the room, figuring she would either understand or he would explain later.

When Rasheed checked in on Ranya the following morning, he found her looking out of her hotel window at the empty Sunday-morning streets of Birmingham.

Sunlight poured through the glass, casting her in silhouette, and he thought again how beautiful she was, regardless of the time or the day or the season.

She turned to him and smiled. "Isn't it amazing how quiet it is down there? Especially after last night's festivities? And now not a soul moving about."

"Yeah, pretty incredible," Rasheed responded. *Just like you.* He paused for a moment, felt his palms moisten and his mouth go dry. Then he cleared his throat and said, "Ranya, you know, I think we need to find somebody for Gabe."

"Somebody?" she asked absentmindedly. She had turned back toward the window.

"Yeah, you know, he really wasn't himself last night."

Ranya scoffed, "Falling-down drunk, you mean? Yeah, that was a pretty picture."

Rasheed persisted, "Don't you think he must be lonely? You have any friends we could introduce him to?"

"Oh, God, Rasheed," she said, "I have better things to do than play matchmaker for Gabriel. He's a grown man. I'm sure he's perfectly capable of finding someone for himself. And anyway, you know more people than I do and you know him better—why don't you work on that? If you really feel strongly about it, you do something."

Rasheed made a face and groaned, "Oh, I don't know what I'm gonna do with that Irishman."

CHAPTER EIGHTEEN

"There are only the pursued, the pursuing, the busy and the tired."
—F. Scott Fitzgerald,
The Great Gatsby

LESS THAN TWO WEEKS after returning from the Ramallah Convention, Gabriel and Rasheed were sitting at the bar at Houston's, having their customary Thursday-night drinks. Rasheed was in a fine mood, Gabriel observed, even finer than usual, and it didn't take longer than a couple of minutes for him to find out why.

"So, I don't know if you've heard yet—I don't think it's common knowledge just yet, anyway—but not only has Ranya agreed to join the faculty at our very own esteemed institution, she's going to be on track to become the assistant director of the interventional cardiology fellowship program itself!" Rasheed said, grinning from ear to ear. He clapped Gabriel on the back and asked, for effect, "How impressive is that?"

"Well, pretty impressive, I would say. But I'm sure you're not surprised."

"Well, so, I figure," Rasheed blustered on, seemingly unaware that Gabriel had offered any response at all, "that this would be a good time to propose. Again."

Gabriel's mind was moving slowly, still trying to imagine how it would be to have Ranya on the faculty with them. "Propose what?"

Rasheed shook Gabriel's shoulder. "Marriage, of course!"

Gabriel tried not to choke. He managed to sputter, "Oh . . . yeah. Huh." He promptly flagged the bartender down to order another drink.

Rasheed went on, bringing his hand back to his drink, continuing his musings, "I'm thinking that . . . well, we've been seeing one another for over two years, you know? And two years is a respectable time to be seeing one another, and it's time to move the relationship forward. Don't you think?" He looked at Gabriel expectantly.

Gabriel nodded and cleared his throat. "Yeah, I guess so. I mean, yes. Yes, of course." Then the better part of his mental faculties returned and he recalled one interesting word that Rasheed had uttered a minute ago. *Again.*

"Uh, Rasheed, did you say 'again'? As in, you've already proposed to Ranya before?"

Rasheed waved his hand across the air between them. "No worries there. I did, and she said then that she would think about it. It's been long enough that she's had plenty of time to think about it, and she's probably just waiting for me to ask again, you know? I mean, we're still together after all this time, and she hasn't run for the hills, so that's a pretty good sign, right?"

Gabriel realized that he was staring at Rasheed with his mouth half open. He made his lips move. "Um, well . . . yes. No doubt." He grabbed his glass and raised it in an impromptu toast. "Here's to good luck, my friend."

As soon as it was graceful to excuse himself, Gabriel went home and spent the night studying the ceiling.

The following week, Gabriel was in for yet another surprise when he received a text message on his pager from Ranya. "Tea?" the screen of his beeper flashed at him. *I guess she wants to tell me the good news herself.* He made a conscious effort to steel himself against despondency. He knew from firsthand experience how persuasive Rasheed could be.

He met her at their café, and as soon as he saw her face, he knew it was not good news, for anyone. She did not want to sit down, so they walked across campus together.

It was the kind of infamously humid Nashville day that made breathing difficult. But the burden of the oppressive humidity quickly became a secondary concern in light of the agitated story that Ranya had to tell.

"Rasheed proposed to me, Gabriel."

Gabriel kept silent. It seemed the best course of inaction.

She drew a deep breath. "He proposed, and I turned him down."

Gabriel struggled against the feeling of relief that washed over him. He forced grimness onto his face. Not hard to do. After all, he had had plenty of practice.

"Tell me more," he invited.

What came next was a quick and passionate torrent, more talk than he had ever heard from her in the two years he had known her. Talk about how important her career was to her, how she just couldn't see herself getting married right now, maybe ever; about how hard she had fought to get to where she was as a woman in cardiology, and how far she still hoped to go.

"Gabriel," she stretched her hands out to him, as though pleading for him to understand what, he surmised, Rasheed could not. "I want to be one of the best in the world at what I do."

"Nothing less than the best, eh?" Gabriel was grinning now, and that made her face soften, too.

"Yes. There it is. That's what I want."

"But could you not do it with Rasheed by your side, Ranya?" Gabriel asked, in spite of himself. A part of him had to stand up for his best friend, who, without a doubt, would do the same for him were the tables turned. And he sensed that she did not know Rasheed as well as she thought she did, or—and this was the twist of the knife—she would never have turned him down. No woman in her right mind would turn down the Rasheed he knew.

"Not like that, not the way he would want and expect it to be," she asserted.

"I guess you have conveyed that to him, discussed that with him?"

"I don't think he even knows what he expects from me, from a marriage. But I feel certain that I couldn't give it to him, couldn't live up to those expectations. He's a Palestinian man, Gabriel, and that comes with certain assumptions."

"Are you sure you aren't selling him short, Ranya?"

"I don't know, Gabriel, I don't know!" she fretted, waving her hands. "But what I do know is that I'm not ready. I can't do this. Not now."

"I see," Gabriel said quietly.

"Look, Gabriel," Ranya said, "I don't know another Palestinian woman who has had the chances that I've had. I'm not a refugee, I'm not stuck without citizenship, I'm not trapped in poverty or religious fundamentalism. Thankfully for me, I'm an American citizen, and, like most Palestinian immigrants, my parents, God rest their souls, believed in the importance of education, the power of it to elevate you above everything else. And I'm not about to waste that."

Gabriel had not known that her parents were no longer living. He was struck again by how little he knew about her, really. She paused to catch her breath, and Gabriel nodded his silent understanding, which was enough for her to continue.

"You know," she said, "I can't tell you how many times, growing up, I was told a version of: 'the one thing no one can ever take from you is your education.' So you must see, can't you, how much that means to the progeny of a people who have felt at times—many times—that everything has been taken from them??"

She pushed the curls back from her forehead, and Gabriel's heart ached at seeing the burden that was etched across her lovely brow. He heard the volume of his own voice ascend a notch as he protested, "But my God, Ranya, if anyone could understand that, it would be Rasheed! Did you tell him that?"

He watched her shoulders fall, and felt the knot in his stomach twist ever tighter. "No," she said, "I was too upset and he was too upset."

"Well, I think you should," Gabriel told her gently. He extended his hand in her direction, but stopped short of placing it on her shoulder.

She looked up at him, and the pain on her face was almost more than he could bear. "You're his best friend, Gabriel. So you probably know how hurt he must be right now. I wish it didn't have to be this way. I never wanted to hurt him." Then her voice became a choked whisper. "And I don't want to lose him."

"I don't think you will lose him, Ranya." Then, fighting the lump in his own throat, Gabriel looked directly into her eyes as he told her, "He loves you more than anything." He looked away then. *And so do I.*

The following Friday morning, just before the usual 7:00 a.m. hospital cardiovascular conference, Gabriel and Ranya chanced upon one another while walking toward the same bank of elevators. Gabriel could see that she was in improved spirits; capitalizing on this, he said something trivial to cheer her further, and was rewarded with peals of her delighted laughter. He dearly loved that laugh of Ranya's. Hearing it was like being wrapped inside joy itself.

Seeing an open elevator ahead, he called out, "Hold the elevator, please!"

It was the hand of a heart surgeon that slammed against the elevator door to keep it from closing, and an unmistakable voice that bellowed, "I'd know that Irish brogue anywhere!"

Please, let's not have this get awkward, thought Gabriel as he greeted Rasheed, smiling cordially as he stood to one side to allow Ranya to enter the elevator first. Rasheed had not been able to make it for their usual Thursday night drink since the last one featuring his earth-shattering announcement. So Gabriel was relieved when Rasheed returned his smile now, even though it did seem a bit forced.

Let's all pretend for these few moments that we're all fine, shall we? Just five more floors to go. And as they made trivial small talk about the weather and the busy day ahead of them, Gabriel stood with his hands folded in front of him, rocking back and forth on his heels, trying not to feel claustrophobic in the steel cage that bore them all upward.

Sixth floor. The elevator bells dinged and Gabriel cried, "Here's my floor!" with far more enthusiasm than he had intended.

When Rasheed had held open the elevator doors upon recognizing Gabriel's voice, what he hadn't mentioned was that he would know that laugh of Ranya's anywhere, too, and it was a sound he hadn't heard for days. Once they had wished Gabriel a good day upon his exit to the neurology floor, Rasheed and Ranya proceeded to the cardiovascular conference on the ninth floor, where they sat side by side in their usual spot at the back of the room. The entire room was darkened so that the x-ray and cardiac catheterization films being presented at the front could be easily seen. In the darkness, Rasheed leaned over to Ranya and whispered, "So what's going on with Gabriel?"

Ranya, whose attention was studiously focused on the presentation at the front of the room, shrugged her shoulders dismissively and answered, "Oh, Gabriel being Gabriel, you know."

"Maybe I don't know," Rasheed whispered back. "I never knew he was that hilarious," he grumbled.

Ranya shot him a daggered look.

Rasheed sat back in his chair and sighed. He tried to focus his attention on the films being shown on the screen several rows in front of them, but it was no use. He couldn't sit there beside Ranya, breathing in her jasmine-scented perfume as it mingled with the essences of honey and roses that came from her freshly-washed hair, and not feel his heart pounding. He longed to hold her, even as he fought against the resentment that beckoned to him like a demon just beyond the margins of sanity.

He didn't know how they were going to proceed. But as he sat there beside her in the dark, one thing became clear to him: a life without her was not one that he would suffer gladly.

CHAPTER NINETEEN

اعقِلها وتوكّل

"Trust in God, but tie your camel."
—Arabic proverb

THE NEXT TIME THEY MET at Houston's, Gabriel and Rasheed sat at the bar together in silence for a long while, each lost in his own thoughts.

Gabriel found himself thinking of the early days with Rasheed, when the man who would become his best friend was still healing from a regrettable relationship with a faithless nurse. The denouement had consisted of an unfortunate late-night scene in which Rasheed had entered the x-ray file room to search for a chest film, and instead had found her in the arms of a senior surgeon. The whole of the Boston hospital where they were training found out about it eventually, though not from Rasheed. When Rasheed finally did come around to talking about it, it was Gabriel in whom he confided, Gabriel who listened. And Gabriel who eventually managed to bring him out of his doldrums and back into the sunshine again.

And now it was Rasheed who broke the silence once more. "I don't seem to be having much luck with women in this life of mine, Gabriel," he said, his voice heavy. He put his fingertips to his temples and heaved a great sigh.

Gabriel chuckled. "You're having better luck than I am, I'd say."

"Am I?" Rasheed turned to face him now.

Gabriel gave him a quizzical look. Rasheed's gaze met his, and both friends searched each other's eyes.

Rasheed shifted in his seat and loosened his tie. He began, "Well, listen, old friend, I think we need to talk about the elephant in the room."

Gabriel, who had not slept well since the last time they were sitting in this very spot, looked around the room, and then, belatedly recognizing the figure of speech, looked at Rasheed and waited patiently for what he suspected would come next.

Rasheed answered his unspoken question with one name: "Ranya."

Gabriel banished all expression from his face.

Rasheed continued, "She's *my* girlfriend, right?"

Gabriel reached out and squeezed Rasheed's arm, looking at him meaningfully as he replied, "Always has been."

"Good," Rasheed said. He looked pointedly at Gabriel. "Let's keep it that way, okay?"

Gabriel's grip tightened on Rasheed's arm. "Of course."

"You know," said Rasheed, "she hasn't had the easiest time of it. I try to remember that."

"Oh, yeah?" Gabriel responded, waiting—and wanting—to hear more.

"Yeah. I guess she never told you this—well, why would she, anyway, since she prefers not to talk about it—but her mother was a French professor at the university here, and died suddenly from a pulmonary embolism when Ranya was 16. Then her father, who was a neurosurgeon, died from a brain tumor—glioblastoma—about two years after she graduated from medical school."

"Oh, my God, that's awful," Gabriel said, shaking his head. It was a lot to process; he could only imagine what it must have been like for Ranya. His heart, as always, went out to her. Even more so than before.

After a pause, Gabriel commented, "I never knew Ranya's father was a neurosurgeon. Well, that explains a lot." *Her drive. Her ambition.* "And talk about dying from the very disease that you treat!" *Her distaste for the field of neurology . . . and for neurologists like me.*

"Yep," Rasheed said, throwing back his second shot.

They sat in silence for another minute or so, Gabriel knocking the ice about in his drink, watching what little liquid was left slosh back and forth against the glass. He pondered whether or not to tell Rasheed, then decided he should know, decided it was vital that he know. So he raised his head and said to his friend, "You know she loves you, right?"

Rasheed's eyebrows shot up as he studied Gabriel. "I think—well, I guess—I mean, I hope I do know that," he said at last. "But the question that occupies me more is . . . how do *you* know that?"

Gabriel could feel the heat rising in his face, and he turned away momentarily. He downed what was left of his drink and looked at Rasheed again. "Because she told me so."

CHAPTER TWENTY

"Being deeply loved by someone gives you strength, while loving someone
deeply gives you courage."
—Lao Tzu

February 15, 1999
Monday

RANYA WAS SO PLEASED with Rasheed. He had taken it upon himself to
cook her a Valentine's dinner the night before, all by himself. *Maqloubeh* and
tabbouleh, enough for half a dozen people. Pulling on her scrubs and getting
ready for another day in the cath lab, she smiled to herself as she recalled their
exchange over the volume of food he had produced for last night's candlelit
dinner.

"But, Rasheed, this is a feast!" she had exclaimed, staring agape at the massive
pot that held the rice, cauliflower, lamb, tomatoes, and spices that made up
the *maqloubeh,* the wonderful smells of cinnamon, allspice, and fried pine nuts
wafting from his stove. This was a true labor of love. It took a lot of time and
effort, she knew, to make this traditional dish, the name of which was Arabic for
"upside down." She had delighted in watching him flip the entire thing onto a
large serving platter, a technique not easily accomplished by a single man, but one

he handled with finesse. She imagined he had done this many times in his own family's home back in Ramallah.

Seeing the large dish of *maqloubeh* accompanied not only by equally large quantities of tabbouleh, but also by small plates of cucumbers, yogurt, pickled beets, and green olives, she had commented again, "Wow, Rasheed, this is a lot of food! Are we expecting someone else?"

"Certainly not," he'd sniffed. "Whatever we don't eat tonight, we will have all week." He had smiled at her then. Ranya took this as an invitation to eat with him all week, and she gladly accepted. What a wonderful gift.

Last summer, she hadn't been sure how they would go on, but Rasheed had seemed determined to stay by her side, declaring that he would support her in whatever path she chose to pursue in life—as long as she would be so kind as to leave enough room on that path for him to walk with her. That was not a bad deal at all, Ranya thought. To go through life in the company of a handsome, upstanding, loyal gentleman like Rasheed? One could do worse. And Rasheed was a rising star in the cardiovascular surgery department; she was grateful to know he had her back.

He had told her how much he admired her drive and determination to succeed. She didn't know why that had surprised her; why had she not expected Rasheed to be totally behind her? He had even said that he wanted to respect her need for space to pursue her dreams, if space was what she felt she needed. And he had gone on to tell her, quite clearly, that he just didn't see why he couldn't be there beside her as she did it.

When he had put it that way, she found it hard to disagree. And so here they were. Together again, still.

She checked her reflection in the mirror while brushing her teeth, and caught the furrowing of her brow. She tried to pull herself out of her concentrated reverie and bring her mind into the day before her, but she was still ruminating on more of their conversation from the previous night. They had talked about the passing of Jordan's King Hussein, who had died a week before. They had talked about work, and how she was getting on with her first year as a full-fledged attending physician. Rasheed had told her that she could always come to him with any problem or issue, anything whatsoever, reminding her that two heads were better than one.

And then the conversation had turned to the calendar year itself, and the fact that it was 1999, and before they knew it, they would be celebrating the start of a new millennium. "Pretty crazy, eh?" Rasheed had commented when she brought it up.

"You know, Rasheed, we should do something, go somewhere, this New Year's. They're having a huge party on the National Mall in Washington, DC—why don't we go to that? Actually take the time off together, and just go?"

He had grinned at her, his eyes alight. "Sounds like a lot of fun," he said. "Let's do it."

She hadn't finished her next bite of food when he added, "Maybe we should invite Gabe, too. He sometimes goes home to Ireland for Christmas, but I bet we could get him to DC for New Year's."

She had swallowed hastily, trying not to choke. She stared at Rasheed, hoping to read his eyes, but he was gazing off at some point in the distance, thinking about something beyond her read. Not wanting to let too much time pass, she responded with what she hoped sounded like detached propriety: "Of course he's always welcome. Whatever you think is best."

Thinking back on it now from the isolation of her own apartment, she sighed. She filled her blue thermos with water from the fridge, wondering what really was best, and if she would know it when she saw it. She straightened her shoulders, picked up her bag, and threw open her door to meet the day.

The next time she ran into Gabriel, it was at the Second Story Café in Davis-Kidd Booksellers. He was sitting at a table in the airy indoor patio, mid-day sunlight streaming down upon him from the skylights. The crisp, starched collar of his white Oxford shirt folded neatly over the black wool sweater he was wearing, and Ranya reflected again on how his clothes always seemed to fit him perfectly.

One bite of a red velvet cake remained on the plate in front of him, and behind him, a box of feathered ferns and waxy-green peace lilies lent a lushness that was unexpected for the time of year. As she took another step in his direction, he lowered the book he was reading and made eye contact with her.

She hadn't seen much of Gabriel in the past few months; it was almost as if he had been trying to avoid her. Thus she was surprised at the broadness of his smile and the bright welcome in his eyes as he gestured to the seat across from him, inviting her to join him.

"How are you these days, Ranya? Incredibly busy as ever?"

She smiled at him. "Not too busy for the occasional trip to the bookstore," she said. "Nor are you, I see," she added, glancing at the slim paperback book on the table between them.

He picked up the book and handed it to her. "A great play, well worth your time. Quick as you are, Ranya, you'll easily finish it this afternoon."

She read the cover aloud. "The Field, by John B. Keane."

"Yeah," said Gabriel, "a very Irish story. Full of memorable characters. One in particular—Bull McCabe." He chuckled and shook his head. "You don't wanna get on the wrong side of the likes of him."

Ranya looked at him for a moment, the book still in her hand, then ventured to ask, "Do you ever miss it? Ireland, I mean? I imagine you must."

He looked away from her then and sighed heavily. When he met her gaze again, Ranya thought his eyes were the bluest she had ever seen. The color of the Nashville sky on a cloudless summer day. Why had she never noticed that before?

Still holding her gaze, he answered, "Every single day."

"How do you do it, then?"

He smiled at her. "Well, having good friends helps a lot. So thank you for that. And otherwise," he added, seeming to search for an explanation within himself, "I dunno—you just put your head down and keep going, I s'pose." He shrugged.

"There haven't been that many opportunities for neurologists in Ireland over the past couple of decades—that's why I came here in the first place—so I'm grateful for the opportunity that I do have here in America. And if things should one day change back home, well . . . who knows?"

Then he grinned. In her mind, Ranya had labeled this special expression of his as "Gabriel's grin," and she found that it always lifted her heart when he favored her with it. Still grinning, he pointed at the book she was holding. "And reading lots of good Irish books by good Irish writers doesn't hurt," he said.

"In that case, I should give you back your book," she said, standing up.

Gabriel moved swiftly to his feet to stand with her. "Oh, no, Ranya, that's your book now. You keep it."

Her mouth opened, but no words came out. Gabriel didn't leave room for silence this time, and hurried to explain, "I've already paid for it. If you hate it, then by all means feel free to return it."

He smiled at her then in a way that radiated warmth despite the chill on the patio. "But something tells me you won't," he said, tilting his head to one side. "Hate is not in your nature, is it, Ranya?"

CHAPTER TWENTY-ONE

"All the art of living lies in a fine mingling of letting go and holding on."
—Havelock Ellis

December 31, 1999
Friday

Ranya exited the red-line Metro stop at Woodley Park with Rasheed and Gabriel, and the three of them undertook the walk to Mama Ayesha's restaurant on Calvert Street. It was freezing and she felt every step of it, but it was the turn of the century, so she did not care. Neither did her two companions, judging from their high spirits.

They crossed the Duke Ellington Memorial Bridge, and just beyond it, on the edge of Adams Morgan, loomed Mama Ayesha's, the oldest continuously-running Palestinian restaurant in Washington, DC, opened by Mama Ayesha Abraham in 1960. Ranya had eaten there on many a DC trip, and in her humble opinion, they had the best stuffed grape leaves in the world.

The smells of garlic, olive oil, and stewed lamb wafted out onto the street as they neared the entrance, convincing Ranya that she was starving. The maître d' seated them at an upholstered half-moon booth perfect for three. The restaurant's interior was well decorated, bathing them in colors reminiscent of the red soil of the West Bank and surrounding them with objects and artifacts, like the gold-brocade tapestries on the walls, that reminded Ranya of the pictures Rasheed had shown her of his family's home in Ramallah.

Gabriel perused the wine list, commenting on how extensive it was. He had already announced his intention to steer clear of arak, recalling his earlier inauspicious experience with that particular beverage, and so while Rasheed ordered arak with hints of licorice and anise, Gabriel chose a Spanish red wine from Ribera del Duero instead. Ranya requested one of her favorite drinks, *ayran*, a salty-and-sour yogurt drink that always reminded her of her mother.

By the time their appetizers of hummus, labneh sprinkled with za'atar, tabbouleh, baba ghanoush, and pickled vegetables arrived, they were already congratulating themselves on their decision to come to DC to ring in the new millennium in grand style.

"Yeah, we owe you a debt of thanks again, Ranya, for this excellent idea," Rasheed said.

"And I'm looking forward to the special event at the Lincoln Memorial tonight, the—what's it called again? American Gala?" Gabriel said.

"America's Millenium Gala," Ranya said, "and don't you just know there's gonna be a very long line waiting for us when we get there. We're going to freeze to death!"

"Aah, we can tolerate a little inconvenience for an event that only comes around once a century, don't you think?" Rasheed said.

"Indeed. It'll be a celebration for the history books, I'm sure. And we're going to be a part of it!" Gabriel said. "We'll 'party like it's 1999!' Ha!"

Rasheed laughed and Ranya groaned.

She looked around her to see if anyone—or everyone—else was having as much fun as they were. The restaurant was packed, and all the diners were animated, full of excitement and anticipation. Gabriel was not wrong; it was a party-like atmosphere, to be sure. Sitting there surrounded by the good food and warm ambience of Mama Ayesha's, Ranya reflected on how lucky she was to be there, and in such good company.

And something else occurred to her as she surveyed the room and its occupants, many of whom had features similar to hers and Rasheed's, and could be heard speaking Arabic: how much progress Arab Americans had made, how their image finally seemed to be rising in the eyes of the public.

She nudged Rasheed. "Look around. It's gotten a lot easier to be an Arab American in public, hasn't it?"

Rasheed knew exactly what she meant, as she had known he would. They both chuckled.

"What's that?" asked Gabriel, glancing up from his plate.

"I was just telling Rasheed how much easier it is to be an Arab American in public now," Ranya answered. "Only half-joking, I might add."

"Oh, yeah, I understand," Gabriel nodded. "I've seen all the Hollywood movies too, Ranya. Pretty terrible portrayals of Arabs for decades now."

"But, you know," he continued, "that same industry is still pumping out films about the Troubles in Northern Ireland, and will no doubt continue to do so for many years to come. But forget about the film producers. We have only to look at the Good Friday Agreement that finally took effect in Northern Ireland, just a few weeks ago. I'm telling you, there is always hope."

"That's so like you, Gabe: 'Hope is just around the corner,' yeah?" Rasheed said.

"Surely there is hope to be found in all corners," Gabriel murmured, so quietly that Ranya almost missed it. His eyes sought hers for the briefest of moments, then he glanced away.

Rasheed raised his glass and cheered, "To Gabe, the optimistic magician!"

Whether Rasheed had heard his comment, or whether he was just working off Gabriel's prior affirmation of hope, Ranya would never know, but she caught Rasheed's reference, recalling his earlier characterization of his neurologist friend. Could it have been just over three years ago that they had been sitting in Gabriel's apartment, listening to him wax poetic about his choice and love of neurology as a specialty?

Apparently Gabriel caught the reference, too. She watched him grin that special grin, then raise his glass in return, toasting both of his companions at once: "To my dear plumbers! May you leave no artery unclogged!"

Ranya made a wry face at him.

"Well, look, Ranya, you unplug all the arteries you can, and Rasheed is more than happy to bypass the ones you can't. Couldn't be easier—or more convenient!"

"Well, you can't live without the heart," Ranya said.

"Well, you wouldn't want to live without a brain," Gabriel shot back.

"Okay, okay, you two," Rasheed interrupted, waving a hand to signal a cease fire. "What is this, third grade?" He shook his head and asked, "How did we get to this, anyway? What were we talking about?"

Gabriel picked up his glass again, unfazed. "We were making toasts. So here's another one." His smile widened as he intoned, "*Fad saol agat, gob fliuch, agus bás in Éirinn.*"

"And that means . . .?" Rasheed waited patiently.

"Long life to you, a wet mouth, and death in Ireland." Gabriel winked at Rasheed when he translated the "wet mouth" portion, then tipped his glass to his lips and swallowed after completing the full translation.

"Death in Ireland, eh?" Rasheed looked thoughtful. "Not such a bad idea. One could certainly do worse, don't you think?"

Gabriel nodded his head. "No doubt about that, my friend."

Ranya was reminded of another conversation with Gabriel, the one at Davis-Kidd, when he had expressed how deeply he missed his homeland. She wondered if he would ever return there permanently.

They had all fallen silent, the air heavy with remembrance. Too heavy, it seemed to Ranya. She forced brightness back onto her face and into her voice, breaking the silence. "All right, guys, we have a whole new century ahead of us, and we're not working for once, so enough talk about death for now. More talk about Rasheed's upcoming birthday!" She turned and flashed her biggest smile at the birthday boy.

Rasheed smiled back. "Yeah, that's right; I'll actually have a birthday next year. February 29, 2000."

Gabriel said, "So you're really, what, just six years old or something? Explains a lot about you, Rasheed." There was laughter all around.

"Yeah, well, I'm about to be ten, so you can relax, Gabe. Expect a leap in my maturity."

"Very punny, Rasheed," Ranya said. She leaned forward and gave Gabriel a conspiratorial look. "So we're going to have to figure out what you do for a ten-year-old in a grown man's body." Then she turned to Rasheed with a sudden realization. "You know, Rasheed, that's actually your fortieth birthday—it *is* quite a milestone! For anyone!"

"Um, I don't know if I should bring this up," Gabriel said, "but you know, in Ireland, there is a tradition—well, a superstition, really—that women should only propose marriage to men on Leap Day."

Rasheed's eyes lit up. "Really?"

Gabriel cleared his throat and continued, "Yeah, according to an old legend, St. Brigid of Kildare made a deal with St. Patrick to grant permission for women to propose to men once every four years—on Leap Day. And," Gabriel added, pausing for effect, "any man who refuses a woman's proposal on that day is supposed to give her a gown made of silk."

Ranya knit her brows and rendered her judgment. "That's the nuttiest thing I've ever heard! And anyway, a woman should be able to propose to a man any day she wants."

Rasheed nudged Ranya with his elbow and asked, "So what's stopping you, then?"

Ranya rolled her eyes and swatted playfully at Rasheed's shoulder. "Oh, Rasheed, *Habibi*, we've been over this. Not now, okay?" Then she leaned in and made a show of batting her eyelashes at him. "But you can still get me that gown made of silk."

Rasheed protested, "Whoa! I thought it was *my* birthday we were talking about! So not only will I not get a proposal, but I will be getting *you* a gift as well?"

Ranya put her hand on his and said seriously, "Every day with you is a gift, Rasheed, and I am grateful for every one of them."

Gabriel shook the air with his glass and chanted loudly, "Hear! Hear!"

Later that night, they stood on the edge of the reflecting pool in front of the Lincoln Memorial, having braved the massive line that stretched for blocks down Constitution Avenue. They huddled together for warmth as they strained to hear the band play, awaiting, along with thousands of others, the ringing in of not just a new year but a new millennium, with all the promise of better to come. Ranya noted that the purists of the calendar would point out that the old millennium didn't actually end until midnight on December 31 of the year 2000, and Rasheed noted where the purists could go.

When the clock struck midnight, the immense fireworks display began, and Rasheed pulled Ranya off her feet in a passionate embrace. The cheers of the gigantic crowd rose all around them, and even with her eyes closed, her lips against Rasheed's, Ranya could see the bright flashes of the fireworks dancing across her eyelids.

When she opened her eyes, her gaze fell upon Gabriel, a lone shadow against the brilliantly illuminated backdrop. His eyes met hers, and then he strode toward them, arms outstretched, and wrapped one arm around her and another around Rasheed, hugging them tightly and loudly proclaiming, "Happy new year! Happy new millennium!"

Ranya jumped up and down with Rasheed and Gabriel and the rest of the crowd, everyone smiling and laughing as the hopes and possibilities of a new century loomed before them.

PART TWO

CHAPTER TWENTY-TWO

"Is é an dóchas lia gach anró."
("Hope is the physician of each misery.")
—Irish proverb

September 11, 2001
Tuesday

RANYA WAS CAREFULLY GUIDING a catheter to the opening of her patient's left main coronary artery when she became aware of a commotion in the control room behind her. Doors opening and closing and, once, slamming shut. Murmurs and insistent whispers. She could feel her assistant becoming agitated beside her. Not the quiet and decorum she had made clear she expected when she was in the cath lab.

Without taking her eyes from the fluoroscopy screen that showed the placement of her catheter within her patient's heart, she asked the air, "What's going on?"

A voice belonging to one of the technicians in the control room answered over the lab's ceiling speakers. "The Pentagon is under attack."

"Under attack?!" Ranya now held her hands, which in turn held the catheter, absolutely still, and turned to glance at her assistant, who looked equally shocked and was muttering, "Oh, my God," and shaking her head repeatedly. The patient, who was sedated but not unconscious, stiffened and tried to move. A nurse ran to the head of the table and spoke quietly to him, and he became still again.

"There's a fire there or something. I think the Pentagon's on fire. And so is the World Trade Center in New York City," came the voice of another tech from the control room. "Mark is going to find out—he's gone to watch the news. It's all on TV."

Ranya took a deep breath and muttered, "Okay." Then she repeated, louder, "Okay. Let's finish this case here now, all right?"

Returning her focus to the catheter and the coronary arteries before her, she proceeded to shoot a burst of dye into the left main coronary and its tributaries. The course of the opaque dye revealed a severe blockage. Ranya made the easy decision to open up that blockage with a stent.

She was inflating the stent in the artery when another voice from the control room came over the loudspeaker. "Dr. Abbasi, when you're finished, a word with you, please." This time the voice was Rasheed's. Her back still to the windows of the control room, Ranya put up one gloved hand in acknowledgment, but never took her eyes from her procedure.

Only when the case was finally finished did Ranya turn around to find both Rasheed and Gabriel standing in the control room, and as she peeled off her gloves and walked toward them, she noticed that Gabriel seemed slightly out of breath. She realized that he must have run down several flights of stairs, rather than take the elevators. When she exited the room with him and Rasheed, she found out why.

CHAPTER TWENTY-THREE

"Courage isn't having the strength to go on—it is going on when you don't have strength."
—Napoleon Bonaparte

A LARGE CROWD HAD gathered in the cath lab waiting lounge, all eyes raised to the television screen in the far corner. Ranya stood silently, feeling paralyzed. Rasheed and Gabriel stood on either side of her, Gabriel with his hand covering his mouth, Rasheed's eyes wide, as live coverage of the collapsing towers of the World Trade Center filled the screen and hushed murmurs of disbelief traveled across the waiting room.

The three friends were still glued in position ten minutes later when a cath lab nurse approached Ranya from behind, gently took her elbow, and spoke into her ear. "There's a STEMI case coming in to the lab right now." Ranya wheeled around, looking at the nurse and fumbling with her pager. She saw that it had gone off several minutes ago to alert her to the arrival of a patient with the most serious form of heart attack, an ST-elevation MI, requiring emergency cardiac catheterization. She muttered an apology and ran back to the cath lab, leaving Gabriel and Rasheed standing and staring.

It took every measure of inner strength for the entire cath lab team to get through their roster of cases for the day, but once they did, Ranya promptly paged Rasheed to find out where he was and if he was okay. She did not know why she was asking him that, as she knew that he was right there in Nashville with her, but she felt the need to ask someone, to be reassured that someone she knew and loved was okay on that horrible day, in those horrible moments.

Rasheed informed her that he was at home, still watching the news, and that Gabriel was there with him. He asked her to join them, and told her not to worry about dinner, because they had saved some for her. But as Ranya was making the walk toward her car in the gathering dusk, she stopped in her tracks on the red brick portico.

Libby Gold. Libby Gold's son.

Hadn't Libby said that her older son was going to work for an investment firm in Manhattan? Hadn't she mentioned to Ranya at some point that the firm's offices were in the World Trade Center?

Ranya continued walking toward her car at a quicker pace, now with her cell phone in hand, dialing Libby's number. She couldn't get through, no matter how many times she tried. So she left a voicemail and hoped against hope that when Libby had a chance to get back to her, it would be with reassuring news.

Rasheed was on the phone in his living room, standing behind his plush white leather sofa, trying to organize a blood drive at their hospital for the following day. Ranya was sitting on the opposite end of the couch from Gabriel, and both were still watching the news. Gabriel sat leaning forward, elbows on his knees, hands in prayer position in front of his lips.

Ranya had that feeling of utter paralysis again. She found that she couldn't cry, she couldn't speak, she didn't want to move. She couldn't feel anything other than the crashing waves of disbelief that washed over her again and again. And then, after what seemed a long time, after seeing the towers fall again in yet another replay, she found that what she felt was a deep and overwhelming sadness, a sadness that was all-encompassing. It was a sadness for the many lives lost and the lives still missing, for the senseless devastation, for the hatred that must have fueled such heinous acts, for the hopelessness she felt in the face of the existence of such evil, and last but not least, for the backlash that she suspected would be soon to come.

In the back of her mind lurked the questions that had lived there all day, the internal dialogue that would not rest: *Who did this? Who* could *have done this?* She hoped against hope that this had not originated with some group in the Middle East. But the perpetrators who had been identified so far had Arabic names.

Rasheed hung up the phone and sank down into the plushness of his sofa between her and Gabriel. He threw his head back, letting it rest against the top cushions. A wavy lock of black hair tumbled across his forehead, and he irritably stuck out his lower lip and blew it back. When he finally spoke, the quiver in his voice captured her attention. She could tell that Gabriel noticed it too.

"How could anybody do this?" Rasheed asked, bringing his head forward and opening his eyes again to look at the TV screen before them. "I just can't understand it. So much killing, so much destruction."

Ranya put her head on his shoulder and her hand on his arm. "I don't know," she whispered. "I just don't know." And even as the horror of the day's events washed over her again, she found that she couldn't shake the feeling that she was also watching the reputations of all Arabs and Arab Americans fall with the towers, all the gains made over the past few years buried beneath the rubble. It nagged at her enough that she hesitantly—so hesitantly that she almost stopped herself from asking it aloud—voiced the question to her companions.

"Am I a terrible person to see . . . in addition to this unspeakable human tragedy, all the suffering and loss of life . . . but also the collapse of nearly a decade of work by the Arab-American community to improve our image in this country, to become real and valued citizens of a greater nation? The collapse not just of buildings, but of goodwill, of sanity . . . of hope itself?"

She went on, as if stating the obvious would help somehow—or maybe naming it would make the fact disappear: "I mean, all the perpetrators that have been identified so far are Arabs, right?"

She was asking this last question of Rasheed, but it was Gabriel who answered, quietly but steadily. "You're not a terrible person, Ranya; the people who did this are. You're a visionary—I think you always have been—and I'm afraid you may be right about all of the above. But not," he added with firm conviction, "when it comes to hope. There is always hope, Ranya. We can't always see why or even how it's there, but it is there."

Rasheed chimed in, "Yeah, Ranya, much as I hate to say it, I think you're right. But so is Gabe. Look, we'll be doing this blood drive tomorrow, we'll focus on doing whatever we can to help whomever we can that has been affected by this, and the best thing we can do is what we have always done: our best. Every day, one day at a time." He sighed heavily and added, though noticeably without Gabriel's conviction: "The rest will take care of itself."

When Ranya walked into the large gymnasium that had been repurposed for the blood drive, she spotted Gabriel and Rasheed right away, sitting side by side in the center of a brightly-lit row of cots, tubes running from their arms. Actually, now that Ranya thought of it, the "cots" looked more like poolside chaises, and the fact that both Gabriel and Rasheed were absorbed in their respective reading materials only served to deepen that impression.

Gabriel was reading the green journal, more officially known as *Neurology*, the journal of the American Academy of Neurology, while Rasheed was perusing the *Washington Report on Middle East Affairs*, its front cover visible to anyone who cared to look his way. *Oh, great, Rasheed; nice. Like THAT isn't going to draw anyone's attention.* But maybe, as she had thought before when it came to Rasheed, that was precisely his intention.

She paused and reflected on how incongruous it seemed, these two men who were the best of friends, one fair-skinned and blue-eyed and the other olive-skinned and dark-haired, hailing from different sides of the world and yet so similar in their affection for—and loyalty to—one another, lounging there as calmly as if they had been at the beach on holiday, while dark blood dripped from their veins. Their blood was the same color, she noted, and didn't know why she was pointing out the obvious to herself.

And then her view expanded, and it was not just Gabriel's and Rasheed's blood that was the same, but that of row upon row of cot-bound donors of different ethnicities, different skill sets, different backgrounds, different faiths. But on the inside, all the same.

"Prick us, do we not bleed?" Yes, Mr. Shakespeare, indeed we do, all together now, all for the same cause, and all in the same shade.

It struck her again as surreal and almost funny, that she, Dr. Ranya Abbasi, invasive cardiologist extraordinaire, could be entertaining wonderment at this point regarding the universality of the color of blood. Yet there it was—so simple, so self-evident, and so often overlooked.

She forced herself out of her reverie and walked toward Rasheed and Gabriel with a big smile on her face, gesturing to catch their attention. Both smiled back, waving their respective journals at her and seeming oblivious to everyone else in the room. Rasheed urged her to come over, and when she got to his side, he reported on the discovery that he and Gabriel had made not an hour before.

"Ranya, did you know that Gabriel and I share the same blood type?"

Ranya put her hands on her hips and looked down at them both. "Now, why does that not surprise me?"

"Yeah," Gabriel said, jabbing a thumb in Rasheed's direction, "both B+. Isn't that what I keep telling you, Ranya: be positive??" He looked up at her with laughing eyes while Rasheed guffawed.

"Y'all are too much," Ranya said, shaking her head. She turned and headed toward the registration table. She never relished the process of giving blood, but now she couldn't stop smiling.

Two nights later, Ranya and Rasheed dined at Sunset Grill, both nearing exhaustion from the week's turmoil. Midway through their entrees, Ranya's phone lit up. Immediately recognizing the number, Ranya announced, "It's Libby," and jumped up to take the call.

On the well-lit sidewalk that ran past the restaurant's front door, the leaves were just beginning to change colors, and some had fallen to the pavement. That was all Ranya processed as Libby's voice came to her, choking between sobs: "He reported . . . for work Tuesday morning. He was in that tower . . . when the planes hit. All those floors were totally destroyed. He's gone, Ranya. My Jacob . . . my baby . . . is gone."

Ranya leaned backward, reaching with her hand for the restaurant's brick wall to keep herself from falling. "Oh, my God. Oh, my God, I am so sorry, Libby. I am so sorry." Repeated over and over. Not knowing what else to say. Relying on that red brick wall to hold her up as images of a tall, flaxen-haired, confident young man came flashing back to her. A young man gone forever. Libby's son.

When Ranya finally returned to the table, Rasheed had only to look at her face to know. "Oh, no," he said, extending his hand to hers.

"Jacob. Libby's son, whom we met at the bar mitzvah. He—" and then her voice broke and she could not finish. She took her hand from Rasheed's and placed it over her face, slid it up through her hair. She bit her lips to keep them from trembling. Rasheed waited patiently, silently.

When she found her voice again, it was hoarse and strained. "They will be sitting shiva here in Nashville. At Libby's house, I would think—I'll get more details tomorrow. But obviously I want to be there with her."

Rasheed straightened his back and said quietly, "I will sit with you."

CHAPTER TWENTY-FOUR

"Blessed is the season which engages the whole world in a conspiracy of love."
—Hamilton Wright Mabie

Early December 2002

IT HAD BEEN A DARK YEAR, and as Ranya had feared, reprisals were swift to come, and societal fractures appeared and began to magnify with the passage of time. But another Christmas was on its way, another new year, and that never failed to give Gabriel cause to hope. As he stood with his friends in front of one of the grand entrances to Nashville's Opryland Hotel, taking in the more than three million Christmas lights that adorned the complex at this time of year, hope indeed seemed once again within their grasp. They were in need of some light, to be sure, and for now, this was doing the trick.

Several yards from one of the hotel's many circular drives was a beautiful Nativity scene, and as they walked toward it, Ranya turned to Gabriel and said, her breath forming the tiniest of clouds in the cold night air, "Isn't it lovely?"

"Yes, it is," Gabriel said.

Then she posed her second question to him. "You know who the world's most famous Palestinian is, Gabriel?"

Gabriel saw Rasheed give Ranya a knowing smile.

He wasn't sure he knew where they were going with this. He shook his head. "I don't know. Who?"

"Jesus Christ, Gabriel!"

Gabriel stiffened, feeling defensive. He put his hand to his chest. "Well, I'm sorry," he said, "but I really don't know."

"No, I mean Jesus Christ, the one and only—as in, the Lord and Savior, the Prince of Peace," Ranya said.

She gestured with an open palm to the ornate Nativity before her. "Jesus of Nazareth. Born in Bethlehem. Raised in Nazareth. Crucified in Jerusalem. All in the land we know as Palestine. Every Bible tells the story. I mean, here we stand in front of the Nativity, the very promise of peace on earth, and at the center of it is a Palestinian! Why doesn't anybody ever think about that??" She stamped her boot on the ground, gloved fists stuffed into her coat pockets.

Rasheed added, "And he, too, was born under occupation. Roman occupation, at that time. He was also a refugee."

Gabriel raised his eyes to the night sky and laughed out loud with revelation, drawing the attention of passersby. He felt as though an entire world had just opened up to him. While it was true that none of the 9/11 attackers had been Palestinian, there was ongoing violence in the occupied territories even now. There had never been a greater need for the Prince of Peace to grace his homeland with another miracle.

"Wow, you're right. You're absolutely right," he said to Ranya. Then he looked at Rasheed in wonder. "Why has no one ever thought of that?"

The corners of Rasheed's mouth rose. "Ranya has."

Rasheed put his arm around Ranya's shoulders and they all walked back toward the main entrance. Their faces were softly illuminated by the glow of a million twinkling lights of every color. Gabriel counted his good fortune, not for the first time, and not least of all because he knew he couldn't be in better company.

Their destination was the Jack Daniel's restaurant that beckoned to them from within the vast and glittering complex of the Opryland Hotel, which was an indoor city unto itself. When Rasheed had first expressed his eagerness for dining there, Gabriel had readily agreed, but Ranya had wrinkled her nose and quizzed him, "Really?"

"But, Ranya, they have the best burgers this side of Heaven," Rasheed had protested.

"I thought that was Houston's that had the best burgers."

"Well, they do, too."

"Those burgers will be the death of you, Rasheed."

"Oh, but what a way to die, Ranya, *Habibti*," Rasheed had answered, giving her arm a squeeze. It had seemed to Gabriel that they smiled as one.

The restaurant was cozily decorated with wood paneling and black-and-white images from the Jack Daniel's distillery in nearby Lynchburg, Tennessee. In between Christmas jingles, Willie and Waylon's rendition of "Mamas Don't Let Your Babies Grow Up to Be Cowboys" played on the overhead sound system.

Aaah, Nashville. Gabriel had to admit, he had developed quite a fondness for the place. And for a certain pair of its residents. And wasn't that the damnable agony of it?

As Ranya and Rasheed chatted, Gabriel reflected once more on the outdoor manger scene. It occurred to him that there was every likelihood that, historically speaking, the Mother of God bore more physical resemblance to Ranya than to the ghostly-white Renaissance-era depictions that had grown so popular.

When the dinner plates arrived, Gabriel turned his attention to Rasheed, noticing how the sea-green irises of his friend's eyes flashed brilliantly in the warm lights of the restaurant, adding a glow to the broad, relaxed smile he wore as he conversed with Ranya. Gabriel couldn't believe it had never occurred to him before, never occurred to him to ask, in all the years they had been friends.

"Say, what's the story with your eyes, Rasheed?"

Rasheed looked up from the colossal mess of his oversized burger. He had been reaching for the ketchup bottle, but now stopped his hand in midair.

"What's wrong with my eyes?"

Ranya looked now at Rasheed's eyes, first with the examining gaze of a physician, then with the admiring look of a lover. She patted him on the arm. "Nothing at all wrong that I can see, *Habibi*—quite the contrary." She smiled at him. Then they both looked questioningly at Gabriel.

Gabriel said, "I mean, they're green. Why are they green? How can they be green?"

Rasheed set his hand down on the table again and stared at Gabriel. "What on earth, man? Is there something in your Jack Daniel's? My eyes have always been green."

Rasheed looked at Ranya. "Has he been smoking something?"

Gabriel, growing frustrated, made it plainer, pointing to Ranya now. "Her eyes aren't green," he said. "I mean, I admit, I don't know that many Arabs in general or even that many Palestinian Arabs in particular, but you're the only one I know whose eyes are green—or any shade other than brown or black, for that matter."

Rasheed and Ranya both laughed. "Oh, okay, now I get it," Rasheed said. "You know, I never know where you go in that head of yours, Gabe. But I see you're not aware of what some call the 'Crusader effect.'"

"And don't forget the Phoenicians," Ranya added.

"Yeah," Rasheed agreed. "See, Gabe: Palestine, Lebanon, Syria—all the Levant countries with ports on the Mediterranean—have been . . . visited, shall we say? . . . by a number of different seafaring cultures over the millennia."

"Some did more visiting than others," Ranya muttered, "and some overstayed their welcome."

"Well, yeah," Rasheed continued, "so the end effect is that you'll run across Arabs who have lighter eyes, red hair sometimes, and even blond hair and blue eyes. In fact, one of my first cousins is a redhead."

"Huh," Gabriel mulled this over, "so not unlike Ireland as a place that has seen its share of would-be conquerors and passersby."

"Yep," Rasheed said. "So can I eat my burger now?" He took a large bite, chewed and swallowed. Then he grinned. "You know, it's not impossible that I could even have some Irish blood running through my veins!"

Gabriel raised his glass. "And a lucky man you'd be if you did—I'll drink to that!"

CHAPTER TWENTY-FIVE

"A dreamer is one who can only find his way by moonlight, and his punishment is that he sees the dawn before the rest of the world."
—Oscar Wilde

June 2003

"Can you believe another year has come and gone in this hospital, and in less than a week we'll be witnessing yet another changing of the guard?" Gabriel said to Rasheed over Thursday night drinks. "Sure I don't relish the thought of yet another new class of interns taking over the hospital—how is it that we keep getting older while they keep getting younger?"

Hunched over the bar, he was feeling the weariness in his bones, but was glad to see his friend in good spirits, as energetic as ever. He'd never known a heart surgeon—or any surgeon, for that matter—who didn't seem to burn with an all-consuming energy; a necessity, he supposed, for the trade they were in. And that inner burning eventually either flamed out, leaving a bitter core, or blazed brilliantly forth, propelling them to greater and greater career heights.

It seemed Rasheed was on the latter path, thankfully; his meteoric career trajectory had escaped no one's notice, and Gabriel was happy for him. He had just been named Assistant Chief of Cardiothoracic Surgery—maybe the youngest one ever—with the position to take effect this July 1. It was just a matter of time, Gabriel thought, before Rasheed would become the Chief of that department.

As for himself, Gabriel had received numerous teaching awards by this point, but the administrative powers-that-be in his own department had not seen fit to translate that into meaningful leadership promotions, in spite of Rasheed's discreet lobbying on his behalf.

Maybe Gabriel was too outspoken for their tastes, too conscientious when it came to pointing out medical errors and lapses in compassionate and proper patient care. Attention to the financial bottom line was important, but not more important than the empathetic, diligent care of each and every patient, regardless of background or ability to pay. To his mind, that was the essence of the oath he had sworn to uphold.

Rasheed laughed in response to Gabriel's rhetorical question, which he chose to answer anyway. "They don't get younger, my friend; they stay the same and we keep moving on in years. But at some point we're no longer 'getting' older; we're just old." Rasheed leaned against him from the adjacent bar stool, giving him the sly look of a co-conspirator. "But we're not there yet," he whispered.

"And anyway," Rasheed straightened up, raising the volume of his voice a notch and tilting his glass at Gabriel, "your legendary teaching skills are only surpassed by your skills as a clinician. Those new interns are lucky to have you."

Once again, Rasheed was a mind reader. "Too bad the department heads don't seem to think so," Gabriel muttered.

"Yeah, well, those guys are fools," Rasheed said.

They sat in silence for a moment, then Gabriel sought a redirection. "So, with Libby deciding to retire early and the position of cath lab director being vacant, there are at least two openings in the cardiology division, right? I'd think Ranya would be more than eligible to fill any of those positions. Seems like she would have her pick."

Rasheed's face was hard to read. "We'll see," he said. "Rumor has it, they're bringing someone in from Boston to fill at least one of those roles. They certainly didn't ask me my opinion; I can tell you that right now.

"But Ranya's day will come," Rasheed continued. "I have no doubts about that."

Rasheed took another sip of his whiskey, then gave the conversation a jarring turn by asking casually, "So when will we get to meet your new girlfriend?"

Gabriel's stomach did a quick flip. He stared at Rasheed. "What new girl-friend?"

"The one you're gonna have when you finally get off your sorry ass and get a life." Rasheed's tone managed to be friendly, caring, and chiding all at once.

Gabriel heaved a large sigh and ran a hand through his hair. "Oh, God, I don't know, Rasheed. I think I'm going to swear off women all together."

"What, will we be calling you 'Father Gabe' now? Ah, Gabriel, you may be an angel, but you're not a priest," Rasheed said. "Although," he needled, "in the Greek Orthodox tradition, our priests can be married and still be men of God, so maybe you should consider it."

"You heathen," Gabriel said.

"Seriously, though," Rasheed said, "there are lots of lovely women around the hospital, and if they're not to your liking, there's always that new online dating thing. You might want to try it."

Gabriel studied him for a long moment. Finally, he said, "Okay. Maybe I will." He turned back to his drink, then stared at his distorted reflection in the mirrors behind the bartender. "Maybe I will," he repeated, more softly, and tipped the glass to his lips.

"I'll just warn you, he's not the friendliest customer."

Ranya stood beside Gabriel outside the door to his patient's hospital room and nodded as Gabriel spoke to her in hushed tones, detailing not only his patient's history but his demeanor. The bottom ends of their long white coats brushed against one another as she took her stethoscope from one of her side pockets and hung it around her neck.

From what Gabriel had told her, Mr. Shetfield had had a minor stroke and was recovering well, but it seemed probable that he would have another one if they couldn't fix the cause, and the likeliest culprit was the small hole in his heart, a patent foramen ovale, which yesterday's echocardiogram had revealed.

Gabriel had called Ranya to see if his patient might be a candidate for one of the clinical trials she was running, one that was testing the effectiveness of a device that could close the hole and thereby, hopefully, prevent any future strokes. Ranya had to agree that he did seem a perfect candidate.

Mr. Shetfield's bed was in the far corner of the room, and the bed curtain was drawn. A small beam of summer sunlight made its way through the shaded window and formed a circle on the white tile floor. The faint smell of cigarettes that lingered on the air around the bed told her that Mr. Shetfield was a smoker, and the muddy work boots on the floor beside his plastic bag of belongings told her something more.

Ranya let Gabriel go first, and stood at a respectful distance while he peered around the curtain and asked his patient if it would be all right for the cardiologist to see him now. She heard Mr. Shetfield grumble something, which, when Gabriel began pulling the curtain fully back, she took to be a yes. As soon as he laid eyes on Ranya, he spoke more loudly. "So where's the cardiologist?"

Ranya calmly stepped forward with her hand outstretched. This sort of attitude was always tiresome, but that didn't negate her obligation to those who needed her care. "I'm the cardiologist, Mr. Shetfield—Dr. Ranya Abbasi, and it's a pleasure to meet you."

Mr. Shetfield, instead of taking her hand, turned to Gabriel, looking up at him with a smile that turned her stomach. "Look at you, keeping such company." To her ongoing disgust, he winked at Gabriel and made a point of looking Ranya up and down. "Although, with looks like that, can't say I blame ya."

Gabriel's hands clutched the bed's side rail, and Ranya saw his knuckles go white and his face turn red. She folded her arms across her chest, hoping to project a no-nonsense pose to Mr. Shetfield, and Gabriel cleared his throat. Given the look on his face, she was surprised at the measured calmness of his next words.

"Mr. Shetfield, we don't tolerate that sort of talk around here."

The sternness of Gabriel's face brooked no room for argument. Ranya made a concerted effort to keep her own expression as neutral as possible as Gabriel continued, "Now, Dr. Abbasi is the most highly qualified cardiologist I know, and if you'll let her help you, you might just avoid another stroke. And as I've told you, the next stroke could be even worse, much worse."

Mr. Shetfield looked away from Gabriel and stared at the wall, then glanced up toward the television, and finally back at Gabriel. Not meeting anyone's eyes, he mumbled, "Sure, fine."

Gabriel straightened and moved away from the bed, extending his arm as an invitation to Ranya to take over. In that moment, a thought came to Ranya which surprised her: she found she was glad it was Gabriel who was witnessing this encounter, and not Rasheed.

CHAPTER TWENTY-SIX

اتق شر الحليم اذا غضب

"Beware the levelheaded person if he is angry."
—Arabic proverb

March 19, 2004
8:30 p.m.

RASHEED SAT NEXT TO RANYA at the far end of the bank of computers that dominated the main floor of the brightly-lit medical library. He was off that night, but since Ranya was on call, he had come by to meet her for dinner, and now they were catching up on email. His position as Assistant Chief of Cardiothoracic Surgery had meant an increase in his administrative responsibilities, and there seemed to be no escape from the avalanche of emails that threatened to bury him on a daily basis.

Rasheed was finally nearing the end of the list of new messages in his inbox, just as the library's series of overhead announcements began warning of its impending closing time, when Ranya's pager went off beside him. Her brows furrowed as she identified the number. "Hmmm, looks like the cardiac surgery unit." She glanced at Rasheed, who was as puzzled as she was.

As there was no one around them, Ranya dialed the number while still sitting beside Rasheed, enabling him to overhear the conversation. The echo technician on call answered, informing Ranya that he had been called to perform an echocardiogram on one of the patients who had undergone open-heart surgery that day.

Apparently the patient's blood pressure was dropping and her heart sounds were becoming difficult to hear with a stethoscope. The tech said that he could clearly see on the ultrasound images that fluid was building up around her heart, filling the pericardial sac and putting the heart under so much pressure that it was no longer pumping effectively. "So you think she has cardiac tamponade," Ranya summed up.

"Yes, ma'am," answered the echo tech.

"And who is the attending?"

There was a pause on the other end of the line. Rasheed and Ranya exchanged glances. Finally the technician answered, "Dr. Stephens, ma'am."

"Uh-huh. And has anyone called Dr. Stephens?" Ranya was looking openly at Rasheed now. Dr. Bradley Stephens, the current Chief of Cardiothoracic Surgery—and Rasheed's boss—had developed a bit of a reputation of late, and it was not a favorable one. Rumors spread quickly throughout a hospital like theirs, and the rumors had it that Dr. Stephens had developed a drinking problem.

The echo tech replied, "Yes, it seems the nurses here have done so, but Dr. Stephens is not returning his pages."

"I see. Okay, I'll be right there. Please keep the echo machine where it is beside the bedside."

"Yes, ma'am."

Ranya hung up and turned to Rasheed. "Don't you guys leave the pericardium open when you do open-heart surgery?"

"Yes, most surgeons do, precisely because there's an increased risk of cardiac tamponade if you close it."

"Well," Ranya grunted, already on her feet, "looks like Stephens must've closed it. And now he's nowhere to be found. Go figure."

"I'll come with you," Rasheed volunteered, his stride matching hers as they hurried through the library turnstiles.

Ranya had already phoned the cath lab on their way to the cardiac surgery unit, and once they arrived, Rasheed was glad she had alerted the cath team. Even he could see, on the ultrasound images that the echo tech pulled up for them, how the patient's heart was struggling to fill with blood.

Ranya took one look at the situation, confirmed that the images did indeed show cardiac tamponade, and asked for the patient to be taken emergently to the cath lab.

In the cath lab, Rasheed watched from the control room as Ranya readied a long pericardiocentesis needle, preparing to plunge it into the patient's chest to access the pericardium and draw off the fluid building up there. Rasheed could tell from the motion of her elbow when she hit her mark, and when she drew back on the large syringe, it filled instantly with bloody liquid.

Rasheed leaned into the control room microphone so that Ranya could hear him over the speakers inside the lab. "Ranya," he said with urgency, "I know you might not usually do this, but could you run a quick fluoro, just a couple of images? I have a hunch."

"All right, Rasheed, you and your hunches," she replied. "Coming right up."

They both looked at the x-ray screens, and Ranya was the first to speak. "Rasheed, do you see that?" she called into the air above her.

"I sure do," he replied. He heard his voice booming through the microphone, even louder than he had intended.

They were both staring at the evidence screaming at them from the screens: an image of a suture needle that had been left in the pericardium. Rasheed knew it would have to be removed surgically, and as soon as possible.

Rasheed turned to the cath lab technician beside him. "Would you call the OR, please?"

A moment later, the technician, phone to his ear, pivoted to Rasheed and said, "The OR will be ready. They are asking who the surgeon is?"

"I am," said Rasheed, and stomped out of the room to get ready to scrub. He let the door slam behind him.

At the peer-review inquiry that followed a week later, Rasheed and Ranya answered questions about that night's fateful events while Brad Stephens looked on, his belly forming a pillow over his belt, which his crooked tie had not the length nor the gumption to meet. When they were finished, Stephens stood up and complained, "This is really much ado about nothing. Happens to everyone at some point or another. And the patient is fine. Just fine."

Enraged, Rasheed jumped to his feet. "This beggars belief!" he thundered. He stabbed at the air with his forefinger, pointing it in Stephens' direction. "The only reason the patient is 'fine'—if you can call it that," he bellowed, "is because Dr. Abbasi drained her pericardium and I *re-opened her chest* to remove the needle that *you* left there!"

"All right, all right," the hospital administrator interrupted, waving his hand at Rasheed and gesturing for him and Stephens to sit down. "I think we have an accurate picture now of the sequence of events. Dr. Stephens, can you explain why you did not answer any of your pages that night?"

Stephens' blotched face turned another shade of purple. He looked down at the floor, then folded his hands across his copious waist. "I must not have heard my pager go off," he mumbled, shrugging his shoulders. Then he looked up, hopeful. "Maybe the battery was dead."

Rasheed felt as though his own head would explode. He kept his seat, but twisted in it and stuck his neck out as far as it would reach toward Stephens' face. "Or could it be," he said slowly, struggling to contain his fury, "that you were indisposed?"

There it was. Rasheed had said it aloud—and in front of the peer-review board, no less—what everyone had been thinking, whispering, for months. The reason behind Stephens' growing waistline, and his growing negligence.

The hospital's Chief of Staff asked gently, "Dr. Stephens, could it be . . . do you think it's possible . . . that you may need help?"

Rasheed thought Stephens was going to cry, so far and so quickly did his shoulders fall. Stephens was crumpled over in his chair now, face in his hands. When he looked up, steepled hands before his lips, the pain on his face was nearly unbearable, particularly given how Rasheed had known him in better days.

"Yes," Stephens said, voice choked, "that is possible." He nodded his head. "Yes," he repeated, "probably so." He heaved a great sigh then, and put his face back in his hands.

"Okay. Okay," the Chief of Staff said, soothingly but with resolve. "There are resources for you. We can get you to the right people. Thank you for letting us do so. In the meantime, I'll assume that no one will be opposed to Dr. Haddad becoming interim Chief of Cardiothoracic Surgery in Dr. Stephens' place, effective immediately?"

No one was opposed.

CHAPTER TWENTY-SEVEN

"For what you see and hear depends a good deal on where you are standing:
it also depends on what sort of person you are."
—C.S. Lewis,
The Magician's Nephew

June 30, 2005
Thursday

GABRIEL STOOD WITH RANYA in the doorway of Rasheed's new office, waiting to accompany Rasheed to his own party. It had taken the hospital administration a bit longer than a year to discover what Gabriel had known all along: that they would not find, in their search for a cardiothoracic surgeon to fill the Chief position permanently, a better candidate than the one already in front of them. It was only a matter of formality.

So, on the eve of yet another new medical year, Gabriel stood on the plush maroon carpet of the large corner office with Ranya beside him, watching Rasheed remove the final item from the final box: a painted wood carving of Handala. This was the famous, yet fictional, refugee boy, the creation of Palestinian political cartoonist Naji Al-Ali. Handala appeared in every one of Al-Ali's cartoons, many of which Gabriel had seen displayed on the walls of Rasheed's own home.

He recalled Rasheed telling him how Al-Ali had once written that Handala was his signature, an icon to protect him from making mistakes; how Al-Ali had also written that this cartoon boy embodied a promise, above all, to remain true to himself, even as the world around him shuddered with corruption and injustice.

Gabriel watched now as Rasheed placed the wood carving on his black desk, making Handala the crowning feature of his newly-decorated office. After setting the carving down, Rasheed stood back and looked at Gabriel and Ranya meaningfully. "To keep me honest," he said.

Gabriel sat in the back seat of Rasheed's black Audi A4 as he drove them to the party celebrating his new promotion. It was being held at the posh Belle Meade home of the hospital's Chief of Staff, but Gabriel was not looking out the windows at the overly manicured lawns and mansions he had passed many times before; he was contemplating the sheerness of Ranya's sleeves as she sat in the passenger's seat in what he was certain was the most elegant little black dress he had ever seen. He was memorizing the subtle shine of her thin gold bracelets as they dangled from her slender wrist, accenting the warm undertones of her olive skin.

And the shimmer of her earrings, also gold, as they drew a short line from her lovely earlobes to her swan-like neck. Her neck . . . he shifted in his seat and stopped himself. He tugged on the collar of his white Oxford shirt, which suddenly seemed tight and stifling inside his suit coat, and looked out the window. They were finally turning into the driveway.

Rasheed entered the party to cheers from his colleagues. As he was fielding well-wishers, Gabriel slipped over to the bar, followed by Ranya.

"This is quite a turnout for Rasheed, isn't it?" she said, after securing a bottled water.

"Indeed it is—he's the man of the hour," Gabriel said. "But he deserves it, you know?"

Before Ranya could respond, she was accosted by a platinum-blonde woman teetering in burgundy-red stiletto heels and wearing an obscene amount of make-up. Gabriel had a guess as to who she must be, having heard Ranya complain more than once about the insufferable Dr. Sandra MacIllwain, the woman who had been selected for the position of cath lab director—a position that many, himself included, felt should have gone to Ranya.

"Congratulations to Rasheed!" she screeched at Ranya.

Gabriel observed the subtle clenching of Ranya's jaw, the amazing way she managed to grit her teeth while simultaneously attempting to smile. "Thank you, Sandra," Ranya replied, with more graciousness than was deserved, in Gabriel's opinion.

Ranya turned to Gabriel and opened her mouth to introduce him, but before she could utter a word, Sandra pre-empted her with the statement, "Must be nice to have your boyfriend become Chief of CT Surgery, right?"

It didn't task Gabriel's powers of observation to note the vast insincerity of her smile—or the offensiveness of her remark and its effect on Ranya.

Turning her focus to Gabriel before Ranya had time to react, she asked, too loudly, "And who is this handsome devil with you?"

Ranya's face was turning an even deeper shade of red, and to spare her from further interaction with this unsavory character, Gabriel stuck out his hand and offered, "Ah, hello there, I'm Dr. Gabriel O'Brien. Neurology."

"Well, I didn't expect to meet a neurologist at a cardiac surgery party, but we get all kinds around here, don't we?"

Gabriel raised his eyebrows as she actually displayed the audacity to wink at him. She extended her hand to him, palm down, as if expecting him to kiss it. "I'm Sandy MacIllwain," she purred. "Cath lab director," she added imperiously, glancing at Ranya.

It was by the grace of God that Rasheed walked up just then and requested a drink at the bar. He pulled out his handkerchief and wiped the sweat from his brow. "Oh, hello, Sandy," he said dismissively, literally looking down at her in spite of the added height of her stilettos.

Rasheed spoke to Ranya while grabbing his drink, explaining that there was someone to whom he wanted to introduce her.

Seizing his chance, Gabriel announced, "Ah, yes, there's someone I need to greet as well," and excused himself, wondering how on earth the administration had selected such a creature for what should have been Ranya's position. Probably some of the same loons who kept passing him over. Who knew with those fools? Maybe it boiled down to something as insignificant as the color of her hair.

CHAPTER TWENTY-EIGHT

"It is the chiefest point of happiness that a man is willing to be what he is."
—Erasmus

March 2006

"Uh, yes, Dr. O'Brien, there's a prior authorization sheet here for you to sign, and the case manager wanted to talk to you about the plan, and there's something about coding that someone wants to talk to you about, too."

Ranya was about to walk away from the computer station where she had been signing off on charts, but upon hearing Gabriel's name mentioned by the young neurology resident who stood beside her on the hospital phone, she paused. She pretended to study the computer monitor in front of her, and scrolled up and down on the screen, looking at nothing while hearing everything.

She could make out Gabriel's voice on the other end of the line: "Oh, good grief, okay, okay. I'll be right up."

The resident hung up the phone and, looking tired and agitated, went over to let the case manager know that Dr. O'Brien was coming up. Ranya knew what would be next, and in moments her supposition was confirmed: Gabriel came marching down the hallway, his long white coat billowing about him, his jaw set. He slowed down when he saw her, and gave her a slight wave along with a slight smile. Then he was all business again as he looked at his resident and at the case manager, waiting for explanations.

Ranya was watching and listening openly now as the case manager told both Gabriel and the resident (who was surely hearing this for at least the second time) that a request for transfer of one of their patients to a skilled nursing facility was being denied by an insurance company, so Gabriel would need to get on the phone with the company's medical director to explain the medical necessity of the transfer. She also added—with unwise timing, in Ranya's opinion—that several of Gabriel's notes needed further documentation "elements."

"Elements?" Gabriel asked, his face darkening further. "Sounds like something more pertinent to the periodic table than to a patient's chart."

"Uh, yes, doctor, to establish level of care for reimbursement on some of your patients, we need a certain number of elements to be detailed in the admission exam." She handed him a laminated card with writing so small that Gabriel had to squint to read it. She pointed at a line on the card. "Here, for example, you'll see a guide for this diagnosis code, and we just need you to put a little more into your documentation so we can bill properly for that." Next she pointed to the computer in front of which Ranya was still sitting. "The new electronic medical record system can help you with that, with prompts and fields to fill out on every admission note."

Gabriel looked from the case manager to the computer, from the computer to the card, and then back at the case manager again. His resident moved away, looking for an escape route.

"This is truly unbelievable," Gabriel told her. "I spend more time doctoring charts than I do doctoring patients. And yesterday I spent 40 minutes sitting on hold, waiting to speak to some other string of bean counters to get yet another procedure approved for one of my clinic patients! Is there no end to this?!"

"I'm sorry, Dr. O'Brien, but we just need this done as soon as possible, if you wouldn't mind."

"Oh, for heaven's sake. Just give me the number to call," Gabriel grumbled, extending his hand and pressing his fingers together repeatedly. He looked over at Ranya and rolled his eyes. Ranya's pager went off.

She stood up, ceding her chair to Gabriel, and lingered nearby while she answered the page; she hadn't yet told Gabriel what she had wanted to say. But she recognized the call-back number as belonging to the emergency department, so knew the call had to come first.

Sure enough, an emergency-medicine resident answered on the other end of the line and informed her, "We have a patient here with an NSTEMI, Dr. Abbasi, and he asked for you by name."

"Oh, and who would that be?" she asked, wondering which of her established patients was back in with a heart attack now.

"Um, let's see, it's . . . it's a Mr. Shetfield. James Shetfield."

Gabriel, close enough to overhear, raised his head to look at her. She raised her eyebrows at him in response.

"I'll be right down," Ranya told the ER resident.

She turned to go, then remembered and looked back at Gabriel, whose head was again bent over the computer terminal. "Hey, Gabriel?" she caught his eye.

"Yes?"

She waved two fingers at the computer monitor and then back at him. "Stay strong," she said, and winked.

He flashed a forced smile at her. "I'm trying, Ranya. I really am."

The curtain to Mr. Shetfield's room in the emergency department was only half-drawn, and Ranya's gaze could make out the right side of his face and the beige wires that ran from the electrodes on his chest, abdomen, and wrists to the electrocardiogram machine at his bedside. She knocked on the metal doorframe to announce her presence, then came around the curtain, drawing it fully behind her to shut out as much of the emergency-department hustle and bustle as possible. "Mr. Shetfield? It's Dr. Abbasi."

"Hey, Doc, good to see you again, but wish it were under better circumstances, you know?"

Ranya sat down on one of the room's two emerald-green hospital stools and rolled over to his bedside. "Hey there, Mr. Shetfield, fancy meeting you here," she answered his banter.

A nurse shoved the completed ECG into her hand and left the room. Ranya glanced down at it, then returned her attention to Mr. Shetfield. She had gotten to know him far better than she had ever thought possible in the intervening years, gotten to see a softer side of him, the result of a rapport established through stubborn patience, persistence, and the determination to do what was right for him.

She would never forget the day she knew that he recognized this. They had come to the end of one of their clinic visits and she was turning the knob on the door to leave the room. He had called after her: "Hey, Doc?"

She had steeled herself, preparing mentally for one more demand, and turned back to him, only to see him smile—a genuine smile—and hear him say, "You're not so bad, you know. Thanks for all you're doin' for me."

The next visit had been more amiable, and the next even more still, until they had fallen into a mutual appreciation and understanding that neither could have expected at the outset. And now here he was, with a heart attack—one that was, thankfully, likely to be minor.

She asked him about his symptoms, and told him the lab results had shown he was having a heart attack, which he already knew. They talked about his need to quit smoking, which he also already knew. And then she advised him on her recommended course of action, which was to take him to the cath lab to see if coronary stenting was needed.

"Well, only if you're the one doin' it, Doc."

She assured him that she would be—she would see to that. "We'll get you taken care of, okay?"

"I know you will, Doc. Thanks."

CHAPTER TWENTY-NINE

"It often occurs to me that we love most what makes us miserable. In my opinion, the damned are damned because they enjoy being damned."
—Patrick Kavanagh,
Tarry Flynn

July 2006

IT WAS THE LAST SUNDAY OF JULY. High above Ranya, the tops of the shagbark hickory trees swayed in a light breeze that never seemed to reach the ground. The sounds of crickets and cicadas swelled and surrounded her in a cacophonous natural symphony, and the clean, soapy scent of the crepe myrtles in full fuchsia bloom traveled across the late evening air. The flickers of fireflies had just begun to signal the nightly voyage of a thousand tiny globes of yellow light rising from the infinite blades of grass that stretched across the ample lawn.

She was sitting with Rasheed and Gabriel on the back patio of Rasheed's West Meade home, enjoying the fruits of his latest backyard grilling adventure. He had grilled several lamb chops to perfection (and a piece of salmon for Ranya), Ranya had made tabbouleh, and Gabriel had contributed his garlic mashed potatoes.

Ranya gazed off into the distance, admiring the winking golden glory of the Black-eyed Susans that covered the hillside. She was thoroughly enjoying her salmon and the serenity of the evening, largely tuning out Gabriel and Rasheed as they conversed, until she heard her name. Gabriel was addressing her directly: "So I'll be going to Ireland in September for about a week, Ranya, and I think you and Rasheed should join me. It'll be a great time to see the country. We'd have great *craic*."

"Crack?" Ranya asked, certain she had heard incorrectly. Surely Gabriel didn't do cocaine. But who knew what Europeans found acceptable.

Rasheed laughed, apparently knowing what she was thinking, and spelled it out for her. "He means we'll have a good time, basically."

"Oh, yeah, yeah, I'm sure we would, Gabriel," Ranya assured him. "What takes you to Ireland this September? Just a trip home?"

"I've been invited to present at a meeting of the Irish Cardiac Society."

Rasheed evidently couldn't help himself, because he blurted out, "What's a neurologist doing presenting to a cardiac society?"

Gabriel looked straight at Ranya when he answered. "They want me to talk about the treatment of stroke in the acute heart attack patient."

Ranya patted Rasheed's shoulder and gave Gabriel her broadest smile, then said, "Gabriel, we wouldn't miss it for the world."

Gabriel was determined not to allow himself to think about all he wanted to show Ranya once they were in Ireland; he was determined just to get through the rest of the dinner there on the patio with her and Rasheed. But before they had a chance to finish eating, Rasheed's pager went off. Minutes later, after answering the page, he was apologizing: "I'm sorry, guys; looks like I gotta go in. Emergency case." Then he added, sweeping his hand broadly across the table and managing to encompass most of the back of his house in this single gesture, "Please take your time; make yourselves at home."

Ranya assured him that she would take care of things. Gabriel was certain that Rasheed already knew this, and was simply displaying that native Arab sense of hospitality that he seemed to take to its most formal level when he was in a hurry.

After Rasheed had gone, Ranya engaged Gabriel in conversation about Ireland—always their favorite topic, it seemed. They touched upon everything from the predictably unpredictable weather, temperate though it was, to the recent state funeral of Charlie Haughey.

Gabriel couldn't resist any longer, and began telling her about all the places in Ireland they could visit once they were there, both the high-traffic touristy areas with their unbeatable scenery as well as the lesser-known places with magic of their own to offer. They could even go to Michael Collins' birthplace in West Cork.

"Oh, wow, Gabriel, wouldn't that be something?" Ranya murmured reverently. "To see where he was born. And he died not far away, right? We could go there, too?"

"Béal na mBláth, yes, that's where he died. Yes, we could go there, too. We'll see how much time we have, you know?"

They began to clear the plates, and Ranya shook her head in wonder and asked, "Gabriel, can you believe, all this time, and I've never actually been to Ireland?"

Gabriel smiled. "That's exactly why I invited you, Ranya." *That and so much more.*

Inside Rasheed's house, Gabriel helped Ranya clean up. He placed Rasheed's dishes in Rasheed's sink and stood two feet away from Rasheed's girlfriend as she washed plates and handed them to him to dry. He tried hard to avoid letting his fingers touch hers as he took the wet dishes from her, but sometimes, when she passed him small items like glasses or silverware, her fingertips brushed against his ever so briefly, ever so lightly. He fought for self-control each time.

When he opened the cabinets to put away some unused tea cups, he hesitated a moment, then turned to her and asked, "Will we be needing these?" He held his breath, painfully aware that he had just invited himself to a nonexistent after-dinner tea party.

Seeing Ranya realize that she should extend an invitation to him made him feel foolish and embarrassed with himself, and he stood there frozen with the tea cups in his hands. It seemed ages before she replied, "Oh! Oh yes, of course, Gabriel, would you like some tea? I know where Rasheed's kettle is; I'll get it right on. Just a sec."

It was too late at that point to stop her as she bustled about the kitchen, grabbing the red kettle and filling it hastily with water, turning the dial on the stove, rifling through a corner cabinet for tea bags. She turned to him and put out her hands, and like a dope, it took him too long to ascertain that she was motioning for the tea cups that he was still holding.

He felt his cheeks burning, and handed her the cups. He was grateful for the dishes yet to be put away, for he immediately turned back around and set to finishing that task, knowing that she could not see his face, and hoping that would buy him enough time to compose himself.

He had managed to remember himself by the time they sat down for tea at one end of Rasheed's long dining table of solid mahogany. He had already returned the conversation to Ireland, that safe space they shared, and Ranya seemed eager to press him on some of the finer details of Irish history. At one point she commented solemnly, "The Irish seem to have a remarkable capacity to endure."

You have no idea, he wanted to tell her. It had been ten years now since he had first met her, and every one of those years had been the best and the worst of his life. But instead he quipped, "You know, sometimes I think it's just the fatalism of the chronically oppressed." Then he added, giving her a look full of meaning, "You and Rasheed would know something about that, too, I'd imagine."

She regarded him for a moment, nodding. Then she looked down at her watch and said, "Yeah, and speaking of which—Rasheed will probably be back any time now."

He saw that she meant to stay, to be there when Rasheed returned home. He did not want to be there for that. And so he excused himself for the night. Excused himself with as much grace as he could muster; excused himself while excuses were still possible.

CHAPTER THIRTY

"An áit a bhfuil do chroí is ann a thabharfas do chosa thú."
("Your feet will bring you to where your heart is.")
—Irish proverb

September 2006

GABRIEL WAS STANDING BEHIND Ranya as the three friends made their way through the security checkpoint at the Nashville airport, preparing to embark on the first leg of their trip to Dublin. He watched as Ranya shuffled through the metal detector in her socks. He himself had dutifully removed his jacket, belt, and shoes, and stood ready to push his bin onto the belt of the x-ray scanner when he heard a commotion in front of him. Rasheed, who was behind him, craned his neck to see what the fuss was about.

In front of Ranya, a slightly disheveled woman was complaining loudly to her husband that two TSA agents had informed her she was carrying an item that was not allowed in carry-on baggage. "Now I'm gonna have to go all the way back to the ticket counter, get them to find my luggage, and go through all this again, just because—"

And this, to Gabriel's enduring shock, was where the diatribe took a really weird turn. The woman turned around to point at Ranya and continued, "—just because of these towelheads and, and—" sweeping her arm in Rasheed's direction now, "camel jockeys! But oh, they let them get through, and yet I have to strip my clothes off just to get on a plane!"

Gabriel's jaw dropped. Rasheed took a step forward, but Gabriel put a hand on his arm. They both watched Ranya bristle and step toward the hysterical woman. In a calm but firm voice, she told her, "Look, I don't know whom exactly you think you're referring to, but I had to go through the same security procedures you did, just like everybody else here."

The woman's face turned violaceous. She had not expected to be confronted by one of the subjects of her rantings, Gabriel guessed—and she had certainly not expected said subject to speak not only perfect English, but English with the soft but unmistakable accent of the American South.

The woman was looking apoplectic, in fact, sputtering and at a complete loss for words. Her husband, poor man, stepped forward then and apologized profusely for his wife's behavior. He asked Ranya what flight she was on. Gabriel knew he was probably just trying to make small talk, but he also knew that it wasn't his imagination that the man looked relieved when he found out they were not on the same flight. Gabriel himself shared that relief.

Thankfully, the rest of their journey passed without further incident, and during the last hour of their flight into Dublin the following morning, the first view of Ireland appeared below them. Thin wisps of cotton-white clouds floated above the fields upon fields of green, and as the plane continued its steady east-ward course toward Dublin, the beauty of his country's pastoral landscape lay suspended for a moment in its own singular time and space beneath him.

It was a view that never failed to catch Gabriel's breath and hold it still; it was a vision that inspired both pride and reverence, and his thoughts were confirmed by Ranya's exclamation from the window seat in front of him, where she sat beside Rasheed. "I've never seen anything like it! It's so green—I can see why they call it the Emerald Isle! So lovely!" she said, and to Gabriel, the excitement and awe in her voice were almost palpable.

As their plane began to circle around to position for landing at Dublin Air-port, Gabriel leaned forward and spoke to Ranya, directing her attention to the landmarks below, pointing out to her the River Liffey that formed the city's centerpiece. Indeed, he told her, the Liffey was Dublin's original *raison d'être* when the city was founded over a millennium ago by Viking settlers.

Rasheed had leaned over and was looking out Ranya's window with her, and as the plane came around, Gabriel pointed out to both of them the river's opening into the Irish Sea at Dublin Bay, surrounded on three sides by dense clusters of buildings. Steel and glass glittered and flashed across the city in the early morning sunlight, and they could clearly see the two Poolbeg chimneys, their slender industrial columns rising like antennae from the Poolbeg Stacks on the south bank of Dublin Port.

The contrast of Dublin's urban reality with the gently rolling, verdant fields that lay toward the west and through the Midlands always seemed to him a metaphor for something quintessentially Irish: how naturally beautiful the land was, how legendarily nice and hospitable the Irish people themselves could be, and yet . . . there was a harsher edge to contend with, wasn't there? An inescapable hardness born of centuries of seemingly endless miseries and the collective summoning of the will necessary to overcome.

He tried to quiet his mental ramblings and prepare for landing, but found any semblance of peace elusive. Although he had tried to catch some sleep on the overnight flight, it had been to no avail; he never slept well on planes anyway, and sitting behind Ranya and Rasheed the whole time, watching her head of curls rest first against his friend's shoulder, then against the window, and back ... sleep had been impossible.

And now, the enthusiasm Ranya expressed as they readied for landing was mirrored by what Gabriel felt within his very bones, combined with the mixture of relief and nervous anticipation that always accompanied coming home. For this homecoming, there was even more on his mind than usual: his upcoming talk to the Irish Cardiac Society, for one, but even more, his hope that he could do his country justice by showing off the best of it to his friends. He wondered what he had gotten himself into. This time, he was bringing people he really cared about with him. This time, he was bringing Ranya with him.

As they deplaned and made their way bleary-eyed toward passport control, Gabriel tried to shake himself awake and longed to rid himself of the wired-yet-exhausted feeling he had after the long and sleepless journey. The breakfast and coffee on the plane had been wanting, and now his stomach grumbled at him and his foggy mind complained as he waited in line to be processed.

When his turn came, he stumbled forward and presented his Irish passport at the window, trying to prepare himself to answer cordially whatever questions might come his way. The passport official took one look at him and at the etching of the delicate gold harp that adorned the cover of every Irish passport, and smiled warmly, waving him through and saying, "Welcome home."

CHAPTER THIRTY-ONE

"The History of Ireland in two words: *Ah well.*"
—Niall Williams,
History of the Rain

ONCE GABRIEL HAD GIVEN his talk in Dublin, there was time for him to show Ranya and Rasheed a little of the city. Upon encountering the words "*Céad míle fáilte*" at the entrances of many a pub, Ranya inquired after their meaning.

"That's Irish for 'a hundred thousand welcomes,'" Gabriel informed her.

Rasheed smiled. He turned to Ranya and said in Arabic, "*Meet elf marhaba.*" Then turning to Gabriel, he explained in English: "'A hundred thousand hello's.' It's the exact same sentiment."

Ranya was grinning broadly now. "Any way you look at it, that's a far better reception than we received at the Nashville airport!"

Gabriel said, "Yeah, Ranya, again, I was so sorry to see that happen to you. It isn't easy to be an Arab in America now, is it?"

Rasheed commented, "It isn't easy to be an Arab anywhere." Then he pointed toward one of the pubs and smiled. "Except maybe there. Let's go in and avail ourselves of some of that famous Irish hospitality."

They headed toward the west coast of Ireland the next day, stopping in Galway, where Ranya had decided to go shopping. Rasheed had gone with her. For some reason, the thought of Ranya shopping amused Gabriel to no end, but the thought of Rasheed going along too was more than he could handle. He had thus returned early to their designated meeting place on Eyre Square, and standing there in the last light of day, he inhaled the sea air and thought about the journey ahead and the drama behind while he waited for his friends to return from their shopping escapades.

He leaned his head back momentarily, glancing up at the darkening sky as the lights of the city began to come on around him. He looked back across the green of the square, at the university students milling about, the couples chatting, the tourists scurrying to dinner reservations. Ah, Galway! It was always fantastic to be visiting Galway.

Just a couple of days earlier, he had given his talk to the Irish Cardiac Society in Dublin, to great acclaim. He had spoken to a packed auditorium, but as far as he was concerned, it was an audience of one, and everything he had said was directed to her, all content put through what he imagined and supposed her filter to be. All seen through the eyes of the one person whose gaze he had studiously avoided, if only for the sake of being able to complete his presentation without losing all hope of concentration.

When his Palestinian friends finally returned, Gabriel noted the bounce in Ranya's step and the vivacity in her face, combining to radiate a cheerfulness that lit up his entire corner of the square. He grinned at the couple, needlessly inquiring, "So, a successful shopping excursion, I presume?"

Ranya placed her right palm on the air between herself and Gabriel, fingers splayed so he could catch the golden gleam of her new ring.

"The Claddagh!" he said, then pursed his lips appreciatively, proclaiming its meaning with his next breath: "Love, loyalty, and friendship."

He noticed not just its presence, but its placement: the direction of the tip of the heart in the center of the delicate band that encircled her right ring finger. It was a tiny golden heart held between two engraved hands and topped by an equally tiny, bejeweled crown, and the tip of that heart pointed down Ranya's finger toward her, indicating that its larger, living counterpart was taken. Had the tip of the heart been pointing outward, toward the tip of her own finger and by extension toward the rest of the world, it would have signified that she was available. But this was not the case.

He swallowed hard as he thought about where that ring would come to rest one day, on her left ring finger, and his heart thudded with the sudden certainty that when it did come to rest there, it would be for Rasheed.

He turned then to Rasheed and complimented him on springing for such a beautiful ring.

Ranya opened her mouth to correct him, but Rasheed beat her to it. "Oh, no, she bought that for herself. Not that I didn't offer, but she insisted." He shrugged his shoulders at Gabriel, as if to ask, "What's a man to do?" But the light in his eyes and the angle of his chin revealed his pride in Ranya—and, undoubtedly, in the direction of the little heart on that gorgeous ring.

Ranya was ebullient as they walked down the busy streets, under the multi-colored triangular flags that hung between the buildings of Galway's busiest thoroughfares, and eventually came to stroll along the banks of the River Corrib, its dark, rushing waters dotted with peaks of white foam and devoid of all reflection under the gathering clouds. While they stood watching the great river, Ranya turned to look up at Rasheed in a moment of brightness and gushed, "Oh, the Irish! They are wonderfully kind, aren't they?"

Gabriel rolled his eyes and, pretending to look wounded, asked in return, "Haven't I been trying to tell you this?"

Rasheed laughed loudly and pointed at Ranya's newly-purchased Claddagh ring. "Well, I imagine they would be, when you are shelling out big bucks for jewelry like that, *Habibti.*"

In his hotel room that night, Gabriel thought of Ranya. He tried hard to remember when he had ever thought of anything or anyone else when the quiet of the night came to stay, and came up empty. There must have been such a time, a time without Ranya, but that time was lost forever to him now.

He smiled to himself as he replayed the scene in his mind, her asking him the meaning of the Irish saying that was part and parcel of so much of the signage above pub doors and in shop windows, all hoping to catch the attention (and the coinage) of passing tourists. "*Céad mile fáilte,*" the signs cried out invitingly. A hundred thousand welcomes. And Rasheed pointing out what was essentially the same well-known saying in Arabic. How Ranya had looked at the two of them, her beautiful eyes lighting up with sudden comprehension and expressing her unspoken wonder at yet another cross-cultural connection.

When the three of them had said good night in the hotel lobby that evening, she had signed off with a wave of her hand and the light comment, "Okay, Gabriel, you've had more than enough of me for one day, I'm sure!"

How could he tell her that there would never be enough—enough welcomes, enough hellos, enough good nights, enough good mornings, enough days, enough years, enough Ranya? A hundred thousand lifetimes, and there would never be enough.

So he thought about her, and he thought about her new ring. The Claddagh. Love, loyalty, friendship. He wondered which would triumph in his own life. Because sure wasn't it tearing him to pieces, God help him.

But Gabriel, a back-of-the-mind voice reminded him, *the mantra of the Claddagh is all-inclusive of the three. It is not a question of "or." It is a mandate of "and."*

The next day, they traveled to the Cliffs of Moher, where Gabriel delighted in his friends' astonished reactions to the breathtaking majesty that greeted them there. He had warned them that no amount of description or preparation could ready them for the spectacular sight of the marvelous sandstone cliffs rising over 700 feet from the wild waters of the Atlantic, an expanse of jagged green against a riot of vivacious blue.

They joined the other tourists who walked along the path at the edge of the earth, with the frightening drop to the ocean on one side of them, and the calmer waters of Galway Bay in the far distance behind them.

The wind carried giant pillows of white clouds across the slate-blue sky, creating a perfect backdrop for the photos they were all snapping in rapid succession. Ranya pointed to the round, imposing stone tower to her right, near the highest point of the Cliffs, and, yelling above the wind to be heard, asked Gabriel if he knew what it was.

"Oh, yeah, of course—that's O'Brien's Tower," he yelled back.

"Ha! You have your own tower now, Gabe?" said Rasheed.

And thus Gabriel found himself explaining what he knew of O'Brien's Tower, how it had been built in the nineteenth century by a local landowner as a viewing area for the tourists that flocked to the Cliffs even at that time. That the landowner had had the same surname as his could be attributed to the vastness of the O'Brien dynasty from which he, too, was descended.

"A dynasty, Gabriel?" Ranya asked.

"Founded in the tenth century by the great Brian Boru, King of Munster, and eventually High King of Ireland," Gabriel said.

Ranya turned to Rasheed and commented, "There are tribes in every country, it seems."

Gabriel countered, "Maybe, yeah, but the Irish ones are the best." He winked at both of them, and they laughed in return.

They made their way to the grassy patch in front of O'Brien's Tower, where Rasheed spread both arms wide and spun in a circle. He was grinning like a madman while he completed his three-hundred-sixty-degree turn, and, smiling widely at Ranya, called out, "Not the sort of view you see every day, right?"

Ranya turned to Gabriel then with bright, happy eyes, and said, "I love it here."

The Cliffs of Moher. Photo by Keith M. Sturges.

CHAPTER THIRTY-TWO

"I feel more and more the time wasted that is not spent in Ireland."
—Lady Gregory

THEY CAME INTO COUNTY Kerry at sunset, with the MacGillycuddy's Reeks casting their purple mountainous shadows upon the horizon. Ranya felt as though her eyes would never get enough of the lush, green carpets of grass that surrounded them and went on for as far as sight could see, folding themselves under the mountains in the distance. Gabriel, who was driving, announced with a flourish, "We are now entering the Kingdom of Kerry."

"The Kingdom of Kerry?" Ranya and Rasheed repeated in unison.

"There's the Kingdom of God, and the Kingdom of Kerry, and, as the saying around here goes, 'One is not of this world and the other is out of this world,'" Gabriel explained.

Ranya discovered the truth of this statement where most truths were to be found, and that was off the beaten path. The next day, they took the Skellig Ring, a less-traveled route that branched off the Ring of Kerry to reveal the part of the Iveragh Peninsula where one could see the two Skellig Islands. They happened upon an unpopulated footpath that took them directly down to the water's edge. Ranya stood beside Gabriel as he pointed across the Atlantic waves that glimmered magnificently in the sunlight before sending their salt spray up from the craggy coastline.

"Those are the Skelligs," he said of the two rocky islands that thrust forth their peaks from the ocean and toward the aquamarine sky. "The smaller one is known as *Sceilig Bheag*, or Little Skellig, while the larger is *Sceilig Mhichíl*, Skellig Michael—and it's home to a remarkably well-preserved early Christian monastic site."

Something about the two majestic rock formations, their haunting peaks jutting out of the Atlantic Ocean in defiance of the explosive, white-capped waves that sought to consume them, their jagged grayness a study in isolation and a statement of endurance through the relentless eons of sun, wind, and rain, captivated Ranya and begged her not to turn her back on them. She was loathe to move on and follow the others back up the path, feeling as though leaving this place would result in an undefinable yet monumental loss, a surrendering of this irreplaceable scene to the banality of the everyday.

Her heart ached at the thought of ever having to turn away. How could one return to life as it was after seeing this? She knew then that she would hold this place in her mind forever; on the worst of days, in the worst of times, this was where she would return.

They walked uphill with their backs to the Skelligs—Ranya repeatedly turning to look over her shoulder to catch her last glimpses of them before they disappeared from view—and when they reached the top of the lane, Rasheed decided he had found an angle for a photograph that he apparently had missed before. He ran into a nearby field to capture the light that he said was "just so."

Gabriel stood beside her on the hilltop, hands in his pockets, the wind ruffling his hair as they waited. He looked tall and confident standing there, and it occurred to Ranya that he seemed at his very best here in Ireland, as though he possessed a newfound confidence that she had never even realized he had lost. His brogue was thicker, his manner easier, his brow less furrowed.

Looking from him to the vast expanse of natural beauty that surrounded them, she felt overcome with the magnificence of it, with the momentousness of being there, with him, after a decade of talking and thinking and reading about Ireland. The fields around her reverberated with even more than Johnny Cash's forty shades of green, and she had seen how the sky looked when the clouds disappeared: it was the vivid blue of ten thousand smiling Irish eyes, shimmering in the triumph of the sunshine. Eyes like Gabriel's. She turned to him and heard herself blurt out, "Goodness, Gabriel, it's so beautiful here it makes me ache." She held her hand to her heart and asked, "How do you stand it?"

Gabriel's face transformed as he stood there, otherwise motionless, staring at her wordlessly. Those blue eyes of his met hers and her heart skipped. Then he looked over her shoulder, looked past her into the countryside, as if searching for something unseeable, unknowable, and very far away. He inhaled deeply and exhaled heavily, closing his eyes as he did so. She grew bolder and asked, "Do you ever think of returning, Gabriel? Back here, to Ireland?"

Gabriel opened his eyes and looked directly into hers, giving his answer without hesitation: "Every day."

Ranya held his gaze for a moment, then turned to survey the beauty before them once more, the remarkable seascape having become a rolling, luscious green landscape in a matter of footsteps. She nodded her head, and said, "Yeah, I can imagine so. It's like paradise."

"It's not paradise, Ranya," Gabriel said softly. "It's just home."

The Skelligs in the distance, as seen from Glen Pier. Photo by Keith M. Sturges.

CHAPTER THIRTY-THREE

"Too long a sacrifice
Can make a stone of the heart."
—William Butler Yeats,
"Easter, 1916"

LATER THAT DAY, THEY STOPPED at a little shop in Kells on the Ring of Kerry. While Rasheed combed through racks of wool coats in another room, Gabriel watched as Ranya browsed the various knick-knacks arranged neatly on the glass display shelves. The shopkeeper came in and greeted her and Gabriel: "'Tis a beautiful afternoon, isn't it?"

Gabriel smiled at him and replied, "That it is. It's been a fine day."

Having made her way to the front counter now, Ranya caught the shopkeeper's eye and waved. "Hi," she began, then pointed to the decorated decks of playing cards, all sporting scenes of the Irish countryside, that were laid out on the counter and available for purchase. "How much are these?" she asked.

Gabriel recalled the Queen of Hearts card that she had a flair for using as a bookmark. Stepping forward as she made her selections, he insisted on paying for the two decks of cards she had chosen, stating that it was the least he could do to provide her a souvenir of her trip to Ireland.

After finally giving in, Ranya thanked him and walked away, disappearing onto the shop's outdoor patio with her camera in hand. Through the window, Gabriel watched her snapping photos of the surrounding scenery. The shopkeeper commented, "So your lady's an American. And what does she do?"

Gabriel felt the all-too-familiar red heat gaining purchase across his cheeks. "She's a heart doctor," he began in response, intending to deny that she was "his" in any way, but found himself interrupted by the storekeeper's exclamation, "I'd say so!"

Thankfully, Gabriel was spared any further conversation on this topic by the grand entrance of none other than Rasheed himself, who unsurprisingly made instant friends with the shopkeeper as soon as he walked in. "Such a nice place you have here!" he boomed.

Gabriel hastily placed the decks of cards within the plastic bag the man had handed him and got them off the counter. The shop owner had turned his attention to Rasheed now, beaming proudly and thanking him for his compliment. "And where are you from?" he asked Rasheed.

Gabriel groaned inwardly and walked outside to join Ranya, signaling to Rasheed on his way out the door that he should speed it up. By the time Rasheed made it outside, Gabriel was already at the wheel with the engine running. As he climbed into the car, Rasheed commented on the merchant's curiosity. "He wanted to know all about where I was from and where I was going—guess it must be my accent."

"Did he also ask you what you do?" Gabriel grumbled.

Rasheed nodded. "Yeah, he did. I told him I'm a heart surgeon. Apparently, he already knew that Ranya was a 'heart doctor,' too."

Gabriel coughed slightly, then remarked, "That is SO Kerry. There are three questions that every Kerry person seems to ask: 'Where are you from, where are you going, and what do you do?'"

They all burst into laughter. Ranya said, "Well, no harm in that. Everyone I've met here in County Kerry so far has been just wonderful—and fun to talk to."

"Ah, well, just keep in mind that I'm a Cork person, Ranya, so you'll have to take what I say about others with a grain of salt. I have my biases," Gabriel said. He turned his head to smile at her. Rasheed had assigned her to the back seat early on in their road trip, because she had been unable to hide her concern, progressively evolving into a certainty, that every car on the road was on the "wrong" side and that a head-on collision was therefore unavoidable each time they passed another vehicle traveling in the opposite direction. She had said she did not think she could ever get used to driving on the left side of the road.

Gabriel had explained that, in medieval times, when knights carried swords and rode horses, riding on the left side of the thoroughfare was preferred so that one could engage in sword fighting with the dominant hand, which was usually the right hand. He had described how the use of the right hand to wield a sword was the same reason behind the clockwise structure of spiral staircases inside many Irish castles, an additional layer of defense that took advantage of how most people's brains were wired. It made it much harder for attackers coming up the staircase to draw their swords.

This had done little to allay Ranya's concerns.

So the view from the back seat was all hers, and as they traveled along the beautiful West Cork coastline now, she had nothing but praise and expressions of awe for the grandeur of the scenery. And Gabriel's heart swelled with her every utterance.

After a while they turned inland and headed for Béal na mBláth so Gabriel could keep his promise to her, to view the monument commemorating the death of Michael Collins. Once there, he pointed out the location where Collins had been shot in the head in 1922, during the Irish Civil War.

Rasheed, ever the voice of common sense, asked, "Now what would a man like that, a seasoned man of war, be doing walking out into the open road in the middle of crossfire?"

Gabriel had no good answer for that, and finally relinquished, "Well, I think there are many different accounts of what happened. I don't think we'll ever know for sure. But everyone makes mistakes, yeah? Even the best of us."

"Yeah, well," Rasheed said, "that mistake turned out to be fatal, didn't it?"

They all stood in silence for a moment, just the three of them on the side of the quiet, empty road, with the large, stone cross of the Collins memorial behind them and a field full of grazing cows across the road in front of them. Gunmetal clouds gathered in the sky above them, but only a breeze through the trees disturbed the stillness until Rasheed spoke again, turning to eye Gabriel and Ranya standing together at his side.

"You know, guys," he began slowly, scratching the back of his head, "I'm not so sure I wouldn't have been on de Valera's side in that war."

Gabriel and Ranya stared at him in disbelief. Gabriel knew, of course, that Rasheed was referring to Collins' primary rival in the Civil War, the famed Eamon de Valera, who later became Prime Minister and finally President of Ireland. He knew that Ranya was well aware of this, too; few of their many discussions on Irish history could have failed to mention de Valera.

For Rasheed to say such a thing at all, much less here, in this revered place. . . he may as well have given the Big Fella a roll-over kick in his grave. Gabriel was speechless.

The rising wind tossed Rasheed's hair as he persisted, "I mean, maybe Collins didn't get the best deal. Maybe they could have held out for more—held out for all of it—and then Irish history would have turned out far differently."

"Oh, God, Rasheed," Gabriel muttered, drawing his keys from his pocket and taking a few steps toward the parked car, "please let's not rehash the entire Civil War here now."

Rasheed shrugged his shoulders. "I'm just saying . . . there are two sides to every narrative."

"Glad to hear you're finally realizing that, my friend," Gabriel said under his breath, still walking toward the car. Then he stopped in mid-stride and turned to meet Rasheed's gaze full on. "But the thing of it is," he said gravely, "they started out on the same side."

CHAPTER THIRTY-FOUR

"When anyone asks me about the Irish character, I say look at the trees.
Maimed, stark and misshapen, but ferociously tenacious."
—Edna O'Brien

THEY MOVED ON TO Cork City, where Gabriel gave them a tour of his alma mater, University College Cork, as well as of the famed English Market, which Ranya declared "depressingly fabulous" after viewing row upon row of fresh vegetables, baked goods, and every imaginable kind of meat and fish inside the vast covered food market that bustled with foot traffic during every open hour.

Rasheed had asked Gabriel to take them to one of his favorite pubs in the city, so after their extended tour of the Market, they stopped by the Mutton Lane Inn. The dark, candlelit atmosphere of the pub lent a feeling of intimacy to the gathering as the three crowded around their chosen table in the far corner.

Just after their drinks arrived—with a club soda for Ranya—Rasheed departed for the loo, and Gabriel was about to explain to Ranya his affinity for this particular pub, one of the city's oldest and best, when a hand on his shoulder commanded his attention.

"Look who it is!" said the petite, blonde woman attached to the hand. *Curses, it's Saoirse. Of all people, of all times.* Adding to this unfortunate circumstance was the presence of the stout, red-haired man beside her, whom Gabriel immediately recognized as Rory O'Donovan, and to whom Saoirse now turned, saying, "I *told* you it must be Gabe!"

Gabriel stifled a groan, swiveled in his seat, and lifted himself up to a half-standing position to greet his ex-girlfriend and their mutual college acquaintance. He turned to Ranya and resigned himself to making the introductions, however awkward: "Ranya, this is Saoirse O'Sullivan—"

But before he could get any further, she corrected him: "O'Donovan." She put her arm around Rory and repeated, smiling, "It's O'Donovan now." *Oh, lovely. So she actually went and married the lout.*

"Ah, yes—well, congratulations to you both!" Gabriel said, forcing himself to smile. "And this," he gestured to Ranya, "is my friend Dr. Ranya Abbasi. Ranya, meet Saoirse and Rory . . . O'Donovan."

The O'Donovans evidently took this as an invitation to join in, for they seated themselves at the same table, setting their own beverages down and crowding Gabriel closer to Ranya.

"Well, don't they make a lovely couple, Rory?" Saoirse gushed, grinning broadly at Gabriel and Ranya.

"Indeed they do," Rory responded, nodding his approval. He elbowed Gabriel and said, "So you've come back now to show us all how well you're doin', have ya?"

Gabriel shook his head and started to say something, but Rory continued, "Not enough that you're a big doctor and specialist now, but you've a beautiful woman on your arm as well! Fair play to ya, Gabe! We always knew you'd go far."

Ranya cleared her throat, and Gabriel caught sight of Rasheed walking back toward their table. He slid over in his seat, putting as many centimeters as he could between himself and Ranya without landing in Rory's lap. By the time Rasheed reached the table, Gabriel could see the questioning look on his face, and he half-stood again, leaning into the table and bumping into Rory in the process, in order to make all the introductions to Rasheed.

Rasheed, gracious as ever, reclaimed his empty seat on the other side of Ranya and began to make small talk with the newcomers, saying how happy he was to be visiting Ireland with Gabriel, praising him for the good guide and the great friend that he was, and then complimenting the country and the people in general. "And how fortunate we are to actually get to meet some of Gabe's old friends now, too!" he added.

Gabriel could tell from the look on Saoirse's face that she was a little confused and was trying to figure out how Rasheed fit into the picture. He could determine no delicate way out of it now, and was trying to decide whether or not to just come out with it when Rasheed did it for him. He could only think later that Rasheed must have thought this a good segue from the general praise for all things Irish, because his dear friend put his arm around Ranya and, leaning close to her, said, "Show them your new Claddagh ring, *Habibti*."

Rory nearly fell backward from his stool, but Saoirse, after the initial rise of her eyebrows, managed to recover quickly, and took Ranya's outstretched right hand, making the appropriate ooh's and ah's regarding the beautiful ring in question. Gabriel could feel Rory staring at him openly now, and unable to stand it any longer, stood up and excused himself for the bar, offering to bring back another round of drinks for the table.

By the time he returned, as he had hoped, both of his old acquaintances seemed to have regained control of themselves, and were engaged in an animated discussion with Rasheed and Ranya. Rory reached out his arm to Gabriel and said, "I was just about to tell your friends here about another one of your wild nights in our student days! You remember that one where we—"

"Oh, now, I'm sure they don't need the details," Gabriel interrupted, putting a hand on Rory's shoulder and shaking it harder than he had originally intended.

Rasheed looked thoroughly amused and said, "I see you were studying hard back then, Gabe!"

Gabriel shrugged his shoulders and said the only thing that came to mind: "Oh, you know, just some of those stupid things you do when you're young. Always seems like a good idea at the time."

Saoirse touched Rasheed's forearm with her fingertips and chimed in, as if to defend Gabriel, "You know, it's true really, the way I remember it, you could hardly get Gabe's nose out of a book back then." She smiled at them all and laughed lightly, adding, "I should know—I tried!"

Rather than being offended by this, as Gabriel imagined a nobler man would be, Rory looked triumphant. He didn't have to say it; Gabriel could read the look on his smug face plainly enough: *Looks like I'm the one who got the girl after all, doesn't it? Not so high and mighty now, are ya, Gabe?*

Gabriel felt his face go red and shifted in his seat, looking down into his drink and wishing he could disappear into it. Saoirse had never been right for him; he'd known that from the beginning, well before she finally accepted it, and now that awkward certainty was revisited upon him, and in front of his closest friends, no less. What a disaster this was.

He could feel all four of them staring at him as he tried to think of a suitable response, but it was Rasheed's voice that rescued him from across the small wooden table. "No surprise there," he said, turning to Saoirse. "Gabe's a real ladies' man; no shortage of interest in him where we are . . . he's spoiled for choice, for sure."

Gabriel looked sharply at his friend, but could detect no hint of irony on his face or sarcasm in his tone. Rasheed continued, spreading his hands wide and speaking to the entire table now, "But he's so dedicated to his profession, and to his patients, that I don't know if he'll ever settle down. To tell the truth, it's those patients who are lucky to have him. So I guess we could say he's married to his job."

Rasheed's impromptu intervention seemed to persuade even Rory, who raised his glass and toasted, "Well, then! To Dr. Gabe and his lucky patients!"

All Gabriel's friends repeated the toast at once, and he murmured his thanks to them. Looking gratefully at Rasheed, he raised his glass and made a solemn toast of his own: "To good friends." He held Rasheed's gaze as he tipped the glass to his lips.

A soft rain fell the following morning, but the sky was clearing by the time they made their way to the port of Cobh. There Gabriel told them about the many famine ships, often called coffin ships, that had left from there during the Great Famine of the mid-nineteenth century, and later early steamers and even colossal ocean liners—including the ill-fated RMS *Titanic*—carrying Irish emigrants, all hoping for a better life. Over two-and-a-half million emigrants from the port of Cobh alone. He mentioned how families would hold a wake for their loved one before he boarded the ship, because they never expected to see him again.

"Wow," Rasheed said. "Can you even imagine?"

Ranya inhaled deeply as she looked around her, seeming to take in the whole coastline with her gaze. She shook her head and said, "Goodness, it's so beautiful here. It must've been pretty bad for anyone to ever want to leave."

After a long pause, Gabriel responded, "You have no idea."

After another moment of shared silence, Rasheed said, "Yeah, well, I'd say starving to death is reason enough." Then he put his hand on Gabriel's shoulder. "It's always hard to leave, though, isn't it?"

Gabriel felt the earlier tensions fade away. He smiled at his friend and fellow emigrant, knowing that Rasheed, of all people, understood.

CHAPTER THIRTY-FIVE

"The musical art often speaks in sounds more penetrating than the words of
poetry, and takes hold of the most hidden crevices of the heart . . ."
—Friedrich Nietzsche

May 2007
Saturday night

WHEN THE DOORBELL RANG, Ranya was standing barefoot in front of her
bedroom mirror, fiddling with her earrings. She looked at her watch. Rasheed
was early for once.

She ran down the stairs to her foyer and pulled the oak door open. But
instead of Rasheed, there to her great surprise stood Gabriel, dressed smartly
in suit and tie. He looked down at her bare feet and apologized, "I'm a few
minutes early, I know."

"Um, well, hello, Gabriel, but . . . early for what? Rasheed and I have the
symphony tonight."

Gabriel, still standing on her doorstep, asked confusedly, "But did he not
tell you?"

Ranya was beginning to lose patience; she still needed to finish getting
ready. "Tell me what, Gabriel?"

"He's been called in for an emergency surgery, some mix-up on the call schedule or something, and he won't be able to take you tonight. But he knows how
much you were looking forward to this, so he asked me to stand in for him."
Gabriel was looking increasingly uncomfortable.

Ranya hoped the disappointment she felt did not show on her face. She suddenly realized that Gabriel was still standing on the doorstep, and remembering
her manners, she invited him in and thanked him for coming, telling him she
would need just a moment to finish dressing.

As he stepped into the foyer beside her, appearing even taller than usual to
her since she was not wearing shoes, she was perturbed to find that her normally
steady speech faltered, and she felt the blush creeping over her cheeks. Disconcert-
ed, she looked away from him and gestured toward the living room, stuttering,
"Um, well, uh . . . please . . . uh, make yourself at home. I'll be right back."

She raced upstairs to finish putting on her jewelry and shoes, still taken aback
at this unexpected turn of events. She wished she had heard the phone, answered
Rasheed's call. Now she wouldn't dare bother him over this while he was in
surgery.

A part of her found it hard to believe that this was what he really wanted, but
then again, she was grateful to him for putting her desires and her happiness above
all other considerations. He knew how much she loved the Nashville Symphony
and how much she was looking forward to this concert in particular.

Of course, she could have gone alone, but she also knew that Rasheed didn't
want her to feel she had to sit alone in the symphony box for over two hours.
Rasheed was just like that; he understood the power of occasion. The perfect
gentleman, that Rasheed. And Ranya understood that this was one of his many
ways of telling her that he loved her.

Downstairs, Gabriel's mind was busy conjuring curses for Rasheed. He had seen how disappointed Ranya had looked at the sight of him on her doorstep, noticed the sagging of her shoulders, bared by the cut of her black-and-red dress. He made a mental note to give Rasheed an earful tomorrow.

But there was something else, another thought, that whispered in the back of his mind as he entered her living room, and it was his impression of Ranya's reaction when he had stepped into the foyer beside her, close enough to breathe in the honeyed scent of her hair, towering over her as he made sure his own polished black dress shoes steered clear of her bare feet.

She had seemed flustered.

Ranya, who had always been one step ahead of him, had been since the day they met, now seemed flustered. It was both intriguing and strangely unsettling.

Looking around him, he realized that, in all these years, this was the first time he had ever been inside Ranya's house. He recalled that she'd bought a nice townhome a few years back. Now, surveying her large living room, his eyes fell upon the Steinway baby grand piano, gleaming under the lights of an elegant chandelier, lid propped open so that the inner strings were on display.

Gabriel had always been fascinated by the inner workings of a piano, and was drawn to examine it closer. He found on its music rack the sheet music for Beethoven's *Pathétique* Sonata, which happened to be one of his favorites. He knew it was an intricate piece, and he had a healthy respect for the technical skill it required. Just as he was marveling at the possibility that Ranya was able to play it, she stepped into the room—shoes on—exclaiming, "Oh! You've found the piano, I see." A sheer black scarf lightly covered her shoulders now, which, he found, only served to add to her mystique . . . and to his desire.

"Do you play, Ranya?"

"Well, it's not there just for show, Gabriel," she retorted. So she had recovered her usual confidence, it seemed.

He laughed and asked, shaking his head in wonder, "Is there anything you can't do?"

She grinned broadly at him and replied, "Yes. I can't drive on the left side of the road."

The new Schermerhorn Symphony Center was a masterpiece of Neo-Classical architecture updated with contemporary touches, an imposing four-story building in the center of downtown Nashville that had been built after much study of European counterparts and with such painstaking attention to acoustic details that it was widely reported that there was not a bad seat in the house. But Rasheed had gotten what Ranya believed to be two of the very best seats in the hall, and those were in Box One of the loge, piano-side. Box One actually jutted out onto the stage, so that its occupants were on the same level as the orchestra, and Ranya always reveled in the feeling of being very nearly a part of the orchestra itself, such was the vantage afforded.

She and Gabriel took the seats that Rasheed had long ago reserved, and Ranya surrendered to the fullness of the experience that was a night out at the Schermerhorn: the sounds of members of the orchestra tuning their instruments before the concert, the length and depth of the hall, the opulent white-globed chandeliers that hung from the high ceiling and lent a cool glow to the muted and calming shade of green that claimed most of the open wall space.

The dimmer lighting of the seating sections transitioned smoothly into the brighter illumination of the polished wood stage, where all eyes would fall, as they always did, upon the conductor's box in the anticipatory moment just before the concert began.

As they were still several minutes away from that point in time, Ranya let her eyes roam over the white boxes and balconies that lined either side of the magnificent floor of the front seating section, watching as black-suited ushers guided well-dressed patrons to their seats. Ranya knew the secret of the chairs on the main floor, now being occupied by symphony guests; she had seen how the chairs could turn over and disappear, like magic, into the floor, so that the main floor became a flat space for the placing of cabaret tables during pop concerts.

Another of the Schermerhorn's engineering feats that never failed to mesmerize her was the way the grand piano could literally rise out of the stage, through a special system of gears and a floor panel that detached from the front center of the stage and could move up and down like an elevator. It went down empty and came back up with the grandest Steinway grand that one could hope to see.

She turned to Gabriel beside her and began pointing out some of these features, not knowing which he might already be aware of, since the Symphony Center had been open for less than a year and she had only ever been there with Rasheed. He nodded and murmured appreciatively, his gaze following hers, his blue eyes lit softly under the chandeliers, the edges of those eyes crinkling as his cheeks rose in a gentle smile.

The house lights went down and the glow of the stage lights remained, highlighting the olive skin of Ranya's face, arms, and hands. They were piano hands, Gabriel realized, noting her long, slender fingers. Of course. He wondered how he had not noticed that before.

The angle of his box seat, slightly behind hers, was such that it afforded him the rare opportunity of observing Ranya within his natural field of view, the same field of view that encompassed the orchestra directly before them. Thus he could regard her without seeming to be staring at her. In the dimly-lit darkness, he studied her raised, rosy cheekbones and the beckoning curve of her lips, his eyes moving to the length of her neck, where stray curls fell from her updo. He marveled at how she had managed to tame her mass of curls so alluringly, and he was overcome by the sudden brazen desire to undo the updo, to set those curls free . . .

He shifted in his seat and forced himself to stop there, to look past her to the instruments of the orchestra, willing himself to single out the French horns, then the flutes, then the clarinets. This exercise clarified his focus and calmed his breathing. Yes, breathing. Breathing in the fragrance of Ranya's intoxicating, jasmine-scented perfume. Oh, God, never again would he be a sane man.

He had tried, for Rasheed's sake, for his own sake, for Ranya's sake, even . . . he had tried to find other women. He had tried the online dating sites; he had chatted with other members of the hospital staff. He had looked through so many online profiles by this point; there were attorneys, PhDs, real estate agents, cheerleaders, teachers, former sorority members, tall ones, short ones, blonde ones, red-haired ones. But all he could see was that not one of them was Ranya.

He silently turned the pages of his program, seeking a distraction, any distraction but the one sitting beside him. He read through the listing of musicians, members of the Nashville Symphony. First violins. Second violins. *Playing second fiddle. Yeah, I know what that's like.* He sighed. Ranya glanced at him, and he straightened in his seat, closing his program and focusing his attention on the stage, where the second violins were keeping up perfectly fine with the firsts.

"Is there anyone as magnificent as Beethoven?" Ranya breathed as they exited the hall.

Gabriel knew this was a rhetorical question, but answered anyway. "Well, I'd say that Tchaikovsky came pretty close."

"Close, yes, Gabriel—but the prince is not the king," Ranya declared with a triumphant smile.

Playing second fiddle. Well, so he could take some comfort in knowing that he was in good company among those second placers in Ranya's mind.

They didn't speak again until they were in the car, waiting in the long line to exit the parking garage. It was then that Ranya said abruptly, "You know, Rachmaninoff is really good, too. I like almost anything by Rachmaninoff."

Gabriel smiled. *Ah, so there is another.*

"In fact," she went on, "his second piano concerto is one of my favorite pieces in all of classical music."

"I like that one, too," Gabriel said, still smiling.

On the ride back, Ranya opened up more and expressed to him what a good time she had had, how much she had enjoyed the concert, and how she appreciated his filling in for Rasheed on such short notice. It was an hour to midnight and they sat in Gabriel's car at the entrance to Ranya's house, saying goodnight.

Gabriel did not trust himself to escort her inside. So he kept his hands, both hands, on the wheel, and turned to her and smiled again. He told her how glad he was to know she had enjoyed the evening, and apologized once more for being a poor substitute for Rasheed. She swiveled in her seat and put her hand out as if to touch his cheek, but instead rested it on his shoulder, only briefly.

"It was wonderful," she assured him, smiling a full Ranya smile, that smile that lit up the room and his heart in concert, her eyes shining, her lips full. This close to him, her hair smelled of jasmine and roses. He inclined his head slightly toward her and closed his eyes.

And in that moment the mental image he had was not of Ranya at all, but of Rasheed, his friend's face contorted in misery when he recounted the late-night x-ray room betrayal back in Boston, his . . . Gabriel's eyes snapped open, and he nodded his head at Ranya. "Delighted to hear it. Hope you have a good rest of the night."

He watched her walk up her front steps, then turn and wave to him from her red-brick patio. Having seen the door finally close behind her, he sat very still behind the wheel of his car for a moment and focused on his breathing. Trying to regain just one single normal breath. Trying to calm the pounding of his heart. Trying to steady his hands, which had not left the wheel. Trying. It had become the summation of his life story. Trying.

When he finally reached for the transmission to put the car in drive, it occurred to him that they had passed Rasheed's test.

CHAPTER THIRTY-SIX

"And now here is my secret, a very simple secret: It is only with the heart that one can see rightly; what is essential is invisible to the eye."
——Antoine de Saint-Exupéry,
The Little Prince

RANYA SET HER PURSE DOWN on her nightstand and pulled off her shoes. She would need a long bath to even begin to recover from this night. After letting the water run, she went to remove her jewelry and the rest of her clothing.

Gabriel had looked, seemed, so dashing tonight. Her thoughts turned to the conversations she had had with him, both on the ride over to the Schermerhorn and during the concert's intermission.

"Yeah, Gabriel, I'm a musician. Many cardiologists are. The heart produces a music all its own, you know. Its own rhythm, its own sounds, even its own tune . . ."

"So the sounds of the heart are as magical to you as the workings of the brain are to me," he had said, giving her a look of deep understanding. He got it. Yes, he got it. And she loved that he got it.

During the intermission, when she had expressed how awestruck she always was when she considered how Beethoven was able to produce such magnificent musical works even as deafness closed in upon him, Gabriel had told her about the blind Irish harper and singer Turlough O'Carolan, who, more than a century before Beethoven, had composed beautiful melodic pieces that were still played and celebrated to this day. He had promised to deliver to her an album of O'Carolan's works.

So musical was Gabriel's brogue itself that there were times, she had found, when she could close her eyes for a moment and bathe in the uplifting lilt of his baritone, and be transported to a bright cobalt sky above endless green fields. She had never known before that a speaking voice could move its listener in the manner ordinarily reserved only for singers of the finest class. But that was it: there was music in his voice and in his brogue, and she never tired of listening to it.

Now, every time he spoke, Ranya saw Ireland, and this vision was accompanied by a yearning that rose in her throat and ached in her heart. For the cool breeze moving small white pillows of clouds against an impossibly-blue sky. For the infinite ribbons of green that connected both ends of every horizon. For the dazzling sparkle of ocean waves, scattering like so many brilliant diamonds against the jagged edge of the earth.

So this is what it was to have music walk beside you.

She sat on the edge of the tub and dipped her fingers into the water, testing the temperature. Looking down, she realized she was still wearing her Claddagh ring. As she turned her hand over to slip the ring off her finger, her heart skipped a beat. She stopped and stared. In her hustle and haste to finish getting ready earlier, she must have put her ring on upside down. For the tip of the heart was pointing outward.

Rasheed called and asked to come over early Sunday morning; when he arrived, he was full of apologies. Ranya could see that he was exhausted and knew that he had probably been up most of the night operating; she quickly reassured him that it was okay, that she understood.

"Hopefully that Irishman didn't bore you to death?" he asked, winking.

"Oh, no, no, it was fine," she reassured him again.

He went on, "I just couldn't bear the thought of sending you alone, and I didn't want you to miss the concert altogether. And I couldn't think of anyone else off the top of my head who enjoys classical music as much as we do."

"Rasheed, after all this time, don't you think me capable of attending a symphony concert by myself?"

"Of course, of course, *Habibti*—that's not what I meant." He shrugged his shoulders and sank back into the couch beside her.

"But you have to admit," he added, smiling widely and putting his arm around her, "it would've been such a shame to let one of those great box seats go to waste."

She elbowed him playfully and he held her closer. "You can forgive me, can't you?" he asked, giving her a look that revealed his confidence in the outcome.

"Maybe," she responded, tilting her chin upward and drinking in the depths of his gorgeous green eyes. He reached out and caressed her hair, lowered his lips to hers.

"I'll convince you," he murmured into her hair.

She allowed herself to succumb to his passion, was even relieved to do so. Being with Rasheed felt so comfortable, so . . . right.

But when he brought her to ecstasy later, it was Gabriel's name that nearly escaped her lips.

CHAPTER THIRTY-SEVEN

"Every night I cut out my heart. But in the morning it was full again."
—Michael Ondaatje,
The English Patient

June 2007
Sunday morning

"LOOKS LIKE GABE HAS a girlfriend," Rasheed announced.

Ranya's heart skipped a beat. "Really?" she asked, concentrating on keeping her voice steady. She was sitting with Rasheed at his breakfast table, and had just removed the tea bag from her glass. She focused now on preventing her spoon from clattering onto the glass table.

"Well, okay, maybe that's going a bit far," Rasheed admitted. "He's only been on a couple of dates with her."

"Oh," Ranya said, hoping she sounded casual. She let her gaze follow the sunlight as it danced off the face of Rasheed's watch and skipped across the cream-colored walls.

"I thought it would be a good idea for us to do a double date with him soon, so we can meet her," she heard Rasheed say.

Ranya tried to ignore the feeling of dread that gripped her stomach and tightened her chest.

"Um, yeah, sure, I guess that's fine," she replied, shrugging her shoulders. "When do you want to do it?"

They all met for lunch the following Saturday at Kalamata's in Green Hills. Veronica was a pretty redhead with clear blue eyes and a freckled face. She informed them that she was pursuing her Master of Social Work degree. Ranya estimated her to be at least fifteen years younger than Gabriel.

"Gabriel says y'all are from Pakistan," she said.

"Palestine," Gabriel quickly corrected her.

"Actually, I was born and raised in Nashville," Ranya said to her, trying hard to be kind. "My parents were Palestinian—from the Middle East, you know."

Veronica's eyes widened. "Oh," she said.

After an awkward pause during which Gabriel shifted uncomfortably in his seat, Veronica volunteered, "Well, I grew up outside Atlanta, but I'm here in Nashville for school, you know." Then she leaned forward and whispered, as if imparting a secret to be shared with precious few, "But I like Nashville better."

"Yeah, sure, Nashville is grand, isn't it?" Gabriel said, smiling widely at the room in general.

"Isn't his accent just the cutest?" Veronica gushed.

"Loads cuter than mine, apparently," Rasheed remarked. Ranya glanced sharply at him.

Veronica turned her attention to Rasheed now. "So you weren't born in Nashville?"

Rasheed stared at her. His accent was not as thick as some, maybe because he had attended the Friends School in Ramallah, but his clearly enunciated consonants and harmonious vowels combined to form what was, to Ranya's ear, the unmistakable accent of a native speaker of Arabic. Certainly not the accent of a native Nashvillian, or a native Southerner, to anyone's ear.

Rasheed looked at Ranya, then at Gabriel, who pointedly did not return eye contact, instead choosing to examine the napkin in his lap. Rasheed finally responded, "Uh . . . no. No, I wasn't born in Nashville."

Gabriel cleared his throat and made a poor attempt at changing the subject. "So how is your food, Veronica? This is Middle Eastern food, you know—Lebanese, to be exact."

"Ooh, I gotta take a picture," Veronica said excitedly. She pulled out a pink pocket camera and snapped two photos of her falafel plate and two of Gabriel's *fattoush* salad. Then she handed her camera to Ranya. "Would you take a picture of me and Gabriel, please?"

Ranya endeavored to smile. "Sure," she said, and even to herself it sounded curt.

Beside her, Rasheed leaned back in his chair, thumbs in his pockets, and goaded Gabriel, "Say cheese!"

"Cheese!" Veronica responded. Gabriel's grin was noticeably absent as Ranya depressed the shutter button.

The next day, while cleaning her kitchen, Ranya received a text from Gabriel. The fact that it was from Gabriel was the first surprise; the second was the question it posed: "What did you think of Veronica?"

"Doesn't matter what I think. What matters is what you think," Ranya texted in return.

She went back to cleaning her stove, wondering if she would receive a reply to that one. When it didn't seem that she would, she recalled what Rasheed had said in the car the day before, after they had left Gabriel standing with Veronica in front of the entrance to Kalamata's. "Well, that's not gonna work out," Rasheed had commented gruffly as they pulled out of the parking lot.

"Nope, can't see that it will," Ranya had agreed.

"I can't believe Gabe can't do better than that," Rasheed said.

And now it occurred to Ranya, as she moved on to washing the few dishes in the sink, that maybe Gabriel did not want to do better than that. Even as this thought occurred to her, she was fairly certain that it had not occurred to Rasheed. At least she hoped not.

She eventually moved on to dusting her baby grand, running a clean cloth lightly over the shiny black finish. She sat down and let her fingers wander over the keyboard, her mind wandering with them. At some point she realized she was picking out the melody to Stephen Sondheim's "Send in the Clowns." Indeed. What elaborate irony.

She closed her eyes, squeezed them shut, but the tears came anyway. All the years washed over her, all the valiant struggles to deny, repress, her feelings. No . . . no. There was no choice to be contemplated. Rasheed had done nothing to deserve this, nothing to deserve any wavering or doubt on her part. How could there be a better man? He was such a decent man, a prince, and he had never been anything but devoted to her.

She found herself wishing she had never met Gabriel, and she wept openly upon recognizing this sentiment within herself. For Gabriel had been so good to her, too. A paragon of propriety, given the circumstances. And it was uncanny the connection they had, how he seemed to know her so well. As though he could see through to her very core, heart and soul, feelings and thoughts, shining upon them an inexplicable understanding, an illumination all his own. That was it: he *saw* her. Even when she could not always see herself.

Enough of this. She sat up straight and rubbed her face with her sleeve to wipe the tears away. The logical choice was clear: Rasheed was there first, she loved Rasheed, she would stay with and remain faithful to Rasheed. End of story.

She walked back to the kitchen to pick up her phone, intending to place it in her purse on her way out. But as she lifted it from the counter, she saw that she had one text message beckoning to her. It was from Gabriel, and had been sent a few minutes earlier. "I don't know what to think anymore," had been his reply.

CHAPTER THIRTY-EIGHT

"Gáire maith is codladh fada, an dá leigheas is fearr i leabhar an dochtúra."
("A good laugh and long sleep are the two best cures in the doctor's book.")
—Irish proverb

September 2007

RANYA WAS TRAVELING QUITE A BIT now for business, giving presentations at national and international medical meetings as a recognized thought leader in the new and rapidly-growing area of cardiac catheterization via radial access. She was a staunch proponent of this new technique utilizing the radial artery in the wrist rather than the femoral artery in the groin as the point of access for a cardiac catheterization procedure. She found the evidence to be compelling, and saw in her own patients how this switch in anatomical access points led to better outcomes, with less potential for internal bleeding complications and faster recovery times.

Armed with the data and the desire to implement the highest standards for her patients, she became an evangelist for radial access not just in her own hospital but beyond. And, truth be known, she was grateful for the opportunity to put a little time and distance between herself and the two men in her life.

To her surprise, however, her frequent travel and rising academic fortunes had brought her into direct conflict with the cath lab director at her hospital, none other than the unsavory Dr. Sandra MacIllwain. Her appointment to the position that many had thought was rightfully Ranya's had turned out to be the first of many causes for astonishment where Dr. MacIllwain was concerned. Her signature red stiletto boots clicking through the hospital corridors, face overly done in garish makeup, MacIllwain was less of a force of nature than an annoying caricature of everything Ranya was not.

Rasheed and Gabriel had assured Ranya that there was no way that Sandy Mac, as they had taken to calling her, would last for long in their hospital. But now she had been perched on her throne for over two years, and Ranya had come to the point where she wasn't sure who would go first, Sandy or herself, so intolerable had the situation become. Not only was Sandy reluctant to implement the new radial access technique throughout the cath lab, insisting that there was no reason to mess with tradition, but she had begun scrutinizing every expense that Ranya incurred on her lecture circuit to promote the radial technique.

It was a conflict regarding one such trip expense that nearly came to blows on a Thursday afternoon outside the doors to the cath lab.

Heels clicking furiously down the hall, Sandy caught Ranya's attention just as she was about to push the circular metal button that would open the automatic doors to the lab. Dressed in scrubs and sneakers, Ranya turned her head, black curls whirling, in response to the insistent calling of her name.

"Dr. Abbasi, Dr. Abbasi."

"Yes?"

"I need to talk to you about this baggage fee."

"What?"

"From your last trip. You checked a bag. The department is not going to be reimbursing you any longer for checked bags. I mean, really. You ought to be able to put everything you need in a single carry-on bag."

"Is that right?" Ranya's eyes widened with incredulity. "Sandy, are we seriously talking about a $25 baggage fee here? You are interrupting my busy day for $25?"

Sandy pursed her magenta lips and jiggled her large hoop earrings. "Every penny counts, Ranya. You have an explanation for why you need to carry so much luggage with you every time you trot off to God knows where?"

Against her better judgment, Ranya decided to engage Sandy. "I'm sure you're aware of the TSA restriction on liquids?"

The corners of Sandy's mouth turned downward with skepticism. "You can take a bunch of liquids in a quart-size bag. What's the problem?"

Ranya could feel the heat rising in her face now. "The problem," she said slowly, trying to keep her voice low, "is that hair like mine requires a bit more product than one can fit in a quart-size bag. Not to mention all the other toiletries I need. Or maybe you have something against mouthwash and hand sanitizer, too?"

Sandy's face turned sour, but her own bleached-blonde pixie cut moved not at all as she jutted her chin out at Ranya and snapped, "Well, maybe you should cut your hair then. Or straighten it. Make it more manageable." She drew out this last word, man-age-able, her voice dripping with scorn and condescension.

Ranya saw red now. She spoke with cold fury, her own voice a steady crescendo as she countered, "Let me get *this* straight: you want me to cut off a manifestation of my heritage and an essential part of who I am, part of my identity? Not a chance. Get lost, Sandy."

Ranya slammed the heel of her hand against the button to open the automatic doors. She gave Sandy her back and walked through them. As she did so, she announced loudly, without turning around, "My resignation will be on your desk tomorrow morning."

When Rasheed met Gabriel that evening for their usual weekly get-together, he reported that Ranya would be joining them shortly. She had never asked to do so before, and Gabriel made no attempt to hide his own surprise, which mirrored Rasheed's. "And to what do we owe this honor, I wonder?" he said.

Rasheed replied, "Knowing Ranya, it won't be long before we find out."

Gabriel had not seen Ranya since his latest dating fiasco; although he knew she was busy and had heard from Rasheed how much she was traveling, still it seemed to him that she had been going out of her way to avoid him. Had he managed to stir some sort of jealousy within her? The better part of him doubted that.

No, he reasoned, with Ranya it was more likely that she couldn't stand to see him embarrass himself further. And in the end he hadn't been able to bear it either; one more date with Veronica had been the final destination of that misadventure. So what was Ranya doing coming here now?

Several minutes later, Ranya plunked herself down beside Rasheed and recounted the afternoon's events with Sandy Mac. Gabriel's jaw dropped in sync with Rasheed's.

"She wanted you to do *what*?" Gabriel asked.

"You're resigning over your *hair*?" Rasheed sputtered.

"Unbelievable," they said in unison.

After a shocked silence, Rasheed ventured, "You know, Ranya, revenge is a plate best served cold. Why don't you sleep on this tonight, think it over?"

"Yeah," Gabriel agreed, "maybe not be so hasty, you know, to do something you may regret later."

"Guys," Ranya sighed, "I know you're probably right, but I just can't stand that woman. Why do I have to keep putting up with such ignorance?"

"I know, I know," Rasheed said. "But consider this, Ranya: if you leave now, she wins."

"And anyway, Ranya," Gabriel added, "when it comes down to it, you are such an asset to that department that Sandy's boss will flip if he finds out that she's the reason for your resignation—and I would wager that Sandy knows that."

Rasheed nodded at Ranya and said, "You know he's right."

"Thanks, guys," Ranya said softly. "That helps." Gabriel watched her hands, which had been tightly clenched, relax; she folded and placed them on the table between them. Her Claddagh ring, still on her right hand, caught the gleam of the lamp that hung overhead.

Gabriel leaned back in his seat. He took a deep breath. "Good ol' Sandy Mac," he murmured, shaking his head. Then, raising his glass and his voice, he toasted gleefully, "Here's to Sandy Mac! May she burn for all eternity!"

"I'll drink to that," Rasheed said.

Rasheed was on the phone in his office the next day when none other than Dr. Sandra MacIllwain appeared in his doorway. Finishing the call, he turned his attention to her and pretended to be surprised.

"Dr. MacIllwain. Good morning. To what do I owe the honor?"

Not awaiting an invitation, Sandy stepped into his office and walked up to his desk. "I'm hoping you can convince Ranya not to resign."

"And why would Ranya resign?"

Sandy's face turned three shades of red, clashing horribly with her lip color-du-jour, which was some version of orange. "We may have had a . . . disagreement. Yesterday afternoon."

"Ah-ha."

"Yes, well," Sandy drew herself up and clasped her hands in front of her waist, concealing—too briefly—the gold buckle of her leopard-patterned belt. Getting no further response from Rasheed, she broke the silence herself, waving one hand carelessly and saying, "Whatever it was, it certainly wasn't important enough to resign over. I hope you can convince her of that."

Rasheed pushed his large rolling chair back and folded his arms across his chest. He regarded Sandy for a long moment. He had always wondered what she was trying to prove, with her outlandish way of dressing and her heavy mascara, her seemingly endless search for points of contention and angst. Or what she was trying to hide. He found her to be Ranya's opposite—and inferior—in every way.

Finally he stood up and walked around his desk, gesturing toward the door. He attempted a polite smile as he walked her to it, murmuring, "I'll see what I can do."

Sandy halted in the doorway. She looked up at him and smiled obsequiously. "Thanks so much. And, hey, put in a good word for me with that handsome Irish friend of yours, okay?" She raised her painted eyebrows and winked.

The smile, thin though it had been, disappeared entirely from Rasheed's face. "Good day now, Dr. MacIllwain."

Rasheed wondered for the hundredth time how she had been appointed Director of the Cardiac Catheterization Laboratory. But he doubted that would last long.

He couldn't wait to relay her request to Gabe. He would choke on his Guinness.

CHAPTER THIRTY-NINE

"I am resolved to rise superior to every obstacle."
—Ludwig van Beethoven

April 2008

SO RANYA STAYED AND TOUGHED IT OUT, and tried to be satisfied with the fact that Sandy, for the most part, stayed out of her way.

She was speaking to wider audiences now, getting invitations from around the world, and becoming a regular feature on the cardiology lecture circuit. In fact, she was entertaining yet another invitation to speak at a major medical society meeting when she received a call from an industry liaison, a representative of a medical device company, offering to sponsor her travel and cover all her expenses not only for her upcoming talk but for several others that she might agree to do "for them" in the future.

"Thank you for your interest," Ranya told him, "but my speaking engagements are independent of any industry influence or sponsorship. I don't accept any sort of compensation from anyone other than my own department. And it's always been my understanding that this is an established policy here at our hospital."

"But Dr. MacIllwain accepts our sponsorship funds all the time," came the reply.

"I'm sorry?" Ranya asked into the phone, blinking twice and pressing the receiver against her ear to be sure she was hearing correctly. "Are you speaking of Dr. *Sandra* MacIllwain?"

"Yes, of course," the industry rep said. "Why, just last week, she gave a talk at a local steakhouse that we sponsored. And I know that her research lab receives funding from us. Probably from others, too."

Ranya's mouth had dropped open. She knew this to be a clear violation of department policy. After a weighty pause, she politely declined his offer a second time, thanked him, and got off the phone.

That evening, Ranya had just entered her home and set her keys and phone down on the small wood table in her entryway when a text message illuminated the screen of her phone. She figured it must be from Rasheed, as it had been a long day and he had promised to pick up something for dinner. He probably wanted to know what she was craving at the moment.

Well, what she was really craving was some clarity. On several counts.

When she looked at the message, however, she saw it was from Gabriel. "Ranya, have I offended you in some way?" the screen flashed at her.

Her breath caught in her throat and she frowned. What on earth was he talking about? She decided on the direct approach and texted back, "What are you talking about?"

The next thing she knew, her phone was ringing. Gabriel was calling her.

She let it ring twice, three times. No, she couldn't get out of answering; that would be inexcusable now and would only make things worse. She answered on the fourth ring before it went to voicemail.

"Ranya, hello, sorry to bother you, but you walked right by me in the hospital lobby this afternoon as if I were a total stranger. Is something wrong? Is there something I should apologize for?"

She was astonished, not only by his description of an incident of which she had no recollection, but by the urgency of his concern.

"What? In the lobby? When? I didn't see you!" she said.

"I waved to you; I was standing by the information desk with Ryan Davis." She knew he was referring to one of the family medicine physicians, a mutual acquaintance.

"I—I'm so sorry, Gabe. I honestly didn't see you. I must have been in my own little world after that phone conversation I had with a device company rep." A part of her was flattered that her attention meant so much to him.

"Wow, well, that must have been some phone call! Care to divulge?"

She hesitated for only a moment, then unpackaged the whole dilemma for him, outlining what the device rep had revealed about Sandy Mac's shady dealings in flagrant violation of department policy, and her own outrage and then contemplation of what her next step should be. Gabriel listened silently until she had finished.

"Ranya," he said, his voice deep and serious, "you have to report this. Turn her in. Lord knows she has it coming to her."

Then he asked, "Have you told Rasheed?"

"Not yet; I haven't had a chance yet." She didn't mention that she expected to have that chance within the next hour or so.

"Well, you should. It'll mean the end of Sandy Mac's tenure here. Hopefully."

"Hopefully," she agreed. She felt an uplifting sense of satisfaction wash over her.

CHAPTER FORTY

"Heat is required to forge anything. Every great accomplishment is the story of a
flaming heart."

—Arnold H. Glasgow

LESS THAN THREE WEEKS LATER, Ranya was called to consult on one of
Rasheed's patients who had gone into the irregular heart rhythm of atrial fibrillation following cardiac surgery. This was not an uncommon occurrence, but
what she was not expecting was to find Gabriel standing at the patient's bedside
when she arrived. He held in one hand a stapled sheaf of papers and was flipping
through them with the other hand.

Ranya smiled to herself. Everyone knew how much he hated the electronic
medical record system; he liked the feel of papers in his hand. He said it distracted
him less from what he was doing and allowed him to keep his focus where it ought
to be: on the patient. Now, as he glanced from the papers to the patient, he looked
pensive.

As she approached the bedside, he looked up at her and flashed a smile, though
it was not representative of his best effort. He began with, "Why, hello, Ranya!
So glad to see you," before going straight to the matter that was clearly of utmost
importance in his mind. He pointed at the patient's IV line and a stern look settled
over his face. "I'm concerned that the amiodarone is going to interact adversely
with my patient's seizure medications."

Ranya was caught by surprise. "*Your* patient? Seizure medications?"

"Yes, I—"

Ranya started her rant. "I thought this was Rasheed's patient. Who put him on amiodarone? I didn't order any amiodarone—"

"Well, I didn't say you did."

She plucked the papers from Gabriel's hands. "Those surgeons always load amiodarone at the first sight of any rhythm abnormality." She rolled her eyes.

As she looked at the same evidence Gabriel had, convincing herself of the patient's current status, he explained, "This is one of my clinic patients whom I've been following for a long time for a seizure disorder, and he happened to need cardiac surgery, which is how he ended up here. I was just checking in on him. I'm glad you're here, as I said before—obviously, he needs a good cardiologist who can set this to rights."

Ranya was too preoccupied to spend much time wondering whether or not he was being sincere or trying to flatter her. She quickly decided on sincere, since flattery for flattery's sake was not Gabriel's style, then turned on her heel and walked toward the bank of computers behind the central nurses' station. She beckoned to him to follow her, returning his papers to him as she moved.

"Let's just have a look at the current medication orders, okay?" she said to him as they sat down together at one computer. She typed and clicked a few commands; then, while waiting for the screen to give her what she wanted, she spun around in her chair and grabbed the patient's telemetry chart, full of information on his heart rhythm since he had come out of surgery. From that she hoped to determine when his atrial fibrillation had begun. While spinning back around, she asked one of the nurses to page Rasheed.

"Ah, yes, let's call in the Man himself," Gabriel quipped.

As they waited for Rasheed, Ranya explained to Gabriel that she hoped to use electrical cardioversion to shock the patient back into normal rhythm, but wanted to do a transesophageal echocardiogram first, out of an abundance of caution, to get some good ultrasound images of his heart and make sure there were no blood clots that could be thrown to the brain and cause a stroke. She looked meaningfully at Gabriel and said, "So we don't end up with another Stroke Code on our hands."

Gabriel gave her his trademark grin and said, "So the cardiologist wants to shock the patient back to normalcy. Why am I not shocked?"

She groaned at his very bad joke.

Then, with unexpected earnestness, he asked, "Did you know that the first portable defibrillator was invented by an Irish cardiologist?"

Ranya groaned again and made a face. "Oh, come on now, Gabriel, not everything can be Irish."

He leaned in and insisted, "No, seriously, it was Dr. Frank Pantridge, from Belfast. Many have called him the 'father of emergency medicine' because of it. And can you just imagine, that first defibrillator weighed 70 kilos and got its energy from car batteries!"

"Wow," Ranya replied, shaking her head. "Okay, I stand corrected."

"And that stethoscope around your neck—" he said, pointing, "it was, in fact, another Irish doctor who invented the first version of it."

"Okay, now I know you're pulling my leg, Gabriel! What do you take me for? We all know that it was Laennec who invented the stethoscope—and he was French."

"Laennec invented a tube," Gabriel scoffed. "It was the Irish physician Arthur Leared, born in Wexford, who took it further and invented the bi-aural version, the one that fits in both ears." He smiled triumphantly and added, "Very similar to the one you are wearing today."

Ranya returned his smile. "Well, then, so we can thank Dr. Leared and Dr. Pantridge when I shock your patient." Then she shook her index finger in the air and said, "But only after I'm certain there are no clots that could go to the brain."

"Well, I do sincerely appreciate your concern for my patient's brain, Ranya," Gabriel said, a hint of the old sternness returning to his voice. "I can assure you that a stroke is the last thing he needs right now."

"A stroke is the last thing any of us need right now!" boomed Rasheed's voice from behind them. "Who is having a stroke??"

Ranya turned around and made no attempt to hide her annoyance. "You know, Rasheed, when you call a cardiology consult, I really wish you would tell your team to hold off on giving any cardiac meds—like this amiodarone—unless it's an emergency."

Gabriel said, "Yes, it's important to consider the effects on his seizure medications, you know."

Rasheed replied, "And has he had a seizure?"

"Not as far as I can tell at present," Gabriel acknowledged.

"Well, then." And with that, Rasheed turned his attention to Ranya, clearly wanting to tell her something else. She had just enough time to consider whether it would be an apology before she spotted their patient's nurse approaching the bedside. Without giving Rasheed a chance to speak further, she got up and walked over to tell the nurse the plan of care that she had already discussed with Gabriel.

Rasheed and Gabe watched her walk away from them, her step indicating that she was in charge now. Rasheed was all too familiar with it. He smiled to himself, then grew more serious as he thought of the sight that had greeted him when he first entered the unit: Ranya and Gabe, side by side, their heads bent together over the telemetry chart, thick as thieves.

He had to admit they worked well together, his two favorite people in the world.

He turned to Gabe and, seeing that his friend's eyes were still trained on Ranya, he commented, "She'll make an excellent replacement for Sandy as Cath Lab Director."

Gabe broke off his gaze and cleared his throat. He glanced at Rasheed and said, "It's done, then?"

"Pretty much," Rasheed said. Then he laughed and added, "Sandy is claiming to everyone that the climate in Florida suits her complexion better."

Gabe smiled and said in a low voice, "Good riddance to her, then."

CHAPTER FORTY-ONE

"Everything should be as simple as it can be, but not simpler."
—Albert Einstein

January 2009

RASHEED WAS BETWEEN OR CASES, and thought he would check in on one of his post-op patients. As he rounded the corner of the nurses' station, he halted in mid-step, for there was Gabe, huddled behind the counter, leaning over a keyboard and holding the handset of a corded hospital phone to his ear. He looked agitated, and as Rasheed came closer, the fullness of his friend's brogue reached him, his words conveying the reason for his agitation.

"Well, Dr. Jenkins, I was just trying to ascertain how you performed a prostate exam on my young female patient with seizures? Not *why* even, but how?" Gabe was saying in clipped tones into the phone. He paused and rolled his eyes at whatever response he was being given, and within the upward roll caught sight of Rasheed. He nodded at him and Rasheed approached, leaned his elbows on the gray counter, folded his hands in prayer position, and rested his chin upon them. The shows that Gabe put on when in defense of patient care were too good to be missed.

"Yes, well, I'm looking at your note here in the electronic medical record, and it says very clearly, 'Prostate exam normal,'" Gabe repeated, cradling his forehead between thumb and forefinger as he did so.

The muted voice on the other end said something Rasheed could not make out, but Gabe's response was loud and clear. "Yes, I know—we have to watch out when using these electronic templates, don't we? That's why I free-type all my notes. Every patient is an individual, and a human being's medical history and physical exam don't lend themselves very well to templates, do they? Seems a gross and tragic diminution of the human condition. But if you must use them . . . at the very least, please proofread before you enter them into the medical record. Remember you have a brain—I'm going to give you the benefit of the doubt and say it's a good one—so use it." Gabe dropped the handset into the receiver.

"So, another fun day at the office?" Rasheed remarked.

"These residents," Gabe muttered in response, shaking his head and waving his hand from phone to computer. He looked up at Rasheed, who waited, knowing there was more. Gabe leaned back in the rolling chair, folded his arms across his chest, and frowned. "It's getting harder and harder every year, Rasheed," he said.

"Yes, they do seem to get younger and younger, as you've said before, don't they?" Rasheed murmured, trying to assuage him.

"Oh, it's not just the residents," Gabe said, shaking his head again. "It's the case managers forever asking for extra documentation, the bean counters tracking every keystroke I make, the constant requests for insurance pre-approvals or prior authorizations or a blessing from God Himself for every procedure. And I swear," he went on, holding one palm up in the air, "if one more moron calls me a 'provider' . . . I'm telling you, I'd rather pour salt on my eyeballs than hear someone call me by that inane and degradingly meaningless term. I am *not* a 'provider'; I am a *physician.*"

Rasheed folded his arms and nodded, sensing that Gabe was just warming up.

"And then there are the never-ending formulary changes," Gabe continued his rant. Using air quotes, he gave a common example by launching into an imaginary conversation: " 'Well,' the pharmacy benefit manager tells me, 'that medication used to be on the $4 list at the local retail pharmacy, but now it's not, and it will cost close to $100 to get the prescription filled.' So I say, 'But there really is no better medication for him, no substitute—we've tried others, and this is the one that works.' And you know what they tell me then, what they always tell me?"

Rasheed had thought the question a rhetorical one, but Gabe was looking at him expectantly, demandingly. "Uh, I don't know," Rasheed replied. "What do they tell you?"

"That's EXACTLY what they tell me!" Gabe leaped out of his chair, hand-slicing the air in front of Rasheed. "'Well, I don't know, Dr. O'Brien.' 'I don't know what to tell you, Dr. O'Brien.' 'I wish I knew what to tell you, Doctor.' 'I don't know, I don't know, I don't know,' *ad infinitum* and *ad nauseam*. Nobody knows, not a single soul, and least of all me!" Gabe slapped the counter with the palm that had previously been chopping the air to shreds. "It's the most insane system imaginable!"

Rasheed, for the life of him, could not think of a single thing to say that didn't begin with "I don't know what to tell you, Gabe." So he remained silent, standing there in his surgical scrubs, letting Gabe grab his bare arm above the elbow, which he proceeded to shake in ever-increasing fury.

"How can I focus on patient care with all of this going on, Rasheed, how can I?? How can anyone? It's abominable!" he sputtered, his face a fiery red now, the blue of his temporal veins matching the shade of his eyes, and his grip on Rasheed's arm beginning to take on the quality of a vise.

"Good heavens, man, calm down, or you'll have a coronary event," Rasheed said, raising his eyebrows. "And then you'll end up on Ranya's table—or worse: mine."

"Oh, and speaking of which," Gabe responded, finally and mercifully taking his hand from Rasheed's arm, for the sole purpose of jutting his forefinger into the nearly nonexistent space between them, "you know what was the icing on today's cake?"

Gabe leaned in further, which Rasheed had not thought possible. Rasheed held his tongue; no way was he going to attempt to answer another of Gabe's rhetorical questions while he was like this.

"I have just been informed," Gabe said slowly, visibly trying to calm himself, "that another patient of mine has been bumped from today's cath lab schedule when he's been NPO since midnight waiting on the procedure—and this is the second day in a row that this has happened!"

Rasheed released his breath, feeling some relief. "Well, for that one, at least, I know whom we can call."

"No, no, don't even think about it," Gabe said, shaking his head and waving his hands. "I'm sure Ranya has a million things to do, Rasheed; I hate to bother her."

"I assure you it won't be a bother," Rasheed replied, having already pressed the necessary buttons on his cell phone. He regarded Gabe as the phone rang, noted how he drew himself straighter and smoothed his tie and the top of his navy-blue sweater. The redness that had consumed his whole face had receded to just his cheeks now, and a few beads of sweat dotted his brow.

Rasheed felt a deep sympathy for him, felt they had to get this turned around soon, in some way, or Gabe would burn out, and what should have been a brilliant career would be grounded before it had ever had a chance to soar.

"Hello?" came Ranya's voice on the other end, and Rasheed leaned forward so that Gabe could hear.

"Hello, Ranya, *Habibti*," Rasheed replied, as Gabe fidgeted beside him. He explained the situation with Gabe's patient, concluding with, "So, I figured, if the cath lab director can't fix it, who can?"

"Of course I will fix it," came Ranya's brusque reply. "What is the patient's name again? Is Gabriel with you right now? Let me talk to him."

Rasheed looked down at his wrist watch. "I have to get to my next case, but I'll have Gabe call you from his phone, okay?"

Gabe was already pulling out his cell as Rasheed was saying his sweet goodbyes and hanging up.

"Well, good, then," Rasheed nodded to him. "See? No problem!" He waved and walked away as Gabe put his own phone to his ear. He made a mental note to speak to Ranya about what they could do for Gabe. Maybe he just needed to get out more.

CHAPTER FORTY-TWO

"Then I looked at the window and thought: Why, yes, it's just the rain, the rain, always the rain, and turned over, sadder still, and fumbled about for my dripping sleep and tried to slip it back on."
—Ray Bradbury,
Green Shadows, White Whale

May 1, 2010
Saturday

RANYA WAS CERTAIN SHE had just made the stupidest mistake of her life. Her four-door Volvo sedan, and she within it, sat in nearly three feet of rapidly-rising water at the exit to the Belle Meade Kroger parking lot.

It had been raining torrentially since the crack of dawn, but never had she expected flooding like this; she had thought she had enough time to grab a few snacks and other items for the Kentucky Derby viewing at Rasheed's house, which was just minutes away in West Meade.

But Mother Nature had other plans, it seemed. Stuck in the street in this swiftly-forming pond of swirling gray water, she called Rasheed, who sounded far more panicked than she was willing to be. He had just finished an emergency case and was stuck at the hospital. He told her to call 9-1-1 and also said he would try to reach Gabriel, who might be in the area since he was also supposed to be at

Rasheed's in time for the Derby. "Ranya, please, you need to get out of that car," he pleaded before hanging up to call Gabriel.

"You don't have to tell me that twice," Ranya muttered, not sure and not caring whether he heard her before the call ended.

Gabriel was headed toward Rasheed's house when he got Rasheed's text. "911. Ranya stuck in H2O outside Belle Meade Kroger." That was maybe five or so minutes from him if he parked his car right where he was and ran.

Cars were stranded everywhere, it seemed, and he knew he had made the right decision to leave his at the top of a hill. Arriving at the bottom of the hill, he saw Ranya attempting to evacuate her car through the driver's side window. Through water that was nearly waist-level, he waded over to her and lifted her the rest of the way out.

Through his now-soaked, white Oxford shirt, he could feel her heart pounding against his chest, felt her wet palms against his neck and back as he pushed his way forward through the ever-rising waters. He felt as much as heard her breath coming in hard spurts that whispered past his ear. "It's gonna be okay," he said, as much to himself as to her. "I've got you now."

Once they were out of the deepest water, he set her down and steadied her arm as they trudged uphill together, the rain pouring down on them. She looked back at her car, now filling with water through the open window. Gabriel followed her gaze. "No use worrying about that now, Ranya; we have to get safe and we have to get dry."

They called Rasheed as soon as they were in Gabriel's car, letting him know that Ranya was okay and that they were on the way to his house, which was the only location that made sense at that point. Rasheed unnecessarily reminded them to feel free to take a shower; one never knew what all had collected in such mucky water.

Gabriel headed for Rasheed's guest shower while Ranya used the master. Hearing the unmistakable sound of shower water running upstairs, he stared at the silver-framed glass stall before him and thought he might die. The rose-water smell of her hair as he carried her, the feel of her heart against his chest. So fresh a memory from the harrowing moment they had shared.

And then he heard . . . no, that was his imagination, a product of his fantasizing. But there it was again, faint yet definite. The sound of Ranya singing upstairs. So she liked to sing in the shower. Whoever would have thought it. And she was a soprano. Of course she was. He really shouldn't be surprised, should he? Or at least, by this point, not surprised at being surprised. He wouldn't be surprised to learn that she had perfect pitch, too. That was Ranya—perfect, perfect. Even her imperfections were perfect.

But what was that she was singing? He thought he recognized the song, at least from the snippets he could catch. It sounded like Stephen Sondheim's "Send in the Clowns."

Yes, yes, he was sure of it now. That was the song. How appropriate.

He wondered if she knew what she was doing to him, if she had chosen it deliberately, or if she always sang it in the shower, or if she even knew she was singing at all. He stood there transfixed in the guest bathroom doorway, mesmerized by the sound of her voice and by the lyrics as they became clearer and easier to follow. When she asked him if he loved farce, he had to admit that, by all appearances, it would seem that he did. But the fault was not hers, of that he was certain.

Ranya in the shower.

He turned on the water to the guest tub and made sure it was ice-cold before he stepped in.

As he toweled down after that brief bout of refreshing misery, Gabriel wondered if Rasheed would be able to make it home, given the number of roads that were becoming impassable. He found that he sincerely hoped so. There was no way he would make it through a night marooned there with Ranya alone.

Prayers answered, Rasheed arrived just as Gabriel was trying to figure out what to wear now that his own clothes were ruined. Rasheed knocked on the bathroom door and threw him a pair of blue scrubs; Ranya, Gabriel soon discovered, already kept a couple of her own pairs there. *How convenient. But really, Gabriel, what were you expecting?*

For two days and two nights, it rained. It seemed as though the rain would never stop. It rained until the Tennessee highways turned into rivers and Tennesseans' basements became lakes. It rained until the staccato patter of heavy raindrops on the roof and against the windows became incessant, and then routine, part of the rhythm of life, the percussion section in a stormy orchestra, the steady, ominous drumbeat of things to come.

It rained until the Opryland Hotel became a giant indoor city under water, a sad Atlantis, images from its interior broadcast on the local television news. Where Ranya and her duo had walked beneath the hotel's directional signposts, five feet of water now stood, so that all that was visible were the tops of the signs themselves.

It rained until the Cumberland River swelled to historic levels, passed flood stage, and overflowed its banks, spilling its liquid fury onto the streets of downtown Nashville, into the bowels of the Schermerhorn Symphony Center three blocks away, wiping out the beautiful Steinway grands and nearly destroying the glorious, multi-million-dollar pipe organ that had been the pride and crowning glory of the concert hall.

Ranya and her men watched the news in horror as entire buildings, including a mobile classroom from a local school, were seen floating down Interstate 24 after Mill Creek completely covered it with its regurgitated excess, with no regard for pavement or property.

They watched as the Grand Ole Opry drowned and floodwaters submerged the entire adjacent Opry Mills complex, until the only structure left afloat was the General Jackson Showboat. As the news reported on various other water rescues, Ranya remembered how fortunate she was that she had escaped her own car unscathed. Never had she been so grateful for Gabriel's presence—and for his dogged dedication to staying in good physical shape.

But even as she recalled her good fortune, she tried hard to forget the feel of her ribs pressed against his wet chest, and the smell of his sweat as she clung to his neck, the strength of his arms enveloping her.

And so for two days and two nights they watched and listened to the rain fall. It came down straight and it came down sideways and it never stopped coming down, and while they watched the rain and the television in utter disbelief, they all voiced how grateful they were for the comfortable cocoon of Rasheed's home, where they got creative in making use of the pantry ingredients he had on hand and prayed that the power would stay on.

During the first night of their stranded state, Gabriel fell asleep on the couch even though Rasheed had given him the guest bedroom and told him repeatedly to make himself at home. But how could he possibly feel at home while the memory of holding Ranya was still so fresh, even as she herself slept upstairs with his best friend? It was madness. So he remained on the couch and stubbornly flipped through infomercials until a fitful sleep found him.

Sometime after falling asleep—it could have been a few minutes or it could have been a few hours, so heavy and dull was his slumber—the sound of gentle footsteps in the kitchen, which was open to the great room, awakened him. He heard a cabinet door open and then water running as he sat up and rubbed the sleep from his eyes. The next thing he heard was Ranya's swift intake of breath as she realized that he was there, still on the couch.

"Gabriel!" she exclaimed in a hushed whisper. "What are you . . .? Oh, I'm so sorry to wake you; I was just getting a glass of water."

She then asked him if he would like some water too, to which he replied in a sleepy mumble, "Oooh, I think we've seen enough of that today, haven't we?" Then he sat up straighter and tried to decline more properly. He spoke softly, assuming Rasheed was still sleeping and wanting to keep it that way. "I'm fine for water, thank you. Please don't trouble yourself."

She was walking toward him now. Reflexively, he moved farther down the sofa to make space for her. But she did not sit down. Standing at the far end of the sofa, she began telling him something about how he should go to the guest bedroom, that the couch was no place to spend the night, that there was no need for him to do that here, and that Rasheed would probably be upset if he found him there in the morning when there was a perfectly good bedroom given over expressly for his use.

But Gabriel's mind was not processing or caring about most of this; he was drinking in the way her red satin night robe moved against her each time she gestured with her hands, and how her dark curls tumbled over her shoulders, even more alluring in their slightly disheveled state.

So apparently she kept a lovely robe like that lying around Rasheed's house too. No surprise there, he supposed. And weren't they done with surprises, as he had decided earlier?

Now she was asking him if he needed anything. *I need you*, his mind replied. He looked down at the Persian rug beneath his stocking feet—Rasheed's rug— and shook his head.

The next thing she said drew his focus to her once more, as if there were ever any question of his focus being elsewhere. She had placed her hand on the edge of the sofa and tilted her head downward before saying, "Thank you for coming to my rescue today—well, technically, I guess it was yesterday—but the point is—"

Even in the dim lighting of the great room, he noticed the flush that came over her face. He sought, as he always did, to save her. He waved his hand to interrupt her. "Oh, no, not at all, Ranya; don't mention it. No need to thank me for that. My pleasure, really," he said, and with these last words, he looked directly at her, seeking her eyes.

She insisted, "No, really, I'm lucky you came when you did. I just want you to know that I know that. In fact, after some of what we've seen on the news today, it's entirely possible that you may have saved my life." And with this final remark, she met his gaze.

"You or Rasheed would have done the same for me," he said.

At his mention of Rasheed's name, she seemed to remember something, and picking up her glass from the end table, she said, "Well, I can't thank you enough. I hope you get some rest now. Good night." And with that, she turned and walked back upstairs, away from him.

Any remaining prospects he might have had for "getting some rest" left with her.

The next night, Ranya convinced him and Rasheed to watch *The English Patient* again with her. Gabriel knew that, along with *Michael Collins,* it was one of her favorite films. And it was better than watching the news, from which they all needed a break.

When the film was over, Rasheed leaned back and commented, "All these people who have affairs—where do they even find the time to cheat? I mean, it just seems exhausting!"

Ranya stared at him.

Gabriel, desperate to prevent an awkward silence, inserted quickly, "Well, that's one way of looking at it. I'm sure they have their reasons."

Now it was Rasheed's turn to stare. And the awkward silence ensued despite Gabriel's best efforts.

Ranya stood up abruptly and announced that she was tired and was going to bed. Rasheed muttered, "Sounds like a good idea," before turning to Gabriel to wish him good night and to urge him yet again to make himself at home.

Once Ranya and Rasheed had gone up to the master bedroom, Gabriel sprawled on the couch again, flipping mindlessly through TV channels, looking to watch anything but the ongoing destruction of Nashville, hoping to be distracted by anything other than the thought of Ranya and Rasheed together upstairs. So his choice came down to Andy Griffith or Hawkeye Pierce, and he chose the latter. The witty-yet-somber alcoholic surgeon seemed to be the perfect companion at the moment, and anyway, the antics of the other colorful members of the magnificent 4077th always made him laugh, and sure couldn't he do with a laugh right about now.

During the commercials, his eyes wandered around Rasheed's living room, taking in all the happy pictures of Rasheed and Ranya, decked out in classy, modern frames and sitting on the mantel, hanging on the walls, decorating the end tables. His gaze settled on the one picture that included the three of them, standing together at the Cliffs of Moher. The angle of the camera had caught O'Brien's tower in the background, and the dark wood frame served to highlight the brilliant greens and grays of the cliffs against the blues of the Atlantic Ocean.

Gabriel smiled in spite of himself, remembering that moment and Rasheed's well-placed jokes. He recalled how he and Rasheed had carried on snapping photos of the woman they both loved as she stood at the edge of the earth, smiling and laughing in the winds of the Wild Atlantic Way. He wondered if Rasheed had caught the unbridled joy that had radiated from Ranya at that time, at that place.

Yes, of course he had.

Gabriel knew that by rights Rasheed could have thrown him out on his ear by now, even for the suspicion of coveting Ranya, but that wasn't Rasheed's style, and Gabriel had tried so hard to remain faithful to his friend. Oh, how he had tried. And he had to think that Rasheed knew that too.

God, what am I doing? Gabriel wondered, for the millionth time. *I should go away, go away and leave them be. Go back to Ireland, where the rains fall softer, and there find what's left of my life.*

But even as the Nashville rain continued its relentless march across Rasheed's roof, Gabriel knew in his heart he would do no such thing. He knew he was the barely-breathing prisoner of an inertia that was all the more inescapable because it was of his own making.

PART THREE

CHAPTER FORTY-THREE

"It occurred to me that there was no difference between men, in intelligence or race, so profound as the difference between the sick and the well."
—F. Scott Fitzgerald,
The Great Gatsby

"Give a man a mask, and he will tell you the truth."
—Oscar Wilde

May 2012

Ranya was struck by THE SILENCE as she entered the darkened hospital room. There in the corner, in the single bed that seemed to hold no one, was a shrunken version of the man she had known and had been privileged to call her patient for the last decade. Even in the darkness—especially in the darkness—the wasting of terminal lung cancer was apparent on his face, which appeared almost skeletal now as he attempted a feeble smile upon her approach to his bedside.

"Mr. Shetfield," she said softly, "hey there."

"Hey, Dr. Ranya," came the throaty rasp.

"May I sit here?" she patted the pale blue bedspread.

He nodded and patted the same place with his own hand.

She sat beside him, facing him, with her hands clasped, then looked down and thought hard, again, about what on earth she could possibly say. But she didn't have to think long, because after a quiet moment, Mr. Shetfield reached out and placed his hand lightly over hers. He looked up at her with a steady gaze, and both his hand and his voice shook as he said, "I want to thank you, Doc."

Ranya took his hand between both of hers, blinked, and swallowed hard, trying to push down the lump in her throat. She shook her head gently. "You don't have to thank me, Mr. Shetfield. It's been the utmost privilege to be a part of your care all these years. I'm the one who should be thanking you."

She came out of the room with tears in her eyes, but wiped them away hastily when she noticed Gabriel's form approaching through the blur of her vision. He looked at her strangely, questioningly. She cleared her throat and straightened her back. "Mr. Shetfield," she said, pointing her thumb over her shoulder at his room. "He's going home to hospice today."

"Uh, yes, that's exactly what I was coming to tell you. I see someone else has beaten me to it."

"Actually, it was he himself. He had the nurses call me so he could say good-bye."

"I see."

Ranya really didn't feel like speaking right now, and bless Gabriel, he always seemed to pick up on that.

"Well, I'll just—I have some charts to sign, phone calls to make," he said, gesturing down the hallway behind him.

Ranya nodded gratefully and turned to go.

"Ranya?"

She turned back.

"I'm so sorry," Gabriel said, his eyes meeting hers, and she knew he understood.

A week later, Gabriel and Rasheed were engaged in their usual Thursday night activity, though now the backdrop had changed to a different location each week, since Houston's had closed years before. Gabriel was once again taking the opportunity to voice his displeasure over the direction taken by American medicine in general, and by their hospital in particular.

He complained to Rasheed, not for the first time, about the hospital administration's use of relative value units to measure his productivity, the RVUs that placed higher value on invasive procedures than on talking to and examining patients; he also bemoaned the corresponding increase in patient volume, the number of patients he was expected to see in clinic every hour.

"I simply cannot take a neurological history, do a thorough neuro exam, and make an assessment—AND recommendations for treatment!—in ten or fifteen minutes," he said, the caramel-colored liquid of his unfinished drink sloshing about in the glass that he set down firmly upon the polished wood of the bar. "Just cannot—and will not—do it. It's mad."

Rasheed remained silent, waiting patiently, which Gabriel appreciated, since he was not yet finished with his litany. "The practice of medicine is now being run by people who know nothing about it, Rasheed," he said somberly. "Businessmen and so-called consultants," he continued, conjuring air quotes as he over-enunciated the word *consultants*, "with profit, rather than patient care, as their bottom line."

He shook his head in disgust, then threw up his hands. "I don't know how much longer I can stand it." The ice clanked in his glass as he raised it to his lips again.

Rasheed nodded his head sympathetically, then halted as Gabriel wagged an index finger at him. "And you—" Gabriel went on with his tirade, determined to spare no one, "—you with your high-paying procedures and interventions and what-not, what would you know about the plight of those of us who actually see real, live, whole patients for a living? Those of us who use our brains day in and day out to figure out the intricacies of patients' complicated diagnoses? Those of us who are more than just vascular plumbers??"

Against the buzz in his brain, Gabriel made out the hint of an inkling that he may have gone too far. Although Rasheed's manner remained easy, his posture relaxed, Gabriel felt the need to apologize. "Okay, look, I'm sorry, Rasheed; I didn't mean anything personal. Of course I know that the patients you see are very much alive, sometimes precisely because of your well-thought-out care."

"That's all right, Gabe," Rasheed said, patting his shoulder. "I can see the toll this is taking on you." And then, in what must have been one of Rasheed's best-ever attempts at deflection, he squeezed Gabriel's shoulder and offered, "Why don't you come to Beirut with me? Then all this will seem *so* much less insane."

Caught off-guard, Gabriel just stared at him. Rasheed's eyes were twinkling, and he was smiling so broadly now he looked nearly maniacal, or maybe that was just Gabriel's addled imagination.

A drawn-out "Whaaat?!?" was the only defense Gabriel could muster at first in the face of such a mad proposition. Finally, regaining his bearings, he added, "You can't be serious."

But Rasheed was serious. He explained that he had been invited to give a talk to the cardiothoracic surgery department at a prestigious university in Beirut in July. Apparently, members of that department had asked him to lecture on the latest surgical heart valve techniques.

"But, Rasheed . . . is it safe to go there now?"

Gabriel left unsaid any reference to the ongoing fallout from the Arab Spring and the recent developments in the Syrian civil war; there was no need to mention it to Rasheed, of all people.

"Oh, yes, yes. Definitely," Rasheed answered, seeking to be reassuring, but it was one "yes" too many, and Gabriel remained unconvinced. Rasheed went on,

"Particularly where we're going to be—probably the safest part of town. And Beirut as a whole has largely avoided all that mess . . . for maybe the first time ever."

He patted Gabriel's shoulder again and added, "But of course you'll be with *us*, Gabe. We won't lead you astray."

"'We'?" Gabriel echoed.

"Ranya is coming with me," Rasheed said, smiling once more. "You should too."

Gabriel drew a deep breath and stared at Rasheed, and fought hard, so hard, not to look more interested in the proposition now that Ranya's participation had been confirmed. But he felt his eyebrows go up and his eyes widen, and knew that he was failing.

He thought it quite likely that Rasheed had, by now, catalogued the special smile he reserved for Ranya, the way his face lit up when she entered the room. And no doubt Rasheed knew Ranya had many admirers; how could she not? But only one of them was his best friend.

Rasheed folded his hands in front of him and steadily returned Gabriel's gaze, awaiting his answer. An invitation was an invitation.

"You know," Gabriel said slowly, looking down at the bar and flattening one palm against it before clearing his throat and continuing, "I've never been to Beirut before, and if I were ever going to go, I can't think of better companions." He was smiling at Rasheed now. "Thank you, Rasheed—maybe you're right; maybe that's just what I need: a little more madness in my life."

CHAPTER FORTY-FOUR

"Beirut gives every visitor the impression that it is his."
—Mahmoud Darwish,
in "A Love Story Between an Arab Poet and His Land"
(interview with Adam Shatz),
Journal of Palestine Studies, Spring 2002

"My experience is that Beirut rarely stays normal for long; but while things are
quiet, I think people, especially those who would not be booted out, deserve clean
streets and bright shop-windows and pretty clothes and open bars. They are, after
all, a select group of individuals, people who each have a story which begins: 'I
just missed being killed on the day . . .'"
—Tony Clifton,
God Cried

July 7, 2012
1:00 p.m.
Saturday

FROM THE ROOFTOP OF the Four Seasons Hotel in Beirut, Lebanon, Gabriel looked out at the calm, bright-blue waters of the Mediterranean, shimmering in the sunshine. From this vantage point, twenty-six floors up, he had only to look in one direction to take in the beauty of the sea, in another direction to admire the majesty of the mountains where the famous Cedars of Lebanon resided, and in yet another to observe the thriving downtown scene. He now understood the saying that Beirut was a place where one could go swimming in the morning and skiing in the afternoon—or was it the other way 'round?

Gabriel remembered a time—not so long ago, it seemed—when Beirut was one of the four "B's," one of the war-torn cities of the world to be avoided at all cost. Bosnia and Baghdad were two more. The fourth was Belfast. And yet here he stood, in the midst of a largely rebuilt and flourishing city, at the top of a fancy hotel that likely hosted an even fancier wedding every night, on the edge of a glamorous crowd of doctors and medical students who pressed into the gigantic lunch reception in Rasheed's honor. They were gathered around the rooftop pool, but none of them looked as though they had any intention of swimming. The lavish reception had been commissioned at the behest of one of Rasheed's acquaintances, a family friend by the name of Dr. Mikhail Khoury.

Gabriel could not help smiling to himself at the scene that unfolded before him from within the crowd of besuited men and statuesque women. There was none other than Dr. Khoury chatting it up with Ranya, who was wearing a stunning floor-length sun dress that showed off her shoulders to advantage. He knew the look of a smitten man, knew it well, maybe better than anyone.

He recalled with some amusement how, when Rasheed had introduced Dr. Khoury to them a couple of days ago, Ranya had courteously stepped forward with her hand outstretched, but instead of a mere handshake, Mikhail had held on to her hand while announcing in his booming bass of a voice, "No! We must do it the Lebanese way!" And then he had proceeded to pull her in and give her three cheek-kisses in rapid succession. Right cheek, left cheek, then right again, all while holding her hand.

"Okay, okay," Rasheed had said, stepping between them and putting both hands on Mikhail's shoulders. With his own special blend of good-naturedness and annoyance, Rasheed said, "I'm sure Ranya has gotten along fine so far without knowing ALL the ways of the Lebanese, my friend."

And so Gabriel watched now as the Chief of Cardiac Surgery at the Beirut university hospital that was financing Rasheed's visit—the very man who had invited Rasheed here to speak in the first place—sought to capture Ranya's attention. *Good luck with that, man.* Dr. Khoury was gesturing dramatically with his hands while his mouth seemed to be going ninety miles a minute, and Gabriel could tell from the inclination of Ranya's head and the somewhat strained expression on her face that she was only trying to be polite.

Seeing that Rasheed was cornered by a group of eager medical students, Gabriel made his decision and stepped into the fray, winding his way around the pool, gently pushing through elegantly-dressed ladies and gentlemen, distinguished professors of medicine and junior faculty alike, all jockeying for position, each in his or her own way. Some things never changed, no matter where in the world one happened to be.

Upon reaching Ranya and Dr. Khoury, he was rewarded with a smile that totally transformed her face, a smile that was nothing like the thin, courteous one she had been wearing for Mikhail Khoury's benefit. He touched Dr. Khoury on the shoulder and complimented him on the reception, at which point the good doctor beamed and thanked him. Gabriel then guided the conversation to an appreciation of Rasheed's talk that morning, the great success of which all were aware and in agreement.

Dr. Khoury, apparently sensing that Gabriel wasn't going anywhere, fixed him now with a measured look and asked, "Is this your first time in Beirut, Dr. O'Brien?"

"Yes, it is."

"And how do you find it?"

"I find it a shame that I haven't had a chance to visit sooner."

Mikhail Khoury beamed again. Obviously unable to resist, he began telling Gabriel of all the many merits of Beirut, how the city was once known as the "Paris of the Middle East," and how, although it had certainly had its share of hard times—no one could deny that, certainly—it was up-and-coming again now; indeed, there was no quashing the Lebanese *joie de vivre*.

"Wouldn't you agree, *Dooktora* Ranya?" he asked, turning back to the original object of his attention.

"Well, of course, *Dooktor* Mikhail, it's always lovely to be among friends in such a fantastic city, and I'm so glad to see how well Beirut has recovered," Ranya said, "but do you worry about the warfare next door in Syria? You know, I've always heard the saying, 'The road to Beirut goes through Damascus.'"

"Mixing metaphors, my dear," Dr. Khoury replied, with a wave of his hand and no further explanation, leaving Gabriel to wonder if the man knew what the expression meant.

Not a moment too soon, Rasheed, having freed himself from his latest young admirers, materialized at Dr. Khoury's side. Khoury, hardly missing a beat, turned and clapped a hand upon his shoulder. "Ah! The man of the hour!" he exclaimed. "Rasheed, I was just explaining to these two that Beirut is a shining jewel once again, safe as she'll ever be."

Rasheed gave a hearty laugh and raised his eyebrows at his fellow surgeon. "I'm afraid that may not be saying much, Mikho."

Dr. Khoury, who had now moved the grip of his large hand to Rasheed's forearm, shook it affectionately and turned back to Ranya with a wink. "He is ever the joker, this one."

Later that afternoon, Ranya and Rasheed offered to take Gabriel for a stroll around the city. He savored the salty air as they walked beneath the rows of palm trees that lined the seaside corniche, with its magnificent views of the Mediterranean and the legendary Pigeon Rocks that rose from the azure waters like ageless sentinels. He was reminded of the Skelligs then, which were a different thing altogether, and yet similar in their power to haunt and captivate. Not unlike the woman who walked at his side.

Throughout their tour, his companions pointed out to him various buildings and sites with storied pasts, many relating to the fifteen-year civil war that had ravaged the city and her inhabitants before its fragile end in 1990. Some of the buildings still bore the pockmarks of bullet holes, reminding him, oddly enough, of the General Post Office in Dublin, which still displayed the souvenirs of artillery fire dating back to the 1916 Easter Rising and its aftermath.

It was uncanny to him, and somewhat incomprehensible, how these cycles of destruction and rebirth seemed to keep repeating themselves throughout history and among peoples as ferociously as though for the first time every time.

There was a kind of civilized wildness to Beirut, it seemed to him, and he got the sense from what his friends were telling him that it was a city that always seemed on edge, always waiting for the next bomb to drop or the next bullet to fly or the next unforeseen and unspeakable catastrophe to come its way. Maybe not so unlike Belfast in that way. But until then—and sometimes even then—that legendary Lebanese *joie de vivre* would reign mighty, an ironic form of fatalism not so far removed from what ultimately enabled that all-too-familiar Irish capacity for endurance.

He noticed that several of the signs they passed were written in both Arabic and French, and that reminded him to ask about the speaking of French that he had often heard throughout the city in addition to English and Arabic, and which surprised him every time he heard it. It appeared that Beirutis could switch languages with nearly every other word. "Oh, yeah," Rasheed said in response to his query, "it's taught in the schools as a second language after Arabic."

"Isn't that interesting, given that Lebanon was held under French mandate for so many years?" Gabriel said.

"Is it any different from English being the language most widely spoken in Ireland?" Rasheed responded. "And I must say, at least here, it is Arabic that you will hear most often."

Ranya said, "Well, but Rasheed, you have to agree, the few decades of French rule don't compare to the eight centuries of British rule in Ireland!"

Ranya turned to Gabriel and said, in a softer tone, "The French influence on Lebanon has been very strong, and there are varying attitudes toward the speaking of French here, all with political and socioeconomic overtones."

Sensing that this was a potential source of conflict between Ranya and Rasheed that he would never have any hope of comprehending, Gabriel let it go at that, and endeavored to change the subject. They had meandered down a number of back streets and side streets now, and he had no idea where they were, and was just about to ask, when the sound of fireworks reached his ears.

How strange, to be shooting off fireworks in the middle of a sunny afternoon. And then, just as strangely, he felt himself stumbling forward—no, he was falling, falling to the pavement, and pulling Ranya down with him.

CHAPTER FORTY-FIVE

إذا خرجت الكلمة من القلب دخلت في القلب ،

و إذا خرجت من اللسان لم تتجاوز الآذان

"What comes from the lips reaches the ear. What comes from the heart reaches the heart."
—Arabic proverb

AT FIRST WHEN RANYA saw the blood, she thought it was her own. Rasheed was shaking her shoulder, bending over her and asking her if she was okay. His voice sounded so urgent.

Stunned, she had no answer at first; then, moving her hands over her body, she replied tentatively, "I—I think so." She realized that she was lying entangled with Gabriel's felled form, and as she began to untangle herself, she and Rasheed turned simultaneously to look at Gabriel, and she saw the fright she felt mirrored in Rasheed's face.

Gabriel was doubled over on the pavement, his hands clenching his abdomen, his face contorted in pain. It was then that Ranya recognized, in a moment of cold horror, that the blood on her hands was not hers, but Gabriel's.

She also noticed that her hands were shaking. Her hands had never been unsteady before. Never.

She drew a deep breath and willed away the tremors so that she could begin to help, to do something, but thankfully Rasheed was one step ahead of her, barking orders in Arabic at the passersby who had rushed to them, and then he and others were lifting Gabriel from the pavement, carrying him forward as she scrambled to follow.

By the time Ranya and Rasheed entered the university hospital's emergency department with Gabriel in tow, shock had given way to alarm as they had ascertained that he had multiple gunshot wounds. One through the chest, one in the abdomen, one in his lower left leg. Maybe more.

A stretcher in the hallway was quickly appropriated, and Ranya held pressure on Gabriel's chest wound as Rasheed engaged the emergency medicine physician. He told him that Gabriel would need emergency surgery. "Yes, yes, of course," came the reply, "but our cardiothoracic surgeon is not in the hospital right now. He has been paged and I know he will be on his way shortly."

Rasheed seemed to be doing a quick mental calculation. A fraction of a second later, he announced, "We don't have time to wait for *Dooktor* Mikhail. This man is bleeding to death *now*. He needs every minute we can give him."

Before the emergency medicine doctor could respond, Rasheed looked at Ranya and said, "I'm going to operate. You're going to assist me."

Ranya opened and then closed her mouth.

Rasheed turned back to his Lebanese colleague. "Take us to your cardiac OR."

The doctor stammered in protest, "No, no, I can't do that. You can't do that."

"Why the hell not?" Rasheed demanded.

"You don't have privileges here. Look, I don't know you from Adam. How do I know you're even a surgeon? How do I know you're not the one who shot him in the first place?"

And that was when Rasheed lost it.

He started yelling in Arabic and in English at not only the emergency medicine physician but at every nurse and technician within earshot, gesticulating with open hands, and ending his tirade with a livid, "Do you need it in French, you bloody Lebanese?!?"

At any other time, Ranya would have been horrified at Rasheed's behavior and unfortunate choice of words, which threatened to turn them into the sole re-ignitors of a regional sectarian war. But they did not have any other time. Gabriel was dying now, right now, before their eyes.

And so from where she had been bending over Gabriel on the now-bloodied stretcher, she drew herself to her full height, locked eyes with the Lebanese physician, and took a step toward him, saying, very slowly and very quietly, "*Donnez-lui ce qu'il veut ou la prochaine victime sera vous.*"

Ranya stood across from Rasheed, and Gabriel lay between them on the cold operating table. Rasheed was working furiously to open his best friend's chest, knowing he had to take care of the chest wound first. Seeing the entry point, he had readily agreed with Ranya's assessment that at least one of the bullets had very likely traveled through the vicinity of the thoracic aorta, the massive blood vessel that was the lifeline from the heart to the brain and the rest of the body.

And sure enough, as soon as he brought the bone saw through Gabriel's sternum, the fountain of blood that met them confirmed their fears. Via the nick in his aorta, the Irishman's heart sent his blood to the ceiling before Rasheed got his gloved hand down on the opening.

"Rasheed, you know better than anyone that unless we get this clamped, he's going to exsanguinate." Rasheed had already called for more blood, and Ranya had never been given to panic, but she was also not a chest surgeon, so she hoped that Rasheed understood that her statement of the obvious was akin to an admission of sheer terror.

Rasheed's hands moved with lightning speed and peerless dexterity, and he never looked up as he replied with the serenity and patience she sought most at that moment: "Yes, I know that."

And then, even more quietly, as he put out his hand for another surgical instrument, he repeated, "God, don't I know that, Ranya."

Nurses were hanging more blood to be transfused and Rasheed had just spread Gabriel's ribs when the loud beeping of an alarm drew their attention to the cardiac monitor, staffed by the cardiac anesthesiologist who had fortuitously come by just as Ranya had begun utilizing her French.

"Asystole!" the anesthesiologist exclaimed now, describing the flat line that ran across the screen.

And there on the table beneath them, Gabriel's heart stopped beating.

Rasheed raised his voice now, commanding Ranya, "Cardiac massage!"

Ranya knew that made sense, but she had never done internal cardiac massage before. All of her work as an interventional cardiologist had been from the outside, through catheters and wires and punctures in the skin. Neat and efficient and under supreme control.

"But, Rasheed—" she protested.

Rasheed calmed his voice, speaking steadily now. "Okay, Ranya, you can do this. I need you to do this while I sew on the connections for the heart-lung machine. Put your hands around the heart and squeeze, in the rhythm of a normal heartbeat as much as you can." He mimicked the motion once with his own hands and she nodded. "You can do this," he said again.

Gabriel's chest cavity was filling with blood, so that Ranya, as she reached down to hold his heart, was nearly up to her elbows in the bright red that already covered her face mask and the front of her blue surgical gown, not to mention the floor, her shoes, and most of Rasheed.

But none of that mattered now. She had to become Gabriel's heartbeat, his only heartbeat, and the one thing that might keep him alive in this terrible moment.

As she pumped with her hands, she began muttering in a verbal cadence that matched the rhythm of her massage, "Come on, Gabriel, you're not gonna get away with leaving us now. You're our guardian angel. You're. Our. Gabriel."

Rasheed glanced up sharply, his eyes lifting upward even as his head remained bent over the table, and his jaw twitched behind his surgical mask. But Ranya did not care. All her cares had become subsumed in the urgency of this one most-important-task. The calm that she always felt in the middle of a cardiac resuscitation, a code, returned to her, enveloped her, and lent her the peaceful singlemindedness that she needed.

Rasheed had just succeeded in sewing on the connections to the heart-lung machine, when suddenly and seemingly out of nowhere, surgeons appeared from all corners. A general surgeon and a vascular surgeon, both of whom Ranya recognized from the reception earlier, arrived at the table. And in short order Mikhail Khoury, a little breathless, appeared at Ranya's side, holding up his gloved hands and saying in Arabic, "I got here as soon as I could."

Ranya gratefully relinquished her spot to him, letting the surgeons do what they did best. She de-gloved and walked behind the curtain at Gabriel's head to see if she could be of any assistance to the anesthesiologist. She had caught the glimmer of hope in Rasheed's eyes when Mikhail had shown up, and that gave her strength.

CHAPTER FORTY-SIX

"Where there is great love there are always miracles."
—Willa Cather

IN THE BEGINNING THERE WAS a woman, and the woman had almond eyes. Her scent was of jasmine and her voice was of honey, and the voice was there with him now. He wanted that voice to be the last voice he ever heard. If there were going to be a last voice, this was the one he wanted it to be. It was the voice that spoke to him now, in his ear, in his head. He must be in heaven.

No, there was something in his throat, something stuck in his throat . . . And there was another voice, too, a man's voice. A man's voice beside the voice of honey that floated to him. Hushed tones, but he knew that other voice too. He struggled to open his eyes but the lids were too heavy for him to lift. There had been an accident, some sort of accident, and he had fallen. Yes, he had fallen. And now an angel was there to take him to heaven. Yes, it was the voice of an angel that he heard. He had always thought so. Always . . .

There was something he must not do, something he must not feel, something he must fight against.

The voices faded, and he was alone. Falling again, into oblivion.

Ranya and Rasheed stayed by Gabriel as often as they could for as long as they could, every day of his recovery. They alternated between standing and sitting at his bedside, between staring into an abyss of despair and daring to see rays of hope with each small change in his condition.

When Rasheed tried to blame himself, Ranya did her best to comfort him, putting her arm around him and telling him he was being ridiculous, that he mustn't hold himself responsible for even a second. But Rasheed kept arguing with her, with himself, and with the universe. "I'm the reason he was even here in the first place. I told him it was safe, that everything would be fine. I never should have brought him here." And he would at one moment hold his head in his hands and shake it, and in the next moment gently reach out to cover one of Gabriel's hands with his own.

Ranya, not knowing what to do, would go to Rasheed, stand beside him, and put her arms around his shoulders, embracing him and trying to absorb some of his pain, even as she struggled with her own.

Mikhail Khoury came by several times to check on his patient and, Ranya knew, to check on Rasheed and herself as well. Each time, he invited them to dinner at his house, but neither of them wanted to leave Gabriel alone while his condition remained critical.

Later she wouldn't remember how many days it had taken, three or four or five, but eventually Gabriel turned a corner and, to their immense relief, began steadily improving, forsaking the darkness in favor of the light. Finally he was conscious enough to have a single sustained conversation, but even that was limited to brief sentences intermingled with long periods of rest.

During one small window of time when Rasheed went out, at Ranya's insistence, to grab a bite to eat, she sat alone by Gabriel's side, fingering the green hospital blanket that covered his bed. *Green. How ironic. The color of Ireland. And the color of Rasheed's eyes.*

She was reminded of a conversation—a heated one, really—that she had had with Rasheed sometime after their trip to Ireland. She had expressed her desire to go back to Ireland soon, and his response had surprised her, to say the least.

"What about Palestine? Wouldn't you like to go there again one day? You haven't been since you were a teenager," Rasheed had said, and the plaintiveness in his voice had been painful to hear.

"I just don't understand it," he had continued. "You never seem to want to visit the Homeland with me, Ranya, and yet you want to go back to Ireland? What's Ireland to you, Ranya?"

Her heart had skipped a beat at this last question, and she had wondered if there was a double intention to it. She had also felt hurt at Rasheed's lack of understanding, his seeming inability to share her joy and desire when it came to the discovery she had made, of a wonderful, lovely, interesting, beautiful part of the world, one that never seemed to leave her mind. Why couldn't he see that too?

But she had tried to remain calm and dispassionate, casual and logical. "Oh, God, Rasheed, not now," she had responded. "I don't want to go to the West Bank right now. Maybe one day, sure—of course—don't we all dream of that? But not now. It's so sad. I couldn't bear to see what's become of it. I just couldn't stand to look at that eyesore of a wall the Israelis are building. Whenever I see pictures of it, it just screams at me: 'We hate you.'"

In spite of her attempt to keep her cool, she felt herself getting worked up. "All the killing, and the oppression, and the tyranny, and the hopelessness, and the never-ending violence. I am so sick of it, Rasheed. All of it."

Rasheed had tears in his eyes then, and she realized that he was sick of it too. And as painful as it had been, it had actually given her hope that they could forge a new life together, free of the drama that never should have been theirs to begin with.

"And as for Ireland and the Irish, Rasheed," she had gone on, finding strength in her position as she voiced it aloud, "the Irish . . . well, the Irish give me hope. Yes, that's it: they give me hope."

To his questioning look, she explained, "Makes me think of what Palestine could have been, you know? Maybe still might be."

"But, Ranya, if people like us won't go back—won't even visit—how will it ever be? How can we expect others to do so? What does the Right of Return mean, after all, if no one wants to return?"

"Well, of course people want to return, Rasheed. Obviously. I'm looking at one of them right now, aren't I?"

"But I'm not doing the same," Rasheed had said, the anguish of defeat creeping into his voice.

And Ranya had thought then that her heart would break, but in her stubbornness and pride she hadn't wanted to let Rasheed see it. "Oh," she had sighed, trying to put an end to it, "I don't know, Rasheed. I just don't know. It just—it just all seems so hopeless."

"There is always hope," Rasheed had countered softly. "Isn't that what your Irishman is always telling us?"

"He's not my Irishman. He's your best friend."

"He's *our* friend." And then Rasheed's face had transformed into the most unexpected of smiles, and he winked at her. "As long as *you* remain *my* Ranya."

She smiled half of a wistful smile at the remembrance of Rasheed's embrace, and was thinking about how she had rested her head upon his shoulder then, when a movement beneath the green blanket startled her, followed closely by the sound of Gabriel's hoarse voice.

"I've been hearing things," he began, then started coughing.

"Gabriel, it's okay, you don't have to talk," Ranya assured him, patting his shoulder. "Take your time."

But Gabriel could not seem to wait; apparently he had something he wanted desperately to say to her. He reached out slowly and took her hand. "You helped save my life. I heard how . . . you held my heart." He coughed and paused for another breath before adding, "You always have, you know."

Ranya felt her own heart pounding, and managed a feeble smile. "Come now, Gabriel, you're delirious."

Gabriel was still holding her hand, and he gave it a weak squeeze. He whispered hoarsely, "I would follow you to the ends of the earth. No matter what happens, I want—I need—you to know that."

Ranya looked away, swallowing hard, blinking back tears. Her gaze wandered toward the door of the room. There she recognized, with a start, Rasheed's graceful figure in the shadow of the doorway. She had no idea how long he'd been standing there.

CHAPTER FORTY-SEVEN

"We've got to live, no matter how many skies have fallen."
—D. H. Lawrence,
Lady Chatterley's Lover

THE NEXT MORNING, RASHEED came to visit Gabe. He came early and he came alone.

To his surprise, he found his friend to have made great strides in his recovery overnight, so that he was not only lucid, but talkative. Rasheed recognized this as his first good opportunity to brief Gabe on his condition and the major surgery he had undergone. Anything else could wait.

Not quite sure where to start, Rasheed began with the part he felt might be most obvious, something he hoped was already known. "So, no doubt you've heard or figured out by now that it was something of a freak accident. Why us—or *you*—nobody knows yet. The police are still working on it, and I have no idea who was doing the shooting. But what I do know is that they were using small-caliber bullets, and that may be the only reason you're still alive."

"Well, I'd say *you* are a big part of the reason I'm still alive, my friend."

"Um, yes, well, about that . . . Gabe, I'm happy to say we were able to patch up your thoracic aorta quite nicely—put in a bit of graft there that will do the trick and should last your lifetime, is my hope. You—we—were so, so lucky that that bullet didn't hit your heart, because, God, it came close. Really close."

"Yeah," Gabe agreed soberly. "But that wasn't the only bullet I caught."

"Right," Rasheed said, being prompted now into what he knew was the more difficult part of his revelations. "There was the one in your bowel, and a very good general surgeon resected part of your small intestine—hopefully you'll never miss it—but it was your kidney that really took a hit."

"Which kidney?"

"Your only kidney."

"I'm sorry?"

"Uh . . . you didn't know you had only one kidney?" This was going worse than Rasheed had anticipated.

"I'm sorry," Gabe said again, this time as a statement. "I must still be under the effects of painkillers or something."

He tried to pull himself up further in bed, and Rasheed moved the pillow up behind his head in sync with his movements. Gabe shook his head and said, "I don't think I understand. Are you saying I somehow lost my other kidney somewhere along the way?"

"No, Gabe, it looks like you have a congenital solitary kidney." When Gabe continued to look at him with a puzzled expression, Rasheed made it as plain as he knew how. "I'm saying you must have been born with only one kidney. Occurs in about one out of every five hundred people."

"But, how . . .?"

"People can get by with just one kidney, you know—that's why renal transplants work." Rasheed couldn't shake the oddness he felt at having to explain this to his friend, his best friend, a neurologist and stellar clinician. It made him realize what a shock all this was to Gabe, and what a toll it was taking. On all of them. But he felt that he had to continue; he couldn't just leave him with part of the story.

"So . . . as I was saying, the one kidney that you do have did, unfortunately, take a hit. Not directly from a bullet, but an ischemic hit—because the blood supply to your kidney was compromised. I mean, with the nick in your aorta, you nearly bled to death—"

"—I *did* bleed to death, though, didn't I?"

Rasheed paused, nodding slowly. "Well, yeah, I guess you did. You know you arrested on the table, and . . ." Rasheed's voice broke unexpectedly. He blinked hard and forced himself to resume, but let the emotion fill his voice now. "You died on us there for a few minutes, Gabe. It's a miracle that we are even having this conversation right now."

Rasheed rubbed his eyes and drew a deep breath before continuing. "But, so, anyway, with the hole in your aorta and the time your heart was stopped—even though it was no more than a few minutes and Ranya did excellent internal compressions—"

"Couldn't ask for better than Ranya when it comes to cardiac resuscitation, could I, eh?" Gabe broke in again, giving a little chuckle that sounded morbidly out of place in the somber room.

Rasheed squared his shoulders and said quietly, "You couldn't ask for better than Ranya when it comes to anything."

There was a heavy silence between them, but Rasheed allowed it to last no more than a moment. "So, as I was saying . . . with all the interruptions in circulation, it's no wonder your kidney suffered. But with her compressions, Ranya was able to preserve the blood flow to your brain even while your heart was stopped."

And then he paused, looking at Gabe sitting halfway up in his hospital bed with his eyes open and seeing and his ears hearing and listening. And Rasheed smiled, even as he blinked to keep the tears from his eyes. Because he remembered then, all at once and in a rush of memory, the words Gabe himself, his best friend and the best neurologist he knew, had spoken so passionately all those years ago: "*We are who we are because of the brain.*"

Rasheed pulled himself together and finished, "So all in all, we did our best to patch things up—had great vascular and general surgeons there, as I've said—and as for the bullet that hit your leg, it just grazed it, so no major damage there, thankfully. But only time will tell how well your kidney will function, you know."

Gabe dropped his head back against the pillow. "Grand," he muttered, closing his eyes. "That's just grand."

When he opened his eyes again, there was a glimmer of the old optimist in them. He looked at Rasheed and attempted a grin. "Well, thank you for saving my brain, then, old friend."

Rasheed reached out and squeezed his shoulder. They sat together in silence for a long while.

CHAPTER FORTY-EIGHT

"Lebanon's revenge was to welcome all her invaders and then kiss them to
death."
—Robert Fisk,
Pity the Nation: Lebanon at War

NEARLY HALF A MONTH after the shooting, Gabriel was finally ready to be
discharged from the hospital. Ranya and Rasheed were there in the room
that morning, prepared to escort him out. The mood was nothing short of
celebratory. It seemed Gabriel's kidney would go on functioning for now,
although not at its peak performance, and would require close monitoring
from a good nephrologist once they got back to Nashville, which they all
agreed they could not do soon enough.

Gabriel's Lebanese surgeons came by to see him off, and, from the edge
of the bed where he sat, looking up at the crowd surrounding him, he took
the opportunity not just to thank them once more, but to reopen a line of
inquiry that he felt had never been concluded to his satisfaction. The story
kept changing, it seemed.

Turning to Mikhail Khoury, who was all smiles, Gabriel began, "So I was
shot because I look like some Western journalist who was critical of Israel?"

"Yes, Dr. O'Brien, that is what the police believe. Apparently it was a case
of mistaken identity." Mikhail shrugged, then added delicately, "You know, it

is entirely possible—maybe even quite likely—that the shooter may never be found."

Gabriel could believe this, given all the different regional players, known and sometimes unknown, who seemed to think of Lebanon as their own private battleground. But he persisted, "And who is this Western journalist that I supposedly look like?"

All were silent. Ranya and Rasheed stood with their arms folded, looking keenly at the Lebanese surgeons, who in turn shuffled their feet and glanced at Dr. Khoury. Gabriel got the sense of a collective breath being held as they all waited to see what the good doctor's response would be.

Gabriel's fellow physician looked him straight in the eye and spoke what everyone in the room knew to be a lie. "I don't know," Mikhail said. Shrugging his shoulders again, he said, "I make it a point not to know. It is better that way, don't you think?"

So this was the Lebanese twist on the old Irish maxim: *whatever you say, say nothing.*

"I see," Gabriel finally relinquished after a long moment during which he and Dr. Khoury studied one another. "Well, I guess I'll never really know then, will I?"

One of the other Lebanese doctors patted him on the arm and lamented, "Such random acts of violence, you know? This sort of thing is very rare, my friend. You were just unlucky."

"How reassuring," Gabriel said.

He turned then to Ranya, who was in her usual position beside Rasheed. There was another question that had remained unanswered. Now he asked it of her, furrowing his brow and squinting slightly as he sought to capture her gaze. "And did I hallucinate this while I was dying, or were you speaking French?"

The room erupted into laughter. Ranya answered simply, "You were not hallucinating, Gabriel."

"So what on earth were you saying?"

"Well . . . um," her face reddened, "if I remember correctly, what I may have done was . . . well, threaten the ER doc with bodily harm."

"Wow, there really is no end to your surprises," said Gabriel, looking down and shaking his head.

Rasheed smiled and said, "Yeah, and if our friend Dr. Husseini, the cardiac anesthesiologist, hadn't shown up right then, I honestly don't know what might have happened. Ranya may very well have torn that doctor limb from limb."

Rasheed placed a hand on Gabriel's shoulder and left it there. "He just messed with the wrong woman, right, Gabe?"

Gabriel, who was still sitting on the side of his hospital bed, coughed and avoided Rasheed's gaze, choosing instead to look straight ahead at the group of Lebanese surgeons standing before him. He smiled perfunctorily at them as Rasheed continued, "But thankfully, Dr. Husseini had been in attendance at my cardiac surgery talk at the university that morning, so he knew that I was who I said I was, and he got us what we needed."

Rasheed addressed his Lebanese colleagues then. "Look, you know, we can't thank you enough for everything you've done, all of you. And I do need to apologize for my behavior in the emergency department. Very rude. Inexcusable."

Ranya added quickly, "Mine too. Please relay our apologies to that emergency medicine doctor. He was only trying to do his job."

"*Ya dooktor,*" Mikhail said, clapping Rasheed roundly on the back, "it's okay. I would have done the same thing had I been in your position."

CHAPTER FORTY-NINE

"But friendship is precious, not only in the shade, but in the sunshine of life; and, thanks to a benevolent arrangement of things, the greater part of life is sunshine."
—Thomas Jefferson

August 2013

"I'M A MATCH, RANYA."

Rasheed was sitting beside her on his white sofa, his long legs outstretched, feet resting on the large ottoman before them. He had been randomly clicking through TV channels, and Ranya had sensed there was something on his mind, something he was trying to work through. But this was the last thing she was expecting.

"What? You? How?" And then in the green of Rasheed's eyes she saw, all at once, all the answers. Her mind flashed back to the blood drive, to the Christmas-time conversation at the Opryland Hotel, to what Gabriel had uncovered without even knowing it.

Rasheed shrugged his shoulders, but his nonchalance was unconvincing. He said, "Guess that Crusader effect was stronger than we thought."

Over the past year, what was left of Gabriel's kidney function had continued to deteriorate, and it had become clear that a kidney transplant would be his only hope of ever coming off dialysis. But to hear that the man sitting beside her was a potential donor was more of a shock than a relief, for as soon as he told her, she knew what else it meant: that he would go through with it. Rasheed would donate one of his kidneys to Gabriel. And there couldn't—shouldn't—be any way of talking him out of it.

"Does Gabriel know?" she asked.

"Not yet. I wanted to tell you first."

"Wow, Rasheed, I don't know what to say. I mean—well, of course, that's great news, but . . . it's just a lot to process, you know?"

Rasheed looked at her with keen understanding. He put his hand over hers. "Don't worry, Ranya; I have all my affairs in order. Nothing is going to happen to me, but if it does, everything will be taken care of. I know you don't need anything monetarily, but still, you'll be taken care of. In every way."

"Oh, goodness, Rasheed, don't talk like that! I'm sure everything is going to be fine. Just fine."

The steady beeping rhythm of Rasheed's cardiac monitor comforted Ranya as she sat by his bedside, waiting for him to wake up. The renal transplant had been a success. Gabriel would live free of dialysis, because of the man lying in front of her now.

She knew that it was time.

She was still holding Rasheed's hand when he awakened. She wanted her face to be the first he saw, and it was. She knew it would take still more time for him to become fully lucid and capable of comprehending what she had to say, but after so many long years, what were a few more hours?

"How is Gabe?" It was the first question out of Rasheed's mouth.

She reassured him that their friend was doing fine, that all would be well. And when she felt the time was right, she led with, "Rasheed—I've been thinking."

He chuckled. "Well, Ranya, when haven't you been thinking?"

She laughed in spite of herself, then continued in earnest, "I think we should get married."

Rasheed stared at her, at first with an open mouth, and then with a guarded look of solemn intent. Finally he asked, "Ranya, are you serious? I mean, really serious?"

"Yes, Rasheed." Her voice broke and she waited a moment for composure to return. "Yes, *Habibi*, I couldn't be more serious."

Then she smiled and added, "That is, if you'll still have me."

"Oh, my God, yes," Rasheed responded, his own voice strained and his eyes squeezing shut before opening again in a shimmer of moisture. "A thousand times, yes," he whispered hoarsely as she embraced him.

Gabriel sat on the side of yet another hospital bed for what he hoped would be the last time, staring at the empty wheelchair that awaited him. Ranya was pulling up the car, and Rasheed remained in the room with him.

Gabriel cast another glance at his friend, who was standing at the window and looking out at the hospital campus below. A stream of sunlight set his figure aflame, picking out the flecks of salt in his full head of wavy hair, the greater part of which was still pepper-black. The sunshine highlighted the luminescent green of his eyes, the very color that had held the hint of Gabriel's salvation.

Those eyes sparkled as Rasheed turned to him now with an all-encompassing smile on his face; Gabriel had noted how ebullient his mood had seemed from the moment he had arrived in the room. Well, after all, each of them had been overjoyed at the success of the operation. Gabriel had thanked Rasheed as many times as seemed decent without becoming embarrassing, but he knew he would never be able to thank him enough. He owed him his life twice over.

Rasheed came over to him now; Gabriel observed the bounce in his step in spite of the pain his friend must still be experiencing from his own operation. Rasheed sat down beside him on the bed and tapped him on the knee. "Gabe, I have something to tell you. Some fantastic news."

Gabriel looked at him expectantly, his curiosity piqued. Rasheed clasped and unclasped his hands, crossed and uncrossed his legs. One knee bounced up and down, slightly shaking the bed. At last he divulged, "Ranya and I are getting married. And I'd like you to be my best man."

Gabriel felt the old sucker-punch again, the immediate and intense wrenching of his gut. And knew that it was not his convalescent status that was responsible. How long had it been since Rasheed had introduced Ranya as his girlfriend just before they all walked into *Michael Collins*? How many years? And still the feeling was the same.

Nevertheless, he managed to meet Rasheed's eyes. Looked long into them. And managed to respond, before the pause got awkward: "Of course."

Of course I will stand beside you . . . both. Of course I could never do, have never done, otherwise. Of course this was how it was always going to be. Of course.

CHAPTER FIFTY

"Again if, as is fabled, there is a lake in Palestine, such that if you bind a man or beast and throw it in it floats and does not sink, this would bear out what we have said. They say that this lake is so bitter and salty that no fish live in it and that if you soak clothes in it and shake them it cleans them."

—Aristotle,
Meteorology (350 BC)

"So we drove on toward death through the cooling twilight."
—F. Scott Fitzgerald,
The Great Gatsby

May 2014

RANYA HAD READILY AGREED to Rasheed's request to travel with him to the Middle East to visit various family members he wanted her to meet before the wedding. No way was she giving him any resistance this time, after all they—he—had been through. If there was a wall to see, she would see it; if there were meaningless pleasantries to exchange, she would exchange them. Their trip would culminate with a visit to Ramallah, and she appreciated that he had arranged a stopover before that at a Dead Sea resort in Jordan so they could enjoy a mini-vacation, just the two of them.

Their flight to Amman was a long one, thirteen hours, and they stayed busy visiting relatives for a couple of days before heading out across a stretch of Jordanian desert to the Dead Sea. Rasheed had distant cousins in Madaba, so they made sure to arrange a stop there, where they paid a visit to the Church of St. George, a small Greek Orthodox church built upon the remnants of an earlier, sixth-century Byzantine church.

And these were not just the remains of any Byzantine church, incredible as that would have been in itself, but this was the church that housed the marvelous Madaba Map, a mosaic that covered the church's floor and contained the oldest surviving map of Palestine and the Holy Land. It originally consisted of two million pieces of colored stone that delineated the topography and cartography all the way down to the Nile Delta and included all the major biblical sites from Lebanon to Egypt. Now, only one-third of it remained, but the creators' intentions could still be seen, the Greek captions giving names of places that still existed.

The map was unique in many ways, not least of all because of the manner in which it was oriented toward the east rather than toward the north. It faced east toward the altar of the church in such a way that the location of the places on the map coincided with their actual compass directions in real life.

The small crowd that gathered around the map spoke in hushed tones, both out of reverence for the church in which they were standing and for the map that was its own minor wonder of the world.

Ranya gripped Rasheed's arm and whispered in his ear, "Can you just imagine how those long-ago pilgrims, the earliest visitors to this church, must have used this huge floor map?"

"Yeah," Rasheed said, "it would have been of vital importance to them as an actual map, to orient themselves on the land where they stood—and where we're standing now."

"Yes!" Ranya said. "They would have relied on it to tell them what direction to go to get to Jericho, or Mount Nebo, or . . . Jerusalem."

And it was Jerusalem itself that formed the centerpiece of the map. *Al-Quds.* The so-called City of Peace, which in reality had only known every possible inverse. Ranya found it to be an especially gripping depiction, and she could hardly believe she was gazing down at a detailed rendering of the Old City that had been accurate in the middle of the sixth century.

There on the floor before them were the legendary gates of Jerusalem. "Look, Ranya," Rasheed pointed out, "that's *Bab al-'Amood.*"

"The Damascus Gate," Ranya said, confirming it by its English name, which referenced the city to Jerusalem's north that was deemed most important then, and now, and nearly always.

"Yep," Rasheed said, "and there's *Bab al-Asbat*—St. Stephen's Gate—and *Bab al-Khaleel,* the Yaffa Gate, the one to which a pilgrim would eventually arrive if he traveled three days along the Yaffa Road from Palestine's port of Yaffa on the Mediterranean."

The Port of Yaffa

"So why is it called *Bab al-Khaleel* instead of *Bab Yaffa*?" Ranya asked.

"Because it's also the gate through which, if the pilgrim were to turn left upon his exit from the Old City," Rasheed turned his body in space to illustrate, "and take it upon himself to cross the biblical Valley of the Shadow of Death, he would eventually come to the ancient city of *al-Khaleel*—Hebron—where the patriarch and prophet Abraham is believed to be buried."

"Ah," Ranya nodded. Rasheed then pointed out to her several other famous Jerusalem landmarks that were illustrated on the colorful map, including the Church of the Holy Sepulchre and the Tower of David, as well as the Cardo Maximus, all painstakingly depicted in centuries-old, locally-sourced stones, pieces of a puzzle that went on forever.

Noting the absence of the Dome of the Rock, such a signature feature of today's Jerusalem, Ranya realized that this map predated the building of the world's most recognizable mosque by at least a hundred years. This further impressed upon her the exceptionality of the Madaba Map for affording its current viewers one very important snapshot in time. Farther to the west were the port of Askalon, the city of Gaza, and others, so detailed that they could have been used as street maps.

So much history, so much of the world's sorrow, lying there in the names at their feet. Ranya could only imagine what it must have been like for those nineteenth-century church builders when they discovered this spectacular mosaic under the rubble of the old Byzantine structure.

But there was something else on the map that caught her eye. It was something that was not just out of the ordinary, but frankly odd.

"Rasheed," she said, touching his elbow, "why are those fish—well, they look like they're swimming upstream."

"Yes, they are," he said. "They are swimming upstream in the River Jordan, trying desperately to escape the salt-clogged Dead Sea."

The fish on the map may have been desperate to escape the Dead Sea, but Ranya and Rasheed went toward it. After they unpacked in the five-star hotel room that featured a large picture window affording a view of the Dead Sea itself, Ranya turned toward Rasheed to thank him for what had been an incredible trip thus far.

They were both standing at the window, taking in the palm-filled landscape that edged the water, and just beyond it, through the haze of the sun and humidity, Palestine in the distance. Ranya became aware that Rasheed was taking deep breaths, or trying to. It was almost as though he were trying to catch his breath in one moment, then trying to calm himself in the next.

"Rasheed, *Habibi,* are you okay?" Ranya asked, patting his shoulder. It had indeed been a long, event-filled day.

"I just . . . feel . . . anxious, somehow," he replied between breaths.

Ranya frowned. It wasn't like Rasheed to have a panic attack. "Why don't you sit down?" She gestured to the bed and sat down beside him.

With an intensity that surprised her, he turned to her, grabbed and squeezed both her hands. Looking deeply into her eyes, he asked, "Ranya, are you one hundred percent sure about this—about us? Are you sure this is what you want?"

Ranya was taken aback and struggled to find words. "But . . . Rasheed . . . this is what you've said you've wanted for years now. Are you saying . . . have you suddenly changed your mind?" She stared at him, studying his face, studying his breathing, which seemed to have normalized.

"Not at all," Rasheed shook his head. He met her gaze full on, and she could feel as much as see the emotion in his eyes. "My mind, and my heart, have never wavered—from the moment I met you, I knew. I have always known. But I wasn't asking about me. I am asking about *you.*"

Ranya straightened her back and did her best to allow him to see what she was feeling, to feel what she was thinking. "Rasheed Haddad, have you ever known me not to know what I want? Do you think I would have asked you if I didn't know, if I wasn't sure? What I want is for us to be married."

Then, after the briefest hesitation, she added, "Don't you want me to want that?"

Rasheed squeezed her hands again. "Ranya," he said slowly, "please understand me." He looked down briefly, then met her gaze again. "I promise you, 'til death and beyond, that I will do everything in my power to keep you happy. I know what I want; I've always known. And that's not what I care about now. I care about *you*. I care that this is absolutely what *you* want. And," he swallowed hard before adding gently, "I want to know that I am the only one you want."

"Rasheed," Ranya answered, hearing the tightness in her own chest reflected in her voice, "there may be others who want me—but you . . . you *have* me." Her voice had thinned to an emphatic whisper. "You always have."

He brought her hand to his heart and closed his eyes, his face relaxing. "Then let's make it happen," he declared when he opened his eyes again, bright and smiling.

That night they dined al fresco on the broad, marble-floored terrace of one of the resort's restaurants. The first sliver of a crescent moon winked at them from the heavens above, which Ranya found fitting, given where they were. The murmurs of conversation from the few other diners and the occasional clinking of cutlery and tea glasses did not disturb the peaceful feeling of the night, but rather enhanced the contemplative mood that seemed to have overtaken them both.

Rasheed had picked up an Arabic newspaper on their way through the lobby, and now he tapped the front page where it lay beside his dinner plate. He took a deep breath, followed by another, much shallower one, and coughed. Ranya looked up sharply from the pita bread she had just begun tearing apart.

"I really worry about what's going on in Syria," Rasheed said.

"Ah, so that's what's on your mind," Ranya said. "Of course. So do I. So does everyone, I would think."

"And Egypt, and Yemen, and Libya, and—"

"And Iraq," Ranya interrupted. "Don't forget Iraq."

"Yes, obviously, Iraq. And Palestine too, of course."

He looked down at his half-finished plate of lamb and hesitated before speaking his next words, which came out slowly at first, then built into a steady crescendo. "You know . . . sometimes I think . . . what would it be like to be able to go home to a place without any strife, without any wars or corruption or destitution or unending sorrow?"

The sadness that she saw in his eyes was nearly unbearable. She answered quietly, "There is no place like that, Rasheed. At least not for very long."

He responded, "I think our friend Gabriel may have such a place."

She couldn't believe he had brought up his name. Here, now. But without a second thought, she heard herself reply, "Then I think you misunderstand what it means to be Irish."

Rasheed raised his eyebrows at her, and a long silence ensued. They finished their main courses without speaking, and it wasn't until coffee had been ordered that Rasheed cleared his throat and said, "It may be that I understand more than you think, Ranya."

He reached across the table and held her hand, squeezed it. She squeezed back in wordless reassurance.

The following evening, Ranya and Rasheed stood hand-in-hand at the place where the River Jordan met its end, at the edge of the Dead Sea, watching the sun descend over the lowest place on the surface of the earth. The smell of salt was overpowering, and the palm trees in the distance behind them stood still in the hot, breezeless air.

Delighted cries of tourists floating in the sea of salt reached Ranya's ears as she followed the direction of Rasheed's hand. He was pointing across the water to the land beyond it, the contour of which she could barely discern through the hot haze. He turned to her and smiled broadly, his green eyes shining in the setting sun. "That's Palestine," he proclaimed of the land beyond the sea.

He had said this before, yesterday, she was sure. And she was also sure that he knew that she knew this, so she doubly appreciated its importance to him. "So close and yet so far," she murmured in response. She noted the somber look that chased the smile from his face then, vaguely darkening his handsome features.

She would later remember exactly how the play of light in the gathering dusk cast shadows under his large eyes, those eyes that resembled the green edges of the sea itself, and how the lines at the corners of his mouth turned upward as he ventured to smile again, his lips pursing as he prepared to say something. It was something left unsaid that she would, for all the times she looked back upon it, always conclude to be of some great importance, and therefore know that all the greater was the loss. For instead of giving voice to speech, Rasheed's next breath was a gasp, a tortured inhalation, and before her eyes, all color drained from his face as he put the palm of his hand to his chest and fell forward.

Ranya went to her knees with him, holding him, shouting his name, then calling loudly for help, for anyone who could hear her. She gently but quickly turned him onto his back and saw that he was no longer breathing. She felt his neck for a pulse, but there was none. She began chest compressions on her fiancé.

Someone rushed to her with a medical kit, but it contained nothing she needed. Someone else announced that an ambulance was on its way, but by that time Ranya already knew that it would be too late. Rasheed was gone. Her fiancé, her *Habibi*, was gone. And when this became indisputably clear, she sank back on her heels, holding his head in her arms and his shoulders on her knees, and wept, her body heaving with every breath that managed to find its way in between sobs.

As she had predicted, by the time emergency medical personnel arrived nearly half an hour later with a stretcher, it was not to continue a resuscitation, but to carry away a corpse.

CHAPTER FIFTY-ONE

"The meaning of life is that it stops."
—Franz Kafka

GABRIEL LET THE METAL CHAIR scrape against the cold floor of the nearly-deserted hospital cafeteria as he sat down to a very late lunch. Halfway through his salad, he dropped his fork and put his head in his hands.

He went over again what he knew, what he had been told. Ranya had said the autopsy had revealed the cause of death to be a pulmonary embolism, a massive one that had straddled and choked off the entries to both of Rasheed's pulmonary arteries, making blood flow to his lungs, and eventually breathing itself, impossible.

That was two weeks ago, but he could still hear the odd detachment in Ranya's voice as she had informed him that Rasheed had not suffered, that it was over in the blink of an eye. And then the tremor—it was almost undetectable, but he knew he had heard it—the tremor in her voice as she had reported that there had been nothing she could do to save him. She had tried. But in the end all she could do was be there with him at his moment of death.

It must have been the long plane ride, she had said. He could almost hear her shaking her head over the phone, and that slight tremor in her voice—he was certain it had returned. Rasheed had not taken her advice to stand and move his legs on the plane; he had been so tired, she said, so tired after weeks of long days in the operating room prior to their vacation. A blood clot must have formed in his legs and traveled to his lungs. These things happened. It made perfect sense.

Gabriel balled his hand into a fist and pounded it into his thigh. *No, it makes no sense. It makes no sense at all.* The only living part of Rasheed that remained was the sole kidney that was keeping Gabriel alive and free of dialysis. *No sense at all.*

He suspected this was not lost on Ranya.

Gabriel didn't know what he was thinking. He knew Ranya didn't drink, had known that for nearly twenty years, and had never even considered asking her after his apparent faux pas that first time. But it was Thursday, and soon it would be Thursday night—a Thursday night without Rasheed.

So maybe it was his grief talking, or maybe it was the guilt he couldn't explain, or maybe it was the emptiness he couldn't face and couldn't bear alone, but whatever it was, it led him to ask the one person left on earth who might understand to join him for a drink on Thursday night.

The conversation didn't last long. The pain in Ranya's voice was more than he could bear, and Gabriel felt far worse after he got off the call than he had before. So that night, at what would have been the usual time, he went by himself and sank into a seat at the bar. He knew it would be best to avoid alcohol with all the transplant meds he was on now, but he was making an exception for tonight, and hoped the transplant gods—and his liver—would forgive him.

He ordered a Jack Daniel's straight. Rasheed would have liked that.

He raised his glass in his own silent toast to his absent friend, and was just bringing it to his lips when a voice behind him asked, "You know why I don't drink, Gabriel?"

Had the liquid been in his mouth by then, Gabriel would have choked. But instead he set his glass down and said only, "Ranya."

She took the seat next to him and repeated her question, her darkest-brown eyes as intense as ever. Maybe more so. "You know why I don't drink?"

His drink sat in front of him, untouched now. He folded his hands and leaned back, saying nothing but looking at her expectantly. Making space for silence.

She looked at him for a long while in that penetrating way that she always had, and then answered her own question, as he had known she would. "Because if I ever got started, I would never stop."

And then she blinked hard and looked away for a moment. Gabriel wanted badly to put his hand on her shoulder. He unfolded his hands and said simply, quietly, "I'm glad you came."

She looked at him again and just nodded, tried to smile. She flagged down the bartender, something he couldn't recall ever having seen Ranya do. She pointed at Gabriel's drink and said, "I'll have what he's having." Gabriel grabbed her wrist so quickly he surprised himself. The bartender was looking at them questioningly.

"Ah, no, she'll have a club soda," Gabriel said, his eyes meeting hers.

The bartender frowned. "Is that what *you* would like, ma'am?"

Ranya cleared her throat and Gabriel took his hand from her wrist as quickly as he had put it there. She nodded at the bartender and said, "Yes, yes, that's what I would like. A club soda. That would be fine."

They sat side by side in silence until her drink arrived. When it did, she raised her glass to Gabriel, who followed suit. "For Rasheed," she managed in a hoarse whisper, blinking her eyes again.

Gabriel took note of her choice of preposition. "For Rasheed," he agreed.

There was no good time to tell her, and he didn't want to leave it up to chance, so he called her directly on her cell late one night. "Ranya, I've decided to return to Ireland."

"You mean for good?" she asked.

"I mean for good or for bad," Gabriel joked poorly.

"When are you going?"

"In a few months."

"I see."

"I'll be home for Christmas," he added, trying again to lighten the conversation, but even to him the jingle fell flat. He winced upon hearing it aloud.

A long pause followed. The past few months had been so hard for both of them. They rarely spoke anymore, and when they did, it seemed they didn't know what to say. Even though, as Gabriel knew in his heart, there was so much to say. So much they had to, needed to, say to one another.

But Gabriel found it so difficult, so awkward, to speak not just of Rasheed, but of anything, in her presence; he found it impossible to summon his old cheerfulness and optimism. It was as though Rasheed's absence had left a terrible vacuum that could not be filled, widened the chasm between them such that it could not be crossed. And there had been nights when Gabriel had lain awake, thinking of all the ways he might cross it, the bridges that he might build, but there was always something else there, the one thing that never failed to rear its head and stand in his way, the obstacle he could never escape and to which he always returned.

It was the sense that, just as they had not betrayed Rasheed in life, so would they not betray him in death either. He couldn't explain it with logic, but he also couldn't deny the power it held over him, and—though he couldn't explain how he knew this either—he was certain that Ranya felt the same way.

He broke the telephonic silence by saying, "I can't stay. You must understand that. It's sucking the very life blood out of me."

He paused, and when she said nothing, he continued, "All these so-called 'advances'—the electronic health records and the like—have made me feel more and more like a glorified data-entry specialist. And I'm tired of being a data-entry specialist. I want to be a doctor again."

He felt the emotion rising in his voice as he went on. *Let it rise.* "I'm on my third life now, Ranya—thanks to you and Rasheed." *There, I said it, said his name.* "Don't I owe it to you both to do my best with it?" He could hear his voice breaking. *Let it break.* "To do what I was born to do?"

He thought he heard a choked sob on the other end of the line. Then once she spoke again he was certain of it. And he felt that the only thing worse than listening to Ranya cry was listening to her trying to hide it from him.

She cleared her throat with more force than necessary. "Oh, gosh, Gabriel, what can I say?" There was one more long pause, a distance unbridgeable, and then Ranya's voice came back to him from a far place, and he swore he could feel the frost of her breath on his ear through the phone. "Well," she said, with a resignation that split his heart, "you do what you have to do."

He wondered what his chances were of ever hearing from her again.

CHAPTER FIFTY-TWO

"Never to travel any road a second time."
—Ibn Battuta

September 10, 2015
Thursday

Rays of sunlight streamed through the lobby as Gabriel walked toward the exit of the medical school building at University College Cork to meet the end of a beautiful September day. Colleagues and students nodded to him as he headed out the doors, but thankfully none stopped him to talk or to petition him, however subtly, for this or that favor, and the fact that none did so made it an even more unusual day here in Ireland. Since he had become the new Dean of the UCC School of Medicine, it seemed as though his time was rarely his own, but perhaps everyone else was taken by the day's fine weather too, anticipating enjoyment in their own activities that were much apart from him or anything he could do for them. And this was just as well, for today Gabriel was preoccupied with the information he had derived from a lunchtime conversation.

His lunch guest had been a visiting cardiologist from Dublin who had brought news from the recent European Society of Cardiology meeting in Barcelona, where, apparently, they had been treated to a lecture by the "world's foremost expert" on the topic of radial artery access for cardiac catheterization. And his colleague had wondered if this were someone whom he might know, given that she came from a hospital in America—in Nashville, Tennessee, in fact—and it was common knowledge that Gabriel had spent a good deal of time there too.

He ran his mind over and around it all day, before coming to the decision that sent him out into the September evening. He still had her email address—assuming it hadn't changed. He pondered over the wording all through dinner. And at last, having washed and dried his dishes in the quiet of his own space, he glanced at his watch one more time before moving over to his desk. 10:00 p.m. It would be 4:00 p.m. in Nashville. Maybe she would even see it with her evening inbox check.

He lifted the cover of his laptop and ran a hand through his hair, letting a thin puff of breath escape over his lower lip as he did so. Thursday nights were always hard for him, still. Probably always would be.

Where to even begin? *Keep it short. Keep it cordial. What salutation to use? None.*

He let his fingers move over the keyboard, and the clicking of the lettered keys reverberated in the quiet corner of his small home office.

From: gobcork@email.com
To: "Ranya (personal)"
Thurs 10 September 2015 22:04
Subject: ESC meeting

Caught wind of the ESC meeting in Spain. An Irish colleague of mine was there. Came back raving about hearing from the "world's foremost expert" on radial artery access. He saw your university affiliation on the program and wondered if I knew you.

```
Guess that makes you the best in the world, doesn't
it? Just as you always wanted.

Proud of you,

Gabe
```

Ranya stared at the screen that displayed the contents of her email inbox. She set her mug of herbal tea down on the black granite countertop of her kitchen bar. It was late; it had been a long day at the hospital, and now it was nearly 10:00 p.m. What time could he have sent it?

Ignoring all the other messages that called for her attention, she hovered the cursor over the only name on the screen that mattered.

She read the message twice, three times, but still didn't know what to think or even what to feel. Was he being sarcastic? Snide, even? No, not Gabriel. That wasn't his style. She had to believe that he was sincere, that he truly was proud of her and her accomplishments. He always had been, hadn't he? Yes, of course. He'd always been in her corner, always been on her side.

She sighed heavily and placed her forehead in her hand. She had missed him, missed hearing from him, missed talking to him and confiding in him. Missed having him on her side. And there was so much going on in her world and in the world at large right now, so much for which she could really use the presence of a stalwart someone on her side. Someone who knew her better than she even knew herself.

Did he miss her too? Yes, clearly he must; she knew that. Else he wouldn't have sent this message. Or maybe he was just being polite? Gabriel was big on being polite.

No, she should quit being ridiculous: he was the Dean of his alma mater's medical school now; surely he didn't have time to send around such messages just in the name of being polite.

Oh, good grief, she was overthinking this. *Go ahead and answer the man already.*

But when she tried to put the words on the screen, she found that she couldn't. Couldn't tell him what she was thinking, the way she used to. Couldn't tell him that it was good—great—to hear from him. Couldn't tell him that she missed him. Couldn't tell him how close she had come to stopping in Dublin on her way home from Barcelona.

She couldn't put words to any of it. Maybe she lacked the will, or the vocabulary, or the courage. Or just the energy. She didn't know.

And then there was that other thing, too. She wanted to provide reassurance that she didn't blame him, but then she wasn't sure that that was true. Rasheed had left her, and then, in short order, Gabriel had left her too. The big difference being that the latter's exit was voluntary. And maybe it was that for which she had yet to forgive him.

She looked across her great room at the framed photo that hung on the opposite wall, the one that kept her company on the darkest nights. Rasheed's bright, broad smile beckoning to her from behind the glare of the glass. The Dead Sea in the background. Waiting for him.

No, if she were being absolutely honest, she did know what was true. If anyone was to blame, it was herself. How could she, the "best-in-the-world" cardiologist, not have seen the early signs of Rasheed's pulmonary embolism? Not have paid attention to what was presenting itself to her, clear as it was now in hindsight?

But then again . . . would it have made a difference if she had? She couldn't have saved her mother from her pulmonary embolism, but could she have saved

Rasheed? Well, now she would never know. So much for all her so-called accomplishments.

She stared at the blank reply-message box on her screen for another brief eternity. In the end, the only response she could muster was: "Thank you." It was all she had left.

CHAPTER FIFTY-THREE

"Ever tried. Ever failed. No matter. Try again. Fail again. Fail better."
—Samuel Beckett

"Where should the birds fly after the last sky?"
—Mahmoud Darwish,
"The Earth Is Closing on Us"

"Dr. O'Brien? We'd just like to know what you think."

Gabriel got the sense that the speaker had already asked him some sort of question before this remark, but he couldn't for the life of him say what it was. He looked down and flipped pages on the report in front of him, then glanced up at the faculty members who sat around the conference table, all staring at him. He turned to one of the more senior faculty and gestured to her with an open palm. "Dr. McCarthy, no doubt you have an opinion on this."

As she began speaking, Gabriel's mind wandered back to its previous state, which consisted of incessant pondering over Ranya's terse reply. "Thank you"? All she had to say was, "Thank you"? Seriously??

Well, that was disappointing, to be sure, but he realized that she must be very busy. His message was probably one of a hundred or more that she had received that day, and given the time of her reply, she was probably just wanting to get through and go to bed. But it left him very little opening for his own reply. He had to admit, part of what he had been hoping for—maybe the greater part of it—was a reopening of the lines of communication between them, the beginning of a correspondence at the very least, even if it was electronic in nature.

He wondered if she would ever consider coming to Ireland, coming for a visit, however brief. He wondered if he could write to her and ask, invite her. Well, no, probably not—not after that response.

Ranya let her keys clatter to the hardwood floor where she stood, checking her email one last time before heading to the Green Hills Y for her evening workout. She stared open-mouthed at the name that popped out at her from the list of messages, begging for her next click.

She willed herself to open other messages first, formulate other responses to other senders, before coming back to his name and his message. Judging from the time stamp, he must have sent it less than an hour ago. She forced herself to open it. No sense in waiting any longer.

From: Gabriel O'Brien
To: Ranya Abbasi
Fri 9/11/15 6:30 PM
Subject: Re: ESC meeting

Ranya,

You are most welcome.

Cheers,

Gabe

Ranya closed the lid of her laptop, bent over to pick up her keys, and walked out the door.

Inside the empty studio at the Y, she began her taekwondo forms. Furiously at first, giving her rage over to every movement of her body, even as it protested against the vigor of the movements. Hard blocks, hard punches, high kicks. As she worked steadily through the forms, from very beginning to most advanced, the rage slowly began to fall away, and the transcendence she sought was at last within her reach.

The mirrored studio's peaceful silence was disturbed only by the sound of her own breathing, and she became lost in her moving meditation, inhabiting a place that was above the sweat pouring down her face and trickling down her spine, beyond the burning of her breath between her ribs and the sting of her hair against her neck when she leapt and landed. A place where the aches and pains of age were meaningless, and the world of cares and sorrows and frustrations receded into oblivion. In her precious transcendence, time stood still, and for a few irreplaceable minutes, she was released from all inner and outer turmoil. She wanted to stay there forever.

From: Gabriel O'Brien
To: Ranya Abbasi
Fri 10/2/2015 4:30 PM
Subject: The Big Fella

Dear Ranya,

Michael Collins is on right now, and I couldn't help but drop you a line. How long has it been since we saw it the first time? Still so powerful after all these years.

Hope you are keeping well. I'm sure you are quite busy. It's been a busy couple of weeks on my end, too.

If you ever think of coming to Ireland for a visit, I trust you will let me know.

Always,

Gabe

    Ranya left her laptop open on the coffee table, letting the screen reproach her as she sank back into her sofa. He had sent the message yesterday, but she hadn't been able to answer it then, and she wasn't sure she would be able to do so tonight, either.

Another Saturday night alone on her couch. It didn't have to be that way. She knew that. Did she want it to be that way? That she did not know.

She got up and turned on the radio; she always had it set to the classical music station, and they were playing Beethoven's *Piano Concerto No. 5*. It was one of her favorite pieces in all of classical music. She took a photo album down from the shelf, brought it back with her to the couch, and began flipping pages.

The second movement of the concerto began, with its stately, poignant lead-in from the strings, and she was reminded of her night at the symphony with Gabriel. Every time she had gone with Rasheed thereafter, it had never been the same. She hated to admit that, but if she were dealing in truth, there it was.

In the next moments before the piano returned, she surrendered to the growing expansiveness of the achingly beautiful music from the strings; and in that expansiveness that tugged upon her very heart, begging it to open, there was hope and promise. She recalled now that she had always found it to be that way with this piece, as with so much of Beethoven's work. And that, too, reminded her of Gabriel. Hope was his right hand. How many times had he implored her to keep in mind that "there is always hope"?

She blinked several times and looked back down at the photo album that lay on her lap. Her fingers rested upon a picture of Gabriel and Rasheed together in Ireland, both raising a pint and smiling for her camera. For her. She remembered how she had snapped the photo and smiled back at them. Remembered it as if it were yesterday. And she also recalled how her gaze had met Gabriel's then, and how they had both quickly looked away. How she had gone over to Rasheed and sat down beside him, as she always did.

She looked up at the wall of her living room, the one that held the smiling photo of Rasheed on the day of his death. *Oh, Rasheed, what would you want me to do now?*

Beside that photo of Rasheed, there was another framed one: the picture Rasheed had taken of the Skelligs on their trip to Ireland. She had lost count of how many times she had revisited that place, that moment, in her mind. Just as she had known she would. But never, not in her most tortured nightmares, could she have foreseen the circumstances.

She had lost everyone dearest to her. Everyone except . . .

As the concerto's second movement slid into the third, she set the photo album aside, wiped her eyes, and leaned forward. Her fingers moved over the keyboard of her laptop, moved so fast she scarcely knew what she was doing. She just knew she had to give voice and chance to her thoughts before any of her countless inhibitions convinced her to stop.

In the love triangle of the Michael Collins story, Kitty Kiernan had suffered the ultimate tragedy in losing both of her beloveds. But the dance of Ranya's fingers across the keys held hope for a different ending.

Gabriel woke up early Sunday morning. Too early. It was 4 a.m. He did not want to be awake at 4 a.m. He hadn't slept well Friday night, either. And all day on Saturday he had kept checking his email for her reply, and hated himself for it. Now he knew he would be checking again. One more time couldn't hurt, and then maybe he could go back to sleep. *Yeah, right.*

A rush of emotions, disbelief foremost among them, flooded him when the sight of her name in his inbox greeted his eyes. From the time stamp, she must have just sent it. With trembling fingers, he hovered his cursor over the message header, took a deep breath, and clicked.

From: Ranya Abbasi
To: Gabriel O'Brien
Sun 4 October 2015 03:59
Subject: Re: The Big Fella

Dear Gabriel,

Funniest thing: recently I was at a medical society
meeting—one of those "networking things"—and we
were split into rotating groups to answer "ice-
breaker" questions (I hate those, as I think you
know). And at one of the tables, the question
was, "What is your favorite movie?" My answer was,
of course, *Michael Collins*, which I figured most
people at that table here in Nashville would have
never heard of, so I added a little, very brief,
explanation of what the film was about—Irish
revolutionaries and the like! ;-) Most people just
looked at me like I was from Mars, but I suppose I'm
used to that by now. But wouldn't you know, when
it came time for the fourth physician in the group
(a white-haired gentleman) to give his response,
he spoke with a British accent! I noticed he had
been studying me when I gave my answer; now I know
why. What do you suppose he must think of me now?!?
Well, who cares.

Beethoven's 5th piano concerto is playing on the
radio now. 91.1, the classical station. You know
how much I love Beethoven ….

How are you? Are you still seeing patients?

-Ranya

Gabriel sat back and let his head rest against the top of his armchair, feeling the unruly strands of his disheveled hair brush against it as he looked at the ceiling. He pressed his eyelids shut, but the tears still came, and with no one to watch, he let them spill down his cheeks. She was back.

CHAPTER FIFTY-FOUR

ما كل جنّي يدخل القنّينة

"Not every genie re-enters the bottle."
—Arabic proverb

October 5, 2015
Monday

GABRIEL WAS IN A JOVIAL MOOD while rounding with the residents and students that Monday morning; in fact, he had to acknowledge that it may have been his happiest mood in years. He saw his generalized cheerfulness reflected in the faces and quick responses of all those who accompanied or encountered him on hospital rounds, and the lesson of how contagious a good mood could be was not lost on him.

He knew that many academic deans didn't keep clinically active, but as he had let Ranya know in his latest reply, he made a point of keeping one clinic day per week and a hospital rotation a few times a year. It was one of the greatest joys of being a doctor, after all: seeing patients. And he had never had any intention of letting that go, and had told her as much.

He rarely relished the thought of checking his email, but today he couldn't wait to do so. Once he had completed rounding and made a requisite couple of phone calls, he asked his assistant, most cordially, to give him fifteen minutes, and shut the door to his office.

But a quick check of his email inbox turned up nothing but disappointment. He looked at his watch. Of course; what was he thinking? She'd likely still be asleep. Better to get busy and then recheck in the afternoon.

It was nearly evening before he had a chance to check again, but his wait was rewarded. She must have sent her reply just before going in to hospital rounds of her own that morning. Excellent.

From: Ranya Abbasi
To: Gabriel O'Brien
Mon 5 October 2015 12:30
Subject: Re: The Big Fella

Dear Gabriel,

Last night I dreamed of Ireland. Must be all this talk of Michael Collins, etc.! But as so often happens with dreams, it was a really odd sequence: a tour of your dear country.

First I was standing on the banks of the lake at Kylemore Abbey, surrounded by Gothic splendor and magnificent scenery (well, where in Ireland isn't the scenery magnificent??). Then I was trying to dip my hand into the water of the lake, but it wasn't the lake; it was the ocean, at that pier where we stopped to marvel at the Skelligs way back when—and indeed, there they were: the Skelligs, beckoning to me, in

all their rough and haunting glory. And just as I was
ready to jump in the ocean and swim to them—ha, ha,
can you imagine?—I found myself standing at Charles
Fort, looking out over the picturesque harbor of
Kinsale in the nearly-blinding sunshine. I looked
over to the left of the fort, and there was a winding
path that followed the curve of the land against the
sea. And there was someone coming up the path, but
I couldn't tell who it was; the sunshine was too
bright. And then I awakened.

Okay, that's enough and probably too much. Gotta
get to work now. Just so you know that Ireland is,
apparently, very much on my mind. Glad you're doing
so well over there and still seeing patients. Now
I'm the one whose turn it is to be proud!

Take care,

Ranya

    Gabriel was momentarily at a loss for words; he reread her message twice. He
wanted to wait to reply, think it over some more, but something told him he
shouldn't leave it too long. He didn't want to risk losing her again, in any way.
And she would be checking, looking for his message in her afternoon or evening
inbox; he was sure of that. So he took a deep breath, and decided to go bold.

Dear Ranya,

What a great tour! Well, you know you can always see
it all in person again. I would be only too delighted

to serve as your guide. You say the word; I'll
be ready. Ireland welcomes you with open arms.

How are you otherwise? How is Nashville?

Yours,

Gabe

The next morning, Gabriel's delight was sustained when his morning
email check revealed a message from Ranya awaiting him near the top of his
inbox. He had been right to respond to her immediately the evening before;
he knew it. He consumed her latest message like a long-hungry man who has
just arrived at a feast.

From: Ranya Abbasi
To: Gabriel O'Brien
Tues 6 October 2015 02:00
Subject: Re: The Big Fella

Gabriel,

Nashville is changing so fast; soon it will become
unrecognizable even to me. Condos and hotels
and new developments of all kinds going up all
over the place. Traffic becoming horrible. Home
prices/values skyrocketing. Crime rate steadily
rising. All the growing pains, I guess, of an "It
City," or a "city on the move," or whatever the
pundits choose to call it. But just between you
and me: I hate it.

Otherwise, work is going really well. I keep traveling to give talks, and I also have a new research
study going. Am happy my radial artery technique has
caught on so well here. Finally! ;)

Best,

Ranya

Well, she was warming up while keeping her distance, in typical Ranya fashion. He could deal with that. Heavens, after nineteen years and all they had been through, he could deal with anything. Anything but the absence of her in his life.

Nineteen years . . . how could it have been that long? And yet it seemed even longer. So often, he felt as if he had known her his entire life.

She would still be asleep now, so his response could wait; he'd think up a good one over the course of the day. He went on to the rest of his email, responding to various business matters and requests, trying to decide whether or not to accept the O'Donovans' invitation to dinner that weekend. No, he might have to go up to Dublin for a meeting then, so maybe he'd get back to them the following weekend. Glad to have a pass.

Just when he was about to sign out of his account and leave for a morning meeting, his inbox surprised him with a flicker and a downward shift in his message list. Another message had been received, and it was from Ranya.

How was that possible? Was she on call? It was 2:40 a.m. for her. And there was a new heading in the subject line.

From: Ranya Abbasi
To: Gabriel O'Brien
Tues 6 October 2015 08:40
Subject: The things people say

Hi, Gabriel,

I'm up after answering a call from the hospital, and couldn't go back to sleep. Keep thinking about something I overheard in the cafeteria yesterday; probably I should let it go, but I can't get it out of my mind. Came from a couple of physician colleagues, no less. They were talking about the Syrian refugee crisis, and how "we can't let those people in here," because they'd "ruin our country" and other nonsense like that. It bugs me so much when I hear anyone talking about Arabs in such a way; I interact with these colleagues all the time, and I wonder if they think of me that way? Well, since I was born here and speak with a Southern accent, maybe they don't. But it still bothers me, you know? The prejudice—and the ignorance!—just seems to get worse and worse here.

Sleepless in Nashville,

Ranya

There was no hesitation at all in Gabriel's response; if it made him a few minutes late for his meeting, so be it.

Dearest Ranya,

We Irish were treated the same in America in days gone by: "No Irish need apply."

From what I have heard and read, the Irish
government are pledging to take 5,000 refugees at
present.

Keep your chin up and be proud of your roots.

Must run to meeting but am thinking of you. Always.

Beir bua,

Gabe

Ranya sat staring at her laptop screen, the blue light of it illuminating the
corner of her living room where she sat, legs crossed, on the far end of her
sofa. She rubbed her eyes and yawned. She really should go back to sleep; the
night wasn't over yet, and there still might be other calls from the hospital,
so she should grab some shut-eye while she could.

But just as she hovered her cursor over the line that would minimize the
window displaying her email inbox, a new message arrived at the top of the
screen. Gabriel was online and had obviously read the somewhat-despairing
message she had just sent. She opened his message without hesitation and
eagerly read his reply. She didn't know why, but it brought tears to her eyes.
Especially that part about keeping her chin up, being proud of her roots. It
was exactly what Rasheed would have said.

She let no more than a minute pass before quickly composing her reply.

```
From: ranyaa@inmail.com
To: Gabriel O'Brien
Tues 10/6/2015 2:50 AM
Subject: Re: The things people say

Dear Gabriel,

Thank you. That is exactly what Rasheed would have
told me. But maybe you knew that?

You know, there are so many times when I think
that if Rasheed were here, he would know just what
to do, just what to say—at times like these, to
people like these—and for so much more and so much
else. I am a poor substitute.
```

And I am tired and lonely here, she wanted to add, but held back, and signed off. Gabriel would have gone to his meeting by now anyway; she didn't expect to hear from him again until later. She closed her laptop and went back into her bedroom, where she threw herself upon the bed and buried her face in her pillow.

Gabriel had been trying to get back to his desk the whole blasted day, or at the very least, to have enough time to himself to check email from his phone, but meeting after meeting had required his full attention. It wasn't until after his dinner meeting that he finally had the opportunity to look for Ranya's reply.

He took off his coat in his home office while watching his inbox messages load. Lots of rubbish at the top, but there toward the bottom, standing out as the earliest of the day's unread messages, was the response from Ranya. A quick conversion of the time stamp told him she had sent it moments after his own message to her this morning. So he had just missed it. He muttered a curse and belatedly opened the message.

Upon reading her note, he realized that it was the first time she had mentioned Rasheed since his death. He took this as a good sign. He came around from the back of the rolling desk chair against which he had been leaning, and sat down in it to stare at the screen once more. Funny thing, but somehow being a foot closer made it more real. He put his fingers to the keyboard and typed.

My Dear Ranya,

Yes, Rasheed would know. He always had a knack for knowing, didn't he? But you know what, Ranya? So do you. The Ranya I have always known and admired would know how to face forward, would know how to keep going with no break in her stride. That Ranya would know this for the nonsense that it is.

So face forward, chin up, and keep your wits about you. And don't let the bastards grind you down.

Here for you—always,

Gabe

They settled into their own rhythm of call-and-response after that, and it was the best part of Gabriel's day to receive a message from Ranya. Some days passed when there was no reply, and those were the worst. He told himself she must be too busy. He made himself hope that was the case.

On Friday of the following week, Gabriel managed to make it off campus in time to get to the English Market before closing. Being there always made him think of Ranya. His mind returned to the one time they had been there together, touring this very market with Rasheed. She had called it "depressingly fabulous," noting the magnificent bounty that the English Market laid before every visitor, a cornucopia of freshness and variety all there for the taking. He wished once more that she were here now. Then it could just be fabulous, and not depressing.

He passed a poster board that sported a photo of Queen Elizabeth II during her 2011 visit to the English Market, and thought to himself how far they had come. A visit from the Queen of England, right here in the "People's Republic of Cork," where she was warmly received and even photographed having a laugh with one very witty Irish fishmonger. He shook his head every time he thought of it. It had only taken a century, but here they were.

Maybe one day it could be the same for the Palestinians and the Israelis. It seemed impossible now, but welcoming the Queen in Cork would have seemed impossible 100 years ago, too. He thought again of Ranya. And of Rasheed, whose kidney labored on quite successfully for Gabriel, allowing him to be here today, to have these thoughts, breathe this air, see these sights, live this dream. Allowing him to connect with Ranya once again.

His path eventually took him by The Chocolate Shop, and the most curious notion found its way into his head: he could buy Ranya some premium chocolates, such as were only found in Ireland, and send them, ship them, to her.

Wouldn't that be fine? But doubt stole in immediately upon the heels of this unexpected idea, and he had to ask himself if Ranya even liked chocolate at all. He had to admit, even after all this time, he did not know. Well, who didn't like chocolate? With his luck, Ranya.

Returning to his house a bit later, he fired off an email to her, one he was certain she'd appreciate, and one that might get him the information he sought.

```
From: gobcork
To: Ranya Abbasi
Fri 16 October 2015 19:30
Subject: Happy Michael Collins' birthday


My Dear Ranya,


As chance would have it, today is the Big Fella's
birthday. He would have been 125 years old today!


Hope you are having a good Friday and that you don't
have to work this weekend. I passed by the English
Market on my way home this evening, and thought of
you, of course. The Chocolate Shop there has some
superb chocolates. Do you like chocolate? I'd be
happy to send you some.


Yours,


Gabe
```

The weather was fine the next morning, and Gabriel's stroll took him to the farmers' market on the Coal Quay. When he passed the lovely handmade bouquets in Hannah and Klaus' flower stall, he of course thought of Ranya again, wondering this time if she liked flowers. He was certain she did; he couldn't imagine that she wouldn't. Which flowers would be her favorites?

How could there be so much basic information he didn't know, never knew, about her? What else didn't he know about her? And would he ever find out?

He was becoming agitated and disgusted with himself, and such a fine day it was, too. He had made himself leave home without checking his email, but now he could resist no longer. He whipped out his phone; paradoxically, maybe that would put a stopper on this madness. And there it was, a reply from the mysterious Dr. Abbasi herself:

```
Sat 17 October 2015 02:35


Dear Gabriel,


Wow. Michael Collins' birthday—yes, of course!
Thanks for the reminder.


Yes, I love chocolate. Who doesn't? ;) But please,
please, don't go to any trouble on my account.


Hope you have a great weekend. Trees are finally
beginning to show some nice colors here; it could
be a beautiful autumn.


Cheers,


Ranya
```

Gabriel smiled to himself. He reread her message again, reflected on it, and smiled again. It could be a beautiful autumn indeed.

CHAPTER FIFTY-FIVE

"Maybe all one can do is hope to end up with the right regrets."
—Arthur Miller,
The Ride Down Mt. Morgan

"Therefore we must be saved by the final form of love which is forgiveness."
—Reinhold Niebuhr,
The Irony of American History

December 24, 2015
Thursday

WHEN RANYA GOT HOME from work that Christmas Eve, there was a package waiting on her doorstep. A medium-sized brown box with a green customs sticker declaring the contents to be "tea, book, chocolate." The handwriting she recognized immediately, even before seeing the return address of the sender.

She couldn't believe it. He had gone and done it, gone and gotten her something for Christmas. And she hadn't sent him anything other than emails—but at least she had done that as regularly as she could.

She set the box down on her kitchen counter and carefully opened it, being sure to preserve the return-address sticker. Inside the box were two other boxes, a slender one wrapped in beautiful gold paper, and a larger one that took the shape of a multicolored cube. Both rested atop a large hardback book. And affixed, with a single strip of gold tape, to the cover of the book was a beige, card-sized envelope.

She lifted out the multicolored box first and held it in her hands, smiling widely as she turned it over and examined it from all sides. Covering the box's white background were images of various tea kettles, mugs, sugar bowls, and flower vases, all in shades of red and yellow. Scattered throughout the images was the cheerful imprint that announced, "Barry's Tea."

He knew her love for tea. And he knew she would remember. That first time they had ever had tea together, when he himself had prepared it. It was Barry's then. And apparently it was to be Barry's now.

She turned her attention to the slender box wrapped in gold. She had an inkling of what might be inside, and when she had removed the gold foil in one splendid piece, her suspicions were confirmed. Under the clear plastic were a dozen chocolate truffles, each a different flavor. They looked decadent.

Next she removed the hardcover book, setting aside the attached card for later. The book was a large, gallery-style volume, with the title *In Great Haste: The Letters of Michael Collins and Kitty Kiernan*. There on the cover was a photo of their hero himself, along with a smaller photo of his intended, Ms. Kiernan.

She flipped through the smooth, glossy pages that contained, evidently, all the available correspondence between the two, including facsimile reproductions of some of the handwritten letters. Amazing. There were some excellent background sections from the editors, too, giving pertinent historical details. Oh, she could tell she was really going to enjoy reading this. And he must have known that too.

Twenty minutes later, she was sitting with a fresh cup of hot tea, one chocolate truffle, and an unopened card before her. Breathing in the wonderful aroma of

Barry's tea, she recalled an Irishman's black-and-white couch, an introductory lesson on hurling, two of the most gorgeous dogs she had ever seen, a room full of vibrant energy . . . and a Nashville that no longer existed, at least not for her.

She sighed and picked up the beige envelope. She could tell from the thickness and weight of it that Gabriel had sent more than just a card. Part of her was eager to read it, and part of her was not. Eventually the first part won out, and as she slid her thumb under the top fold of the envelope, she swallowed hard to release the tightness in her throat.

As she had suspected, inside the beautiful Christmas card was a handwritten letter, on ruled paper that rustled with the feel of fine stationery.

December 13, 2015

My Dearest Ranya,

Happy Christmas! I know you said not to send any chocolate—or anything, really—but it's Christmas, and I hope you will enjoy this just the same. It really was no trouble at all, and even if it were, that would be no matter.

I thought about taking a trip to Nashville for the holidays, surprise you and all, but I didn't know if you would welcome that sort of surprise. The chocolates and the tea will serve you much better anyway, no doubt!

As for the book, I got it at the Winding Stair—a fabulous place you must visit if you're ever again in Dublin—and I know you'll enjoy reading it. Well, I say I know, but you let me know, okay? I can't wait to hear how you find it.

By the way, when I was shopping on Grafton Street, a street musician with a saxophone began playing "Send in the Clowns." Would you believe it? Ranya, I nearly fell over. In fact, I was nearly knocked over by other busy shoppers because I had stopped dead in my tracks, right there in the street, probably leaving everyone around me thinking I'm some sort of eejit—which, who knows, maybe I am. Not sure which one in the song I am now, Ranya—maybe we're each a wee bit of both—but at that moment, on that day, I was once again the one who couldn't move.

And the whole thing got me thinking . . . Ranya, I have a favorite place in Stephen's Green where a large willow tree forms an arch over the two benches at its base, sheltering and protecting them from the rain. And when it rains, as it often does here, sitting there beneath that willow tree is undisturbed bliss. The rain doesn't fall onto the benches; it runs off the leaves onto the ground, sparing the benches and their occupants. You can sit there in a rainstorm and not get wet, yet watch the rain fall all around you. And maybe that is what I should have done. Or maybe, at the very least, I should have been the willow tree over you and Rasheed.

I live in hope. Hope that one day you will forgive me, even if I can never do so myself.

Yours, always,

Gabe

Ranya glanced down at her watch. It would be the middle of the night for him now, and the dawn on Christmas morning came late in Ireland. She would have to wait. She returned to the last page of the letter to read it again, careful to hold it out of the path of her falling tears.

CHAPTER FIFTY-SIX

"There is a luxury in self-reproach. When we blame ourselves we feel that no one else has a right to blame us. It is the confession, not the priest, that gives us absolution."

—Oscar Wilde,
The Picture of Dorian Gray

December 25, 2015
Friday

GABRIEL WATCHED THE STEAM rise from his cup of Barry's tea as he sat by his living-room window, mobile phone in hand. There were phone calls to make, Christmas wishes to impart, presents to deliver, relatives' houses to visit. And he didn't feel like doing any of it.

He stared out the window. It was raining. He watched as drops of water merged into streams that ran down the glass and disappeared onto the exterior window panes, let his mind wander to another place, another time. A Nativity scene that sparked a discussion about Palestine, and the gorgeous, headstrong woman who ignited the sparks, always. He put the fingers of one hand to his lips and smiled, remembering.

He stood up to get his list. People to call. Wouldn't do to miss anyone. Not just good etiquette, which was important; in some ways, it was part of his job. As he walked toward his desk, the phone in his hand started buzzing. Oh, well, at least that would be one down, one to check off the list.

He looked to see who was calling, and froze. His thumb trembled as he hit "answer."

"Hello—Ranya?"

"Hello, Gabriel. Merry Christmas."

"Happy Christmas! My God, it must be three in the morning there! You are in Nashville right now, aren't you?"

"Yes, yes. I'm sorry—am I interrupting anything? I won't keep you—"

"No, no, good heavens, you're not interrupting anything. Couldn't be a better time. I just can't believe—Ranya, it's so good to hear your voice again. What a wonderful Christmas gift."

"Well, speaking of Christmas gifts, I wanted to call and thank you for the ones you sent. And here I didn't get you a thing. I thought the least I could do was give you a call and thank you by phone rather than email."

"I'm so glad you've called. And I'm glad you received the gifts—I hope you like them."

"Gabriel, I love them. So thoughtful of you. I don't know what to say, really."

"Oh, well, again, I'm delighted you like them. And as for not knowing what to say—I'm afraid that makes two of us. Ranya, I've been waiting, hoping, to talk to you for so long, and this is just . . . well, such a wonderful surprise . . . and wouldn't you know it, now here I am babbling and saying nothing!"

"That's okay, Gabriel. I'm pretty exhausted myself, and should go to sleep now. But I didn't want to miss the chance to call you on Christmas morning. So glad I reached you."

"Me too, Ranya. And yes, I understand—please get some good rest now. And feel free to call me anytime. Anytime at all."

"Thanks, Gabriel. Oh, and Gabriel?"

"Yes?"

"There is nothing to forgive."

CHAPTER FIFTY-SEVEN

"I've found myself more and more connected to other places. I've found that a number of places have crystallized in my mind as significant, obviously one is the Middle East, and there is also Ireland . . ."
—Edward W. Said,
as quoted in *The Edward Said Reader*,
edited by Moustafa Bayoumi and Andrew Rubin

FROM: GOBCORK
To: Ranya Abbasi
Thurs 31 December 2015 23:43

Dearest Ranya,

Not long from now, the clock will strike midnight here. Hope you have had a good holiday week. Once again, it was just fantastic to hear your voice on Christmas. Do write soon and let me know how you are keeping.

If Rasheed were here, I'd tip a glass to him and toast him with his favorite toast, *"Fad saol agat, gob fliuch, agus bás in Éirinn.*" Sadly, the first part of that was not to be, and so he is not here; the only part of him that remains (aside from our treasured memories, of course) is the kidney that allows me to have as normal a life as someone like me could possibly have. And maybe, given that, carrying on and striving to ensure that his valiance was not in vain is toast and tribute enough. Wish I could believe that, but really, nothing will ever be enough, you know? Yeah, something tells me that you do.

Not to get all maudlin on you here on New Year's Eve, Ranya, but … God, I miss him. And I miss you, too. Let me know if you might come to Ireland this year—or even if you'd like me to come to Nashville, or to meet you wherever in the world you may be—and we could finally pick up the conversation again in person.

Happy new year to you, and every best wish.

Always,

Gabe

On the first day of 2016, Gabriel resolved, still having not heard back from Ranya, to get a grip. His resolve lasted about as long as his headache, at which point he began wondering if he had scared her off for good. That email couldn't have been so bad, though, could it? Was it? No, he was being ridiculous; Ranya was busy, it was New Year's, she probably had a thousand things to do other than check her email incessantly as he had been doing. He, too, should find some other things to do.

He had dinner out, at the lovely Hayfield Manor, where the happy faces and conversations of the couples all around him depressed him further. A thought entered his consciousness, one he couldn't believe he had never entertained before: what if Ranya really had moved on, both from himself and from Rasheed? He had never really considered it possible, given all he knew about her and how poorly they had both taken Rasheed's death, but why not? Why couldn't . . . Well, she deserved every happiness, of course. He had simply hoped she could have found it with him.

He ordered tea after his meal; he wasn't ready to go home, alone, yet.

He should get a dog again. One couldn't go wrong with a dog in the picture. He wondered why he had waited so long to get another dog after Maggie and Shamrock. He loved dogs. He guessed his life had just been too uncertain for too long. Well, he was back in Ireland now, where he was meant to be. And he was going to get a dog again.

A Glen of Imaal Terrier or a Soft-Coated Wheaten. If the dog were small and friendly enough, he could even bring him to his office at work. Wouldn't that be something? He wondered if he could do that. Well, he was the dean of the medical school, so he supposed he could do just about anything he wanted, as long as it was legal. Eccentric Dean O'Brien and his terrier. The idea was already beginning to grow on him.

He remembered how Ranya had loved his Irish Setters. She would love a Glen of Imaal Terrier; he just knew it. There were probably even puppies from Christmas litters still available. He should email her about it.

Four weeks later, Gabriel pulled out the chair at the oak desk in his home office, having just returned from choosing the puppy he would bring home the following week. It was fair to say he was quite excited, and wanted to share the news with Ranya, even if she hadn't responded to his last two messages. He had decided that she was busy, so soon after the holidays; he was certain of it, knowing her. He also knew her tendency to read messages and let them sit before replying. Frustrating and even annoying at times, to be sure, but that was Ranya.

So when he logged in to his account to type the very brief message about his new puppy, he was overjoyed to find a long-awaited response from none other than the elusive Dr. Ranya.

```
Sat 30 January 2016 14:14

Dear Gabe,

Happy new year!

My deepest apologies for not writing sooner, but
there was a lot I wanted to say, and things have
been super crazy here at work since the start of
the year—patient volume has picked up, I've been
```

asked to speak at five more conferences, and I'm just figuring out how to juggle it all.

But not too busy to read the book you sent me for Christmas—thank you again for that! I have to tell you, though, that I've put off reading the final letters from August 1922; I just don't think I can bear it right now, knowing, as we do, exactly how it ends.

But can you believe that Kitty and Collins wrote to each other nearly every day, and sometimes twice in one day?? I'm afraid I'm an even poorer correspondent than I thought. Apologies for that, too!

You know, I suppose now is as good a time as ever to thank you for indulging my curiosity, admiration, and love of all things Irish, all these many years. I do have an endless curiosity about the world, and not everybody gets that. It may seem, indeed, that my abiding interest in Ireland is more than a little bizarre for a Palestinian American born and raised in the U.S. South, and I've tried hard to understand it myself. Lord knows that Rasheed tried hard to understand it, too, and I'm not sure that he ever did, not completely. But I loved him for trying.

Then I go on to consider all the many things about Ireland and the Irish that resonate with me: a history of tremendous struggle, resilience, perseverance, and eventual triumph. The unparalleled hospitality I experienced in the brief time I was there (and it's not just me: Irish hospitality is legendary the world over) is perhaps unexpected, given all that the Irish have endured over the centuries.

Rather than closing themselves off, the Irish have opened themselves up in so many ways. The world could stand to learn a lot from you all. So many barriers broken and achievements attained, in spite of a history of discrimination here and in your own homeland. It is, after all, the ultimate triumph of the underdog. And that's just scratching the surface.

So thanks once more for showing me the possibilities, for fueling the fire … for giving me hope.

Wishing you the best the new year can bring,

Always,

Ranya

P.S. And check out this story from just before New Year's: www.independent.ie/irish-news/news/irish-have-roots-in-t he-middle-east-and-black-sea-scientists-discover-34319957.html
So maybe I am not crazy after all! What's five millennia between friends?? ;-)

Gabriel sat back and put a hand to his chest, then to the base of his throat. He clicked on the link, and quickly read through the story reporting on the recent scientific findings regarding the makeup of ancient Irish genomes, their links to mass migrations from the Middle East and what was now Ukraine. So maybe Rasheed had been on to something after all. Gabriel had certainly reaped the benefits of those particular genetic twists. He returned to Ranya's message and read it twice more, then put his fingers to the keyboard.

My Dear, Dear Ranya,

I logged on tonight to tell you that I am getting a new puppy—a Glen of Imaal Terrier (look up the Glen of Imaal online; it's such a beautiful spot in the Wicklow Mountains)—and found that my news, as usual, pales beside yours.

You don't have to thank me. From the beginning, it has been my enduring pleasure to be nothing more than a poor sort of catalyst for your flame. If anything, I am certain I have gained far more from our exchanges than you have, and have counted myself a fortunate man since the day I met you. You have brought illumination to my life, in all the best ways.

You write, essentially, of both dissonances and connections, connectedness and separation, gulfs and bridges. I know a little about those things, but I think you already know that. I have lived in the interstices all my life, it seems. So yes, I get it. And I have always admired how you yourself have managed the spaces of unbelonging, with courage and aplomb and the willingness to be a pioneer whenever the situation called for it.

I have watched you navigate the deepest and murkiest of waters under the most varied and difficult of circumstances, on three continents now, and Ranya, believe me when I say: I have never known anyone else remotely like you.

There is a small but vitally important bit of Rasheed in me, but that is not what makes me part Palestinian (if you will allow me, with all humility, to make the claim). Because what does it mean to be Palestinian, to be Irish, to be anything? I think about this a lot, Ranya—have since I met you—have since I met Rasheed, in fact. And maybe that is always the best we can hope for: for the Other to become the One, and the One the Other, until all our differences become our sameness. One under the same stars, united by our common hopes.

It's what I like to think, anyway. And I like to imagine that Rasheed would have felt the same.

As ever, I remain,

Yours,

Gabe

EPILOGUE

February 29, 2016
Monday
Cliffs of Moher

RANYA STOOD WITH THE green-and-white urn in her hands, looking out over the Atlantic from the gray sandstone cliffs that marched on and on like jagged leviathans into the horizon. The wind whipped her hair up and around, as it had done those many years before. But this time there was a tear-stained letter in her bag, and much had passed, much joy, much sorrow, since she had last stood in this place.

But stand there she did, on the verdant grass in front of O'Brien's Tower, at the edge of the earth, thinking of Rasheed. He had picked a good day for this, of course—a gorgeous early sunset and abnormally clear weather. Although the wind was up, the overall weather wasn't terrible, which was remarkable given the time of year. Ranya looked up at the heavens. *You've charmed everyone up there, too, haven't you, Rasheed?*

It was Leap Day. His birthday. He would have been, what, 14 years old today? Or something like that. Gabriel would know. Gabriel would have teased him for that.

She had thought about contacting Gabriel, but it had seemed wrong somehow. She didn't think that was what Rasheed would have wanted. Maybe after she had done what she had come to do. Maybe then it would be all right.

As she looked out at the magnificent view, at the rough silvery rock of the cliffs hewn by the mighty waters of the Atlantic, at the turquoise of the waves as they crested and crashed in pillows of white foam, the winds threw her dark hair back and all around her once more, returning her to the same scene and Rasheed's words at this very spot all those years ago.

"Not the sort of view you see every day, right?"

But it was not Rasheed's voice that she heard now. It was a brogue she would recognize anywhere.

Somehow, in spite of the wind and the waves, his voice held a quiet in it. She turned slowly, unbelievingly, to the man who was now standing beside her. She parted her lips to speak, but no words came out.

"You weren't going to tell me, were you?" His blue eyes regarded her with a mixture of pain and affection. She had seen that look before. On him and on Rasheed. And she no more knew how to respond to it now than she ever had.

They stared at one another wordlessly for a long moment. Then she lifted up the green-and-white urn in her hands and fumbled with the obvious question. "But, Gabriel . . . What . . . How . . . did you know?"

Holding up an envelope that bore his name in Rasheed's handwriting, Gabriel replied, "Probably the same way you did."

He handed her the letter and turned his attention to unwrapping the package he had brought with him. Ranya saw that it was another urn, in orange and white, and as Gabriel lifted it up to hold beside the green-and-white one she still clutched in her hands, she saw in an instant what Rasheed had done. She couldn't hear Gabriel's next words against the crashing of the waves, but she could read his lips, and knew that he had seen it too: "Oh, my God."

Together they marveled at Rasheed's message to them from beyond the grave. There beside O'Brien's Tower, at the edge of the earth, they stood, together, holding Rasheed's ashes within the colors of the Irish flag. And on his rare Leap Day birthday, no less.

Tears fell from Gabriel's eyes, and Ranya realized that she couldn't recall ever having seen Gabriel cry. After all they'd been through, he'd never shown her that. But then again, she'd never really shown him, either.

He looked at her now, raised the crook of his arm to wipe his face as he held the orange-and-white urn to the side, looked at her again. A smile tugged at his lips, and he sought her eyes. "So I guess this is what Rasheed wanted after all," he said, and this time his voice came to her softly through a lull in the waves. He looked out across the cliffs, out toward the vast Atlantic. "*Bás in Éirinn,*" he said, as though to himself, but Ranya remembered too.

She remembered a turn-of-the-century dinner and a brilliant, ebony-haired man with the widest smile and the biggest heart she had ever known. And she remembered a dapper Irishman with a musical brogue and a heart-stopping grin and the bluest eyes she had ever seen. And herself between them, then, and now, and maybe always.

"There's never been anyone else, Ranya," Gabriel said, his voice rising now with the ocean's waves. He straightened to his full height and turned to meet her gaze. "I think—I hope—you know that."

Ranya squeezed her eyes shut and turned her chin up, fighting back tears of her own. At last she nodded, and managed a choked, "Yes." She nodded again, eyes wide open this time, letting the liquid heat pour down her cheeks, letting Gabriel see. And she repeated, "Yes."

Holding his urn beside hers once more to form the tricolor, Gabriel nodded his head, and they smiled together through their tears. Smiles turned to tear-stained laughter as the realization settled and deepened, and their wet cheeks glistened in the final round of sunlight above the Atlantic. Then Gabriel threw his head back and sent all the air in his lungs to meet the Irish sky in a single exclamation: "Thank you, Rasheed!!"

Ranya could have sworn she caught a hint of Gabriel's signature grin when he turned back to her, and the light in his blue eyes now was pure happiness. He reached out and put his free hand over both of hers, which still cradled her green-and-white urn, her half of Rasheed's promise. "Shall we?" he asked.

And with that, they tossed ashes to the air and liberated the past.

About the Author

Yasmine S. Ali, MD, is an award-winning writer and the bestselling author of *Walk through Fire: The Train Disaster that Changed America*. She is believed to be the first female American cardiologist of Palestinian descent. She is the founder of Positive Vibes, a media brand that seeks to promote healthy optimism and the sharing of good news.

Become part of the Positive Vibes community and be the first to learn about Dr. Ali's events and new releases by visiting www.YasmineAliMD.com .

Further Reading

If you're interested in learning more about the Irish or Palestinian history and literature referenced in this book, including some of the books that Ranya and Gabriel were reading, see below:

A Lover from Palestine and Other Poems, edited by Abdul Wahab Al Messiri

Dubliners, by James Joyce

The Disinherited: Journal of a Palestinian Exile, by Fawaz Turki

The Edward Said Reader, edited by Moustafa Bayoumi and Andrew Rubin

The Field, by John B. Keane

God Cried, by Tony Clifton and photojournalist Catherine Leroy

The Graves Are Walking: The Great Famine and the Saga of the Irish People, by John Kelly

The Great Hunger: Ireland: 1845-1849, by Cecil Woodham-Smith

The Hundred Years' War on Palestine: A History of Settler Colonialism and Resistance, 1917 – 2017, by Rashid Khalidi

In Great Haste: The Letters of Michael Collins and Kitty Kiernan, edited by León Ó Broin

Michael Collins: The Man Who Made Ireland, by Tim Pat Coogan

Palestine: Peace Not Apartheid, by former President Jimmy Carter

Pity the Nation, by Robert Fisk

The Son of a Duck Is a Floater: And Other Arab Sayings with English Equivalents, compiled by Primrose Arnander and Ashkhain Skipwith

A Surgeon under Israeli Occupation, by Shawki Harb, MD

Unfortunately, It Was Paradise: Selected Poems, by Mahmoud Darwish

Acknowledgments

THIS WORK HAS BEEN like the writing of a very long letter to so many dear friends. Simply put, this book would never have existed without the help and support of so many, my Irish friends and acquaintances foremost among them.

To Tom Tynan, armchair historian and tour director extraordinaire, and Maura Tynan, his better half: thank you for your hospitality, for furthering my learning of Irish history, for putting up with my artistic eccentricities on both sides of the Atlantic, and for transferring your deep love of Ireland to me and my family. You are truly two of Ireland's finest.

To the incomparable Mary O'Leary, formidable guide and flawless driver on the worst of Irish country roads: thank you for answering so many of my questions, for providing important feedback on the manuscript, for being my "eyes on the ground" whenever I needed a quick location check or recommendation, and for befriending me and my family with such openness and kindness.

To Dr. John J. Ryan, who really does command his dogs in Irish, many thanks are owed for so gamely coming on board with this vast project of mine, for helping me bring authenticity to the Irish characters and settings, for informing and correcting my Irish, for providing invaluable feedback on the manuscript with an excellent eye for detail, for helping me identify key references for my research, for so wisely sending me to The Winding Stair, for introducing me to Barry's tea—fantastic!—and for generally going above and beyond, as is his way. Thank you also, John, for convincing me of the importance of including proverbs (both Arabic and Irish) in their original language, because translations, however good, are never quite the same.

And speaking of translations, I must also thank Dr. Ryan's father, Jim Ryan, and his very helpful Gaelgoir friends, Kevin Johnson and Seosamh Ó Murchú (both at Foras na Gaeilge), for taking the time to find and provide the accurate *seanfhocal* (Irish proverb) translations for some of the more elusive ones in this book, as well as for helping me out with the linguistic history of the Skelligs.

To Tim and Dolores Crowley of the Michael Collins Centre: thank you for the most incredible Michael Collins tour I could ever have imagined—you made a dream come true that day. Unforgettable, and maybe the inspiration for yet another novel.

To Gavin and Brian of Belfast, for alerting me to the history of Dr. Frank Pantridge, and for illuminating the history of the Troubles in the most indelible of ways.

To Dr. Patrick Lavin, whom fate conspired to seat beside me on my first trip to Ireland, for being my very first guide to Dublin and the River Liffey from a bird's-eye view, for graciously allowing me to pester him for years thereafter with my naiveté and endless questions, for giving me a proper introduction to hurling, and for providing insightful book titles and references. Thanks also for that really great cuppa.

To all of you: *Go raibh mile maith agat.*

I also owe a deep debt of gratitude to:

Dr. Kelly Moore, one of the people to whom this book is dedicated, for being such a helpful beta reader, but more importantly, for being such a good friend, excellent sounding board, and stalwart supporter through it all. I have Kelly to thank for urging me to find Ranya's motivation, for always encouraging me in ways that only served to make the manuscript—and myself—better, and for reminding me that 99% of the world's population aren't INTJs.

Dr. Heather Fork of Doctor's Crossing, for reviewing early drafts of the manuscript and for being my invaluable cheerleader through it all—but, most importantly, for teaching me how to live in my True Self. This book would probably have never gotten finished without her support.

Vicki Harden, for being such an amazing, insightful, and persistent friend and beta reader, determined to send me feedback even when she had to type one-handed due to a broken wrist!

Dr. Stacy Davis, for her unrelenting support and encouragement, and for providing clarity in an uncertain world, in no uncertain terms: "You *must* publish this book."

Jen Hall, who, like a guardian angel, wisely kept me from pursuing a path that would have taken me in the wrong direction.

Dr. Holly Urban, for being a constant advocate, mentor, and incredibly helpful beta reader.

Dr. Josepha Cheong, for her invaluable advice during difficult times and her ongoing support of all my efforts, written or otherwise.

Claire Rembecki, for a wonderful conversation about her summer in Ireland, and for the most beautiful description of St. Stephen's Green that I have ever heard. Claire, thank you for permitting me to use your willow tree; may your bliss remain undisturbed.

Dr. Shawki Harb—the original heart surgeon from Ramallah—for providing invaluable input and insight into aspects of Ramallah history and culture, and, most importantly, for being such a dear friend to my family for so many years. *Alf shukr!*

Charlene Harb, for being my piano teacher, friend, and mentor, and for giving me her own copy of Beethoven's *Pathétique* Sonata—and helping me learn how to play it. It's one of Gabriel's favorites because it's one of my favorites, and that is due entirely to Charlene.

Kristen Brustad, for finding and providing an elusive Arabic proverb in the original Arabic, and to Reema for reaching out to Kristen.

The Ramadan family, in particular Siham and Salam, for allowing me to honor Raniyah's memory in this book's dedication, and for always being such wonderful friends and encouragers to my entire family. Raniyah will always be sorely missed, but her courage and beauty live on through all of you.

Kin Clinton, for being such a stalwart source of support and encouragement during the completion of the manuscript and the subsequent search for an agent and publisher. The journey to publication for this book turned out differently than either of us had imagined, but then again, that's so often how life goes, isn't it?

Missy Rodriguez Brower, for swooping back into my life at a time of intense challenge and great upheaval, and convincing me, with her superhuman powers of empathy, of the importance of having a room of one's own. She helped me get that room, and this book was finished in it.

Kim Chunn, my original—and best—ACLS (cardiac resuscitation) instructor: you were at the forefront of my mind as I was writing Chapter Three!

Irfana Anwer, for being such an amazing family friend, supporter, and encourager, for listening to my ideas for this book when it was in its earliest stages and as I was considering publishing it through the traditional route with an agent.

Rania Mallouk, for being so encouraging as a fellow independent author, and for helping to keep the excitement alive for this debut novel.

Fred Ramsey, for allowing us to have one of the most incredible Field Goldens the world has ever seen—our darling Ike, who keeps us in laughter and wonder every single day with his charm, intelligence, and *joie de vivre*. Thank you also, Fred, for your encouragement of and interest in my writing.

Daren Smith, whose phenomenal Craftsman Creative program I stumbled upon seemingly by chance, only to recall later that true coincidence is rare. It's not an understatement to say that Daren and his program helped change my life and turn around my creative business. Daren, thank you for your generosity and all you have done to help fellow creative entrepreneurs.

Patti Hoehn Damesworth, for being such an amazing friend, constant supporter, and true superfan. You are the very definition of Positive Vibes, Patti, and you inspire me in every way!

Carolyn Tucker, always, for her unconditional support and for helping me to think through the timing of this book's publication and release. And for so much more, including understanding the Palestinian tragedy with more empathy than almost any other non-Arab I know . . . Sam, there are no words.

And I can never give thanks enough for my dear family, for instilling in me the twin loves of books and libraries, and for understanding the importance of a well-rounded education. To my Palestinian father, for teaching me to never give up, and to my Syrian mother, for believing in my creative writing efforts from the beginning and for urging me to push forward with this book and its publication.

To Nadia and Khaled, for being the perfect role models to encourage an avid reader (and writer) from a very young age. Nadia, thank you so much for taking the time to be this book's final beta reader and to provide insights into where its market strengths might lie. To Reema, for sharing my love of the best lines and the best stories. And to Samar, for asking me to tell her stories when we were growing up; for casting light on the path when the way looked lost; and for always, always believing in me.

To my four-legged family members, who are still the reason I get out of bed in the morning!

And, most importantly, to my darling Keith, my heart of hearts, love of my life—my very own *Habibi*: thank you for constantly reminding me that writers *write*. It's all for you.

Purchase additional copies of this book, or get the e-book and audiobook, at **LastSkyWriting.com**!

You can also scan the QR code with your phone to go directly to LastSkyWriting.com:

And be sure to subscribe to Yasmine S. Ali's email newsletter, *Positive Vibes*, to stay up to date on all new releases, author events, and subscriber-only discounts! You'll get exclusive content, behind-the-scenes insights, and special offers, and you can subscribe for FREE today!

Subscribe at https://yasmine-ali-author.beehiiv.com/subscribe or scan the QR code with your phone:

20250318111557